Terror Cimbricus

Book 3
The Cimbrian War

JEFF HEIN

RED WOLF BOOKS

Terror Cimbricus

Book 3 of The Cimbrian War

Copyright © 2024 by Jeff Hein

Published by Red Wolf Books

All rights reserved.

eBook ISBN: 978-1-7375539-9-1

Paperback ISBN: 979-8-9920242-0-3

Hardcover ISBN: 979-8-9920242-1-0

No part of this book may be reproduced in any form or by any electronic or mechanical means, including information storage and retrieval systems, without written permission from the author, except for the use of brief quotations in a book review.

This book is a work of fiction. The names, characters, and incidents portrayed in it, while based on historical events and people, are the work of the author's imagination.

Formatting by 341 Enterprise

Cover design by Dusan Arsenic

Torque image by The Crafty Celts.

Available at: https://www.craftycelts.com

Terror Cimbricus

JEFF HEIN

Table of Contents

Dedication.	VI
Germans & Celts Character Tree	VII
Historical Characters List	IX
Map of Europe	XIV
Map of Gaul	XVI
Map of Numidia	XVII
Diagram of the Two Army Structures	XVIII
Epigraph.	XIX
Preface.	XX
Prologue.	XXI
Part I. The King 109-107 BC	
Chapter 1.	01
Chapter 2.	07
Chapter 3.	17
Chapter 4.	23
Chapter 5.	35
Chapter 6.	41
Chapter 7.	51
Part II. The New Man 109-105 BC	
Chapter 8.	61
Chapter 9.	73
Chapter 10.	81
Chapter 11.	85
Chapter 12.	91
Chapter 13.	99
Chapter 14.	103
Chapter 15.	109

Chapter 16.	113
Chapter 17.	119
Chapter 18.	125

Part III Rebellion 107-106 BC

Chapter 19.	135
Chapter 20.	149
Chapter 21.	155
Chapter 22.	169
Chapter 23.	175
Chapter 24.	181

Part IV Betrayal 106-105 BC

Chapter 25.	189
Chapter 26.	211
Chapter 27.	217

Part V Terror Cimbricus 105 BC

Chapter 28.	227
Chapter 29.	237
Chapter 30.	239
Chapter 31.	247
Chapter 32.	251
Chapter 33.	255
Chapter 34.	267
Chapter 35.	269
Chapter 36	273
Epilogue.	277
Historical Notes.	279
Glossary.	283
A Word from the Author.	299
Contact.	300
About the Author.	302

DEDICATION

For my brother Eugene who passed away

during the writing of this book.

He was one of my biggest supporters.

Germans and Celts
(* Fictional Characters)

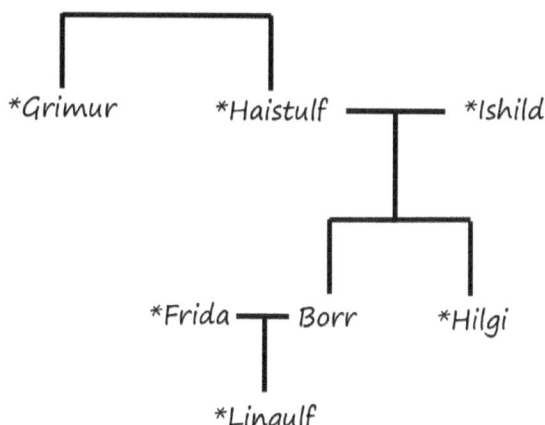

Claudicus – Hunno of the Boar Clan
Caesorix – Hunno of the Raven Clan
Lugius – Hunno of the Bear Clan
*Freki – Borr's Adopted brother
*Hrolf – Borr's friend
*Aldric – Borr's friend
*Ansgar – Commander of Borr's guards
*Gorm – Blacksmith
*Glum – Brewmaster/Frida's father
*Eldric – High priest
*Skyld – High priestess
Teutobod – Chieftain of the Teutones
*Amalric – Chieftain of the Ambrones
*Advorix – Chieftain of the Veneti
Divico – Chieftain of the Tigurini

HISTORICAL CHARACTERS

ROMANS

GAIUS MARIUS – (157 – 86 BC) Marius began his military career under Scipio Aemilianus at the Siege of Numantia. In 110 BC he married Julia Caesar, future aunt to Julius Caesar the dictator. Marius distinguished himself in 109 BC at the Battle of Muthul in the Jugurthine War and went on to defeat the Numidian king in 105 BC. He is on a path that will eventually bring him into direct conflict with the Cimbri.

MARCUS MARIUS – Younger brother of Gaius Marius. Praetor in 102 BC.

PUBLIUS RUTILIUS RUFUS – (158 – after 78 BC) A great-uncle of Julius Caesar the dictator. In 134 BC he served as a staff officer for Scipio Aemilianus during the Numantine War. In 109 BC he fought under Quintus Caecilius Metellus and beside Gaius Marius in the campaign against Jugurtha where he distinguished himself at the Battle of Muthul. In 105 BC he was elected consul.

LUCIUS CASSIUS LONGINUS – (151 – 107 BC) As praetor in 111 BC he was sent to Numidia to escort Jugurtha to Rome to testify in corruption trials. Elected as senior consul in 107 BC with Gaius Marius as junior consul. While Marius would go to Africa to fight Jugurtha, Longinus would go north to confront the Cimbri and their allies.

QUINTUS SERVILIUS CAEPIO – As consul in 106 BC he campaigned against the Cimbrian allies in Gaul and captured the city of Tolosa, where he found the fabled treasure from the temple of Delphi, believed to be stolen during the Celtic invasion of the Balkans in 279 BC. In 105 BC, as pro-consul, Caepio was sent to combine his army with that of that year's consul Gnaeus Mallius Maximus and confront the northern tribes.

GNAEUS MALLIUS MAXIMUS – Elected to the consulship in 105 BC and sent to Gallia Narbonensis to stop the Cimbri and their allies. The proconsul in the field, Quintus Servilius Caepio, refused to cooperate with him due to his status as a Novus Homo, or New Man. The two generals refused to speak to each other leaving them vulnerable to the overwhelming numbers of the northern alliance of tribes.

TITUS & QUINTUS MALLIUS MAXIMUS – Sons of Gnaeus Mallius Maximus who were both killed at the battle of Arausio.

MARCUS AEMILIUS SCAURUS – (159 – 89 BC) Consul in 115 BC and then princeps senatus until his death. Considered one of the most influential politicians in the late Republic and was involved in many negotiations and delegations on behalf of the senate.

MARCUS AURELIUS SCAURUS – Likely not related to Marcus Aemilius Scaurus. Consul in 108 BC. Legate under Gnaeus Mallius Maximus in 105 BC. His separate cavalry command was wiped out at the battle of Arausio and Scaurus was killed personally by Boiorix.

QUINTUS CAECILIUS METELLUS – Another veteran of the Numantine War, he was acquainted with many of the others who served under Scipio. As consul in 109 BC and proconsul in 108 BC he commanded the Roman armies in Africa during the Jugurthine War. In 107 BC he turned the war over to Gaius Marius, his bitter rival.

GAIUS JULIUS CAESAR – In Terror Cimbricus, this Caesar is the father of the Gaius Julius Caesar who became dictator of Rome and was murdered on the Ides of March, 44 BC. Gaius

Marius married this Caesar's sister Julia, making him an uncle of the dictator. Roman naming conventions of the time meant that the entire line of males in a family often had the exact same name, confusing later historians to no end.

TITUS TURPILIUS SILANUS – Roman prefect who was blamed for the massacre at Vaga in 109 BC. His trial and subsequent execution was a major factor that split Marius and Metellus further apart.

TITUS MANLIUS MANCINUS – Roman Tribune of the Plebs during the late Republic.

LUCIUS CALPURNIUS PISO CAESONINUS – Legate to Cassius Longinus and killed at the Battle of Burdigala

GAIUS POPILLIUS LAENUS – Legate to Cassius Longinus. Accepted a humiliating defeat at the Battle of Burdigala and was forced to walk under the yoke with the surviving army.

GNAEUS POMPEIUS STRABO – Later to become a Roman general and a consul in 89 BC, he was known for his role in the social war. His son, mentioned in this book, was born Gnaeus Pompeius and would grow up to earn the cognomen "Magnus", or "the great". Pompey the Great would become a protégé to Sulla and would go on to serve as a successful general earning three triumphs for his military victories. He became a political ally, and eventual enemy, of Gaius Julius Caesar the Dictator, and played a significant role in the turbulent times during the last days of the Republic.

AULUS MANLIUS – Legate to Gaius Marius during the Numidian War in 107 BC.

QUINTUS & GNAEUS GRANIUS – Stepsons of Gaius Marius through his wife Julia.

LUCIUS CORNELIUS SULLA – Just beginning his military career he is elected quaestor and assigned to Marius' army in

107 BC. Sulla will go on to be a major figure in the Cimbrian war and will play a significant role in the end of the Roman Republic.

QUINTUS SERTORIUS – Solider, spy, rebel, general; Sertorius' story is one of the most intriguing during the last years of the Republic. From his first battle at Arausio where he was one of the few survivors of that infamous battle, Sertorius exhibited his bravery and perseverance at every opportunity.

GERMANS AND CELTS

BORR (BORRIX/BOIORIX) – Historical records first mention the leader of the Cimbri in 105 BC when Boiorix defeated the Romans in one of the largest defeats of their history, with a loss of more than 80,000. Nothing else is known of his origins or of him as a person. In The Cimbrian War series, his background is totally invented by the author. The story of his youth begins as a teenage boy around the time the Cimbri were believed to have migrated southward from Jutland (Denmark). Boiorix translates to king of the Boii, which never made much sense to me, as the Cimbri were no friend of the Boii. He would not have been born with the title of king, so, to develop the story, I invented a name. Borr is the name of the father of Wodan the Allfather, and Borr's father Haistulf named him for the creator god Borr. (See glossary) Borr will grow from a boy to chieftain and then king of the Cimbri, Borrix. (The suffix rix meant tribal leader or chieftain and is similar to the Latin word for king, rex). As was common at that time his name was transformed by the Romans to suit their understanding of their world, Borrix was changed to Boiorix, the name that has stood for millennia. At least, that's my version of it.

TEUTOBOD – Leader of the Teutones tribe, he and his people left the area of Jutland around the same time as the Cimbri. They are believed to have accompanied the Cimbri throughout their journey, but it is not clear. Historians differ when and where the Teutones appeared. What is known is that they were involved in the major battles and were fated to cross swords with the Roman general Gaius Marius.

CLAUDICUS/CAESORIX/LUGIUS – Recorded as clan leaders of the Cimbri.

DIVICO – King of the Tigurini, a Celtic tribe and member of the Helvetian confederation of tribes, located in what is now southern Germany and Switzerland. He led the Tigurini during the Cimbrian War and invaded Gaul and Narbonensis as an ally of the Cimbri. He famously made the defeated legions march under the yoke after their defeat at the battle of Burdigala in 107 BC. Fifty years later he would lead a delegation to ask Julius Caesar for safe passage for his tribe through Gaul. Caesar used Divico's past defeat of Roman legions as a reason to deny that request.

COPILLUS – Chieftain of the Volcae Tectosages.

OTHER

JUGURTHA – Adopted son of Micipsa, the king of Numidia. Jugurtha killed both of his adopted brothers to seize the throne, and in the process became an enemy of Rome. Jugurtha was defeated by Gaius Marius and eventually killed. He was familiar with Marius from having served together under Scipio Aemilianus in Numantia.

GAUDA – Half-brother to Jugurtha and rival for the throne of Numidia. Later, king of Numidia.

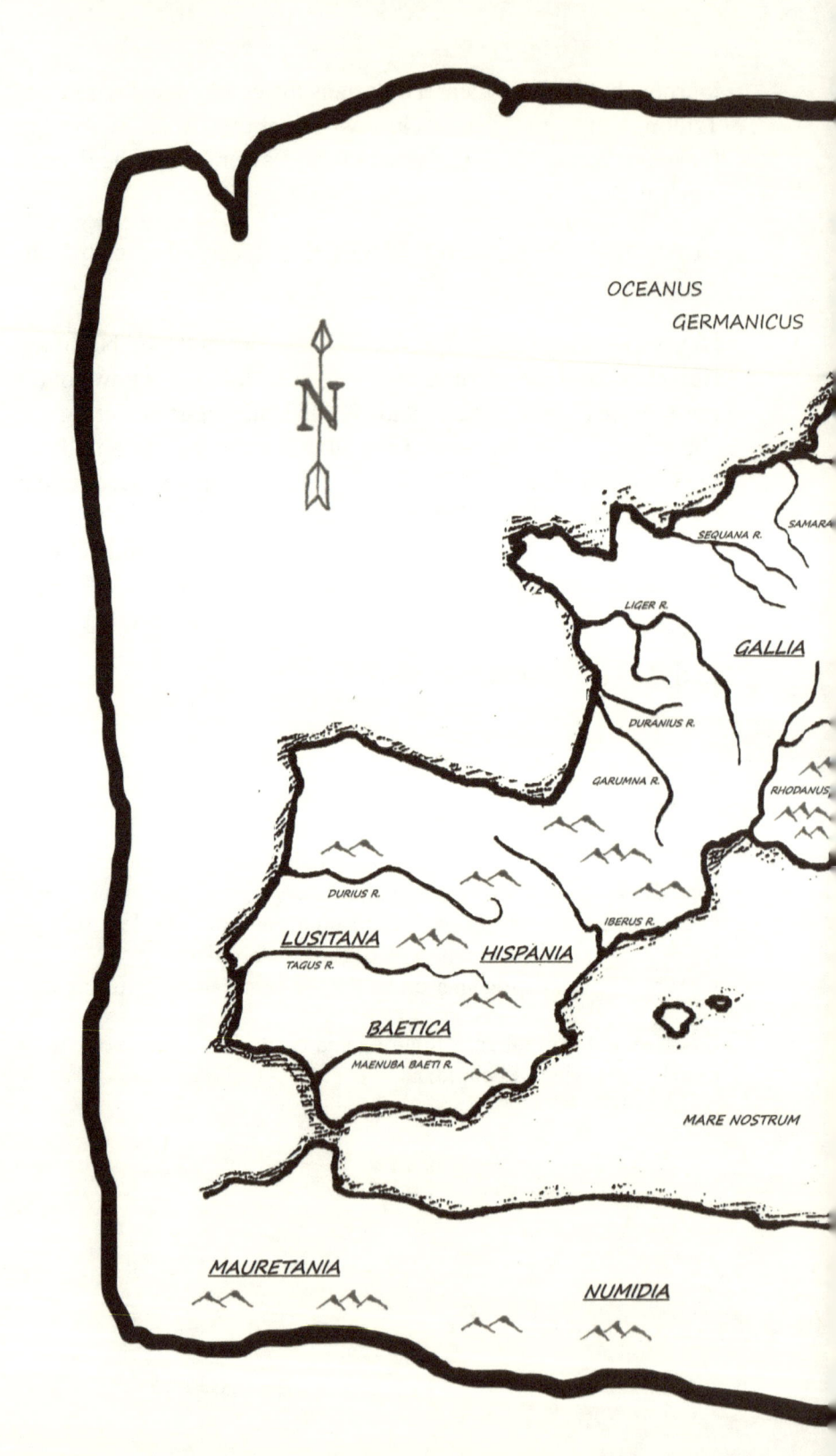

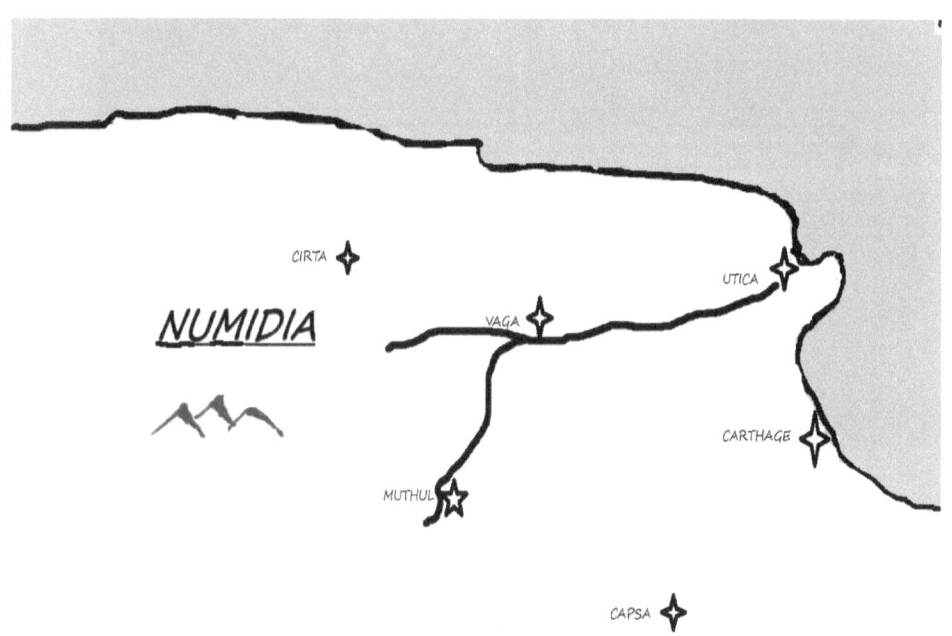

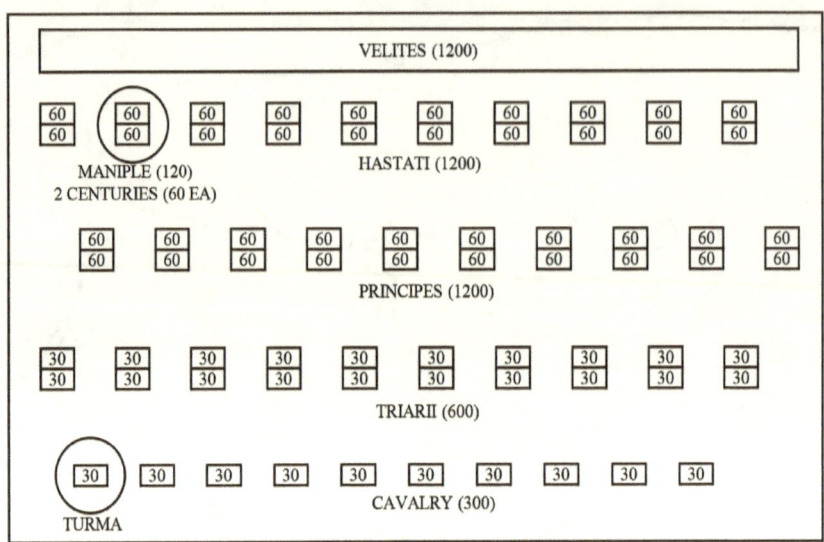

MANIPULAR LEGION (4200 INFANTRY)

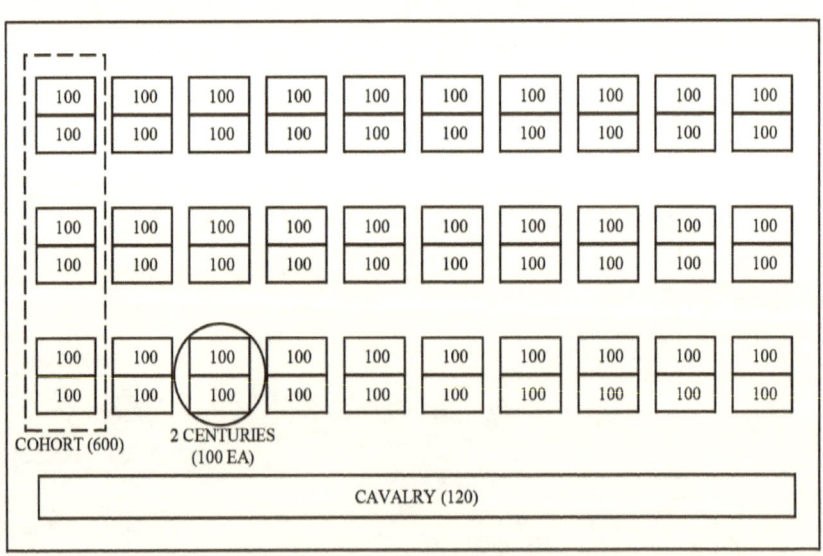

MARIUS' COHORTAL LEGION (6000 INFANTRY)

EPIGRAPH

In the six hundred and forty second year from the founding of Rome, Gnaeus Mallius Maximus and Quintus Servilius Caepio, went against the Cimbri, Teutones, Tigurini, and Ambrones, tribes of Gaul and Germany. These were then closing on the Roman lands via the provinces through which flows the Rhone River. Here envy and discord caused the most damaging dispute between them and brought great shame and danger to the name of Rome.

(Orosius, *History* 5.15 - 16)

PREFACE

In Terror Cimbricus, the Cimbrian War continues as Borr and Marius continue on the separate paths that will bring them to the titanic battle that will shape the future of both cultures.

The reader may sometimes wonder why Marius' story is interwoven with that of Borr and the Cimbri. It is because I wanted you to know who he was, the irresistible force that was Marius. You cannot tell the story of the Cimbri, without telling that of Marius. The man who will eventually collide with the Cimbri and their allies to force the inevitable conclusion of The Cimbrian War.

PROLOGUE

Gaul

109 BC

Whole villages fled in fear of the horde of warriors that approached. Women wailed and hid their children while their men, the pride of the Gallic nations, were slaughtered. All trembled at the sound of the great drums echoing across the hillsides. The whispered name of the Cimbri spread terror throughout the land. The wise had chosen to bend the knee and offer tribute, the rest were crushed under an onslaught that had not been witnessed since the glaciers receded. Like those mighty mountains of ice, the allied tribes had done their damage and withdrawn to the north, leaving in their wake a wide trail of destruction upon the land.

After defeating Silanus the Cimbri returned to Aduatuca, their newly founded city among the Belgae in the north of Gaul. The Ambrones went with them, while the Teutones returned to the Donarsberg. The Tigurini, Raurici, Arverni, and other allies returned to their homes. During their campaign through Gaul, they captured many wagonloads of plunder, thousands of slaves, and herds of cattle and other livestock. The defeated Roman legions provided horses, mules, wagons, weapons, and armor. The tribes' lust for booty was sated, for now.

While the allied tribes walked the warrior's path, those left behind at Aduatuca completed the palisade that surrounded the large oppidum. The gates and towers were strong, and the wanderers had returned early enough to complete the interior buildings and to build their winter cabins outside the oppidum for the many that would not fit inside. Within those strong walls a treasure vault overflowed with the gold, silver, and other valuables they had captured. The armory was filled with Roman and Gallic swords, mail coats, helmets, and shields; taken from the tens of thousands of legionaries and Gallic and Germanic warriors they had defeated.

Large warehouses were filled with bags of grain, barrels of ale, mead, and thousands of clay amphorae of Roman wine. From the rafters hung quarters of salted and dried beef, smoked hams, slabs of bacon and bundles of herbs to be used for medicinal purposes and seasoning food. Crates of turnips and apples were stacked high. Barrels of sea-salt stood beside dried fish, brined olives, pickled cucumbers, and fermented cabbage, which stood beside casks of honey and dried berries of various kinds.

Bales of wool and flax waiting to be spun and weaved into clothing were stacked in one corner, beside piles of woolen cloaks taken from dead legionaries. Iron utensils and tools lay mixed with bronze cooking pots in great heaps. The Cimbri had never seen such riches gathered in one place.

Great caravans crossed the land all summer, bringing the plunder from their campaign back to Aduatuca. Barges floated the Rhenus and other rivers laden with the booty of their victories. The other tribes had taken their share of plunder as well. Gaul had been stripped of its wealth.

PART I

THE KING

109 – 107 BC

CHAPTER ONE

Aduatuca

September 109 BC

I had come to realize that despite the many victories and the vast hoard of worldly goods that we possessed, my people were suffering from a crisis of faith. They had moved so much. They no longer had a permanent place of worship. They needed something that they could see and touch that would put them in contact with their gods. During the great flood, all our holy sites were destroyed. Ever since, our religion had faded into the background of so much else that had happened to us. Our priests and priestesses kept our religion alive, but the people had lapsed in their faith. It was up to me to restore their belief in the gods. Here at Aduatuca the priests had consecrated a sacred grove where they carried out the ancient ceremonies of our people. They placed the sacred wooden carvings of Wodan and Donar in this sanctuary, and it was familiar and comforting to us when we were here. But we had since been joined by many different tribes with many different beliefs. We needed something that all of us could identify with. Something that combined all of us into a single body. I did not wish to favor one faith over the other, I wanted something that would be a symbol of the Cimbri and all the other tribes and people who had joined us. Our cattle were important to us for food and for oxen to pull our wagons and so much more. When we lived in Jutland, they were the representation of our wealth and power. In a time and place when gold, silver, and iron were rare, the animals had been sacred to us, a living symbol of our strength. But that importance had faded during our journey, in the face of so much hardship, and had been replaced by the wagon loads of treasure that we had taken. That reverence for the life-giving cattle was not unique to us, it crossed the cultures of all the tribes, and it would be a way to join us together.

I found Gorm working in his forge, as he always did, in his leather apron and short pants, the glow of the furnace casting rippling red shadows around the open smithy. I recalled how I felt that I had been magically transported to the realm of the dwarves whenever I entered his domain. The smell of charcoal furiously burning in the smelting furnace and the impurities burning off from the molten iron triggered my memories. The heat emanating from the furnace was nearly overwhelming. The sound of his hammer ringing took me back to the happier days that I spent learning the secrets of metal working from him. A boy of about ten or eleven worked the bellows, as I used to. It had been too long since I had visited him. How much had changed in ten years? Yet, much had remained the same. Gorm's forge was an anchor to our past. Only its location had changed. Sweat dripped from his nose to sizzle on the white-hot iron rods he hammered into shape. Muscular arms bulged from a lifetime of swinging his hammer, his skin glistened with perspiration and reflected tones of orange and red from the firelight. His thick hair was pearly-white now and had receded to a narrow widow's peak. He still wore the sides long and tied back with a leather thong.

"Well," he said happily when I walked in front of him. "This is a pleasant surprise. What brings you here?" He grinned and greeted me warmly. He gestured to an assistant and instructed him to continue working the piece that he had been hammering on and we stepped outside.

"I want you to make something for me. Something important. I want you to make a bull."

"A bull," he repeated, confused.

"Yes, a figure of a bull. It must be a thing of beauty, about the size of a calf, but able to travel with us when we move." I indicated the size with my hands. "Something that will inspire awe." I went on to explain the reason for my request and he was intrigued. Gorm, who had been the Wolf Clan's blacksmith since I was a boy, possessed great skill in creating weapons and tools in his forge. He had an innate ability to manage any task he was assigned, no matter the scale, but he was out of his element here. His experience was creating things of utility, not of beauty.

"I will need some help on this," he said. "I don't possess the skill for such a thing."

"I understand. But I trust you to see it through."

Gorm visited the blacksmiths in the allied tribes, asking who might be familiar with the process of casting bronze. Eventually, he was directed to a Gaulish sculptor and metal worker in a neighboring village.

"A solid bronze bull would be too heavy to move easily and require a great deal of bronze," said Vertos. "There is a method to cast a hollow sculpture. It will be much lighter and require only a portion of the bronze of a solid figure. But it will be expensive. I will need help."

"Don't worry about the cost. Hire whoever you need, and keep me informed," said Gorm.

Several weeks later, Vertos invited Gorm to his workshop. A large barn-like structure divided into a shop in front and a work area in the back half. Several tables held ornate bronze castings of animals, gods, and other subjects. There were tables of beautiful jewelry that included brooches, hair pins, finger rings, necklaces, ear rings, torques, and bracelets. Clothing items like leather belts with buckles, and cloak pins covered another table.

They ranged from iron to gold and silver, but all were done with a quality of craftsmanship that far exceeded anything Gorm had seen. He marveled at the beauty of these objects and the skill of the men who made such items while Vertos walked him to the back of the shop, where some of those craftsmen labored at their tasks. On a table stood an impressive wax bull, about one quarter the size of a live animal. "The detail is remarkable," Gorm complimented, running his hands admiringly over the bull. He looked up, smiling at Vertos.

"But wax? How will you cast the bronze?" Gorm had a curious mind and was always eager to learn new techniques.

"First, we made a clay model and fired it, so we had a core for the bull. The clay will be much lighter than a solid bronze cast. We covered the clay model with wax as thick as we wanted the wall of the casting to be. Then the detail was sculpted into the wax coating. This will represent the final look of the cast bull. Next, we cover the wax with another layer of clay that will shape itself to the wax sculpture and create the mold. Would you like to help?"

"Yes," Gorm said enthusiastically. A soft, wet clay was applied carefully to the detailed work in the wax, then more layers were added, building up the thickness required to contain the heat of the poured bronze. Two thin chimneys were constructed along the spine of the bull, one to pour the molten bronze and the other for air to escape. A third was constructed on the belly to allow the melted wax to escape. When the outer layers of clay were complete, the sculpture was left to dry.

"Now we wait," Vertos said. "If we fire the piece too soon, the water in the clay will create steam and cause it to crack and possibly explode."

"How long?" Gorm asked.

"At least a week. Maybe more. The outer layer is very wet.

When it's dry, we will fire the bull. The heat from the kiln will harden the outer layer and melt the wax which will run out the bottom vent and leave a cavity that the bronze will fill. When the wax is gone, I'll plug the vent. Then we will be ready to pour the bronze."

Gorm looked at the mold admiringly. "Fascinating," he said. Vertos beamed at the praise.

Another week passed before Gorm returned to Vertos' workshop. "I fired the mold yesterday and we're ready to pour the bronze," Vertos said, pointing at an iron crucible that sat in a glowing furnace.

Two of Vertos' helpers picked up the crucible with iron bars designed for the purpose and carried it across the room. Everyone held their breath while they delicately poured the molten metal into the gate tube while the displaced air hissed out the vent. Gorm watched the entire process intently. "Three more days to let it cool and harden," said Vertos. "Then we break the mold and clean it up."

JEFF HEIN

CHAPTER TWO

Aduatuca

December 109 BC

My hall was a long building with a stone hearth down the center and raised pallets along each wall where my unmarried retainers slept. Like our other buildings it was built of heavy timbers and mud-covered wattle. Shields hung on the walls with spears and swords, spoils of the many battles we had won. The banners of Roman consuls and tribal chieftains hung from the rafters, darkened by the smoke from the hearth.

I sat in Silanus' *curule* chair, upon the raised dais at the end of the hall, before the hunnos of all the clans. They were gathered for the assembly of elders to elect me chieftain for another year, but they were uneasy. To one side of me stood my brother Freki and my old friend Hrolf, on the other Eldric and Skyld, the high priest and priestess. Behind me my friend Ansgar, commander of my personal guard, stood with his arms crossed before his massive chest. He was a head taller than me, and I was taller than most. His blonde hair was the color of gold, and his bright blue eyes were like the summer sky. In peace, he was a gentle giant, quick with a joke and a smile. He wasn't the brightest of men, but in combat, he was as savage as a bear, and men took to his leadership. A number of hand-picked warriors lined the walls, armed with shields and spears. They were chosen for their size, their lethal skills, and their loyalty. Each of them had been young boys when we left Jutland and had grown up on our journey. They had come to manhood under my leadership, and they were hungry. They wanted the prestige and the rewards that came from being my companions, and they knew that loyalty was the path to their goals. They were a new generation, and they could feel the winds of change.

Eldric, high priest of Donar, rapped his twisted hazel staff three times on the wood planks, commanding the room to silence. The staff was topped with a badger skull that stared blankly out at the gathered leaders. Despite his small frame, the white robed priest possessed a commanding presence with his sharp features and piercing blue eyes. Standing beside him, the priestess Skyld embodied their fears of the mystical things in our world. The old crone stood bent, leaning heavily upon her walking stick, sucking in her lips over empty gums, then pursing them out as if blowing a kiss. Her glazed eyes scanned the room and those present tried to avoid her gaze.

"There will be no election today," Eldric announced loudly. The air seemed to leave the room as the group drew a collective breath. "Today, you will all be witness to a great change. Today, you will witness the ascension of Borrix, King Borr of the Cimbri." The room burst into a babble of voices. My people have never held with the concept of one ruler. A king. The council of elders held an assembly twice a year to hear grievances, pass judgement, discuss events that affected the whole tribe, and make important decisions. But ever since the great flood, the council met each Yule to elect a new chieftain. It was a temporary appointment for unusual circumstances that required power and decisions to be embodied in one man. Today was the day that tradition changed, and it would not come quietly.

Eldric shouted over the uproar. "From this day, and for the rest of his life, Borr, hunno of the wolf clan, and war chieftain of the Cimbri, will be known as Borrix, the king of the Cimbri." Another outburst, this time a roar of voices, cheers as well as protests, filled the hall.

Claodicus, hunno of the Boar Clan, and one of my strongest supporters, stepped out of the crowd and turned to them, waving them down until they were silent once again. "Borr has led us for more than five years. He has always put our people first. He has been a successful leader, and we have prospered. We are no longer the people who were forced to leave our homeland. Once again, we are respected, even feared." He turned toward the dais. "Let us at least hear what he has to say." The hall became grudgingly quiet.

"Thank you Claodicus," said Eldric. "First, let me assure you that the council of elders will remain intact. And they will be able to offer advice that will be considered by the king. But the higher power shall rest with him. Decisions about war and the welfare of the tribe will be his alone. This change is necessary to better lead our people through the coming years.

"Since being forced from our homes twelve years ago, our tribe has known only two chieftains. Father and son. Haistulf and Borr. They have brought us through the most difficult times that anyone alive can remember. Haistulf led us away from the devastation of the great flood and into an unfamiliar world where we learned to survive anew. Borr has become the great war leader that has restored our reputation and earned the fear and respect that is rightfully felt by our enemies whenever word of the Cimbri reaches their ears. Under Borr's leadership we have reclaimed our lost prestige. You only need look around you." Eldric swept his arms wide to indicate the many trophies. "Our herds are healthy, our warehouses overflow with food, we have gold and silver in abundance. Never have we been so strong.

"The gods have marked Borr with their approval, did he not sacrifice his eye, as Wodan himself did?" Eldric gestured at my face. "Donar has marked him with the symbol of the lightning bolt." The crowd murmured with growing approval at his words. "I have prayed at length and communed with the gods, as has Skyld. The priests and priestesses have blessed this decision. Today we have informed you, the council of elders, and tomorrow, on oath day, you shall all swear yourselves to the new king."

"I will not!" came a shout from the back of the hall. All heads turned toward Volker as he shouldered his way forward. Volker was the hunno of the eagle clan. Pointing at Borr he continued. "This man is not worthy to be our leader. Being mauled by a bear does not mean he was chosen by the gods. It is his own sister that has so conveniently provided the prophecy that named him as our leader. Now he wants to be king? Yes, he has presided over several victories, but he himself has doubted his own abilities had anything to do with it. In fact, that is why he went on the vision quest that resulted in his injuries. He has won battles, but at what cost? Thousands of dead. We are on a continuous war footing. We must hold constant vigil for fear of an enemy seeking revenge. He has turned all of Gaul against us with his raiding, not to mention the greatest military power we know, by slaughtering their legions when we should be negotiating with them. He claims that he is seeking a homeland, but how long are we supposed to wander? How long?"

Volker's anger had been simmering for years. He had sworn an oath to serve me, which he was now prepared to break.

He had been speaking to the gathered hunnos, but now he turned back to me. "I challenge you for the leadership of this tribe! I challenge you for Aduatuca and everything within its walls."

My men had all bristled during his speech, but he had not drawn a weapon, so they did not move. After a moment, I slowly rose, returning his glare. "This man has challenged me for leadership of the tribe. I accept that challenge." The sound of my sword scraping through my scabbard's metal throat was the only sound in the room. It was followed a moment later by Volker's. The crowd made room as he took several steps back and I stepped down from the dais. He circled to my left, seeking to take advantage of my blind eye, but he didn't know that I wasn't blind. I only wore a patch to prevent headaches from the light. Inside the hall it was dim, and I could see well enough. I tore off the leather patch and tossed it aside. We circled each other, searching for a weakness, watching for an opening. "Well?" I challenged him. Volker stepped forward quickly and jabbed the point of his sword at my belly, attempting to get past my guard and end it quickly, but I batted his sword away easily. He recovered fast and followed up with a slashing attack aimed at my neck. I danced back and let the blade slice air within a finger's breadth of my skin.

I smiled wickedly at him, which made him furious. He had gambled everything with his speech, and this was his chance. Only I rolled the better dice. Like most of our warriors, he was accustomed to violent slashing attacks, relying on wild overhand swings and superior size and strength to batter their opponent, shatter a shield, or split their helmet. Our people usually fought in large, tightly packed masses that did not allow the room for using fancy sword play, and it was obvious that Volker had only that experience to draw from. I had trained with expert swordsmen of different cultures. I had learned from my uncle and father the basic strokes that Volker was using but had also learned the techniques of the Romans from Vallus, and the strange dance of swords used by my friend Anik, from the far away land of India.

I toyed with him, moving in and out of his reach, moving lightly on my feet and parrying each attack easily. "Stand still and fight!" he roared at me. I parried another overhand slash. With each ringing collision of our blades, he became angrier. Those who at first had seemed to support him, were groaning at each of his attempts, and he was becoming desperate.

Suddenly, I changed tactics. When he came at me again, instead of knocking it aside or stepping back, I caught his blade against my guard and stepped in, forcing the tip downward and around until he lost his grip. The blade flew from his hand and landed in the dirt, and with the same motion mine took his right thumb. His eyes were white with fear, and he was sweating heavily as he tried to stanch the flow of blood from his hand.

"On your knees," I growled at him, then turned to the crowd of onlookers. "This man challenged me for the leadership of the tribe, and I accepted. Is there any doubt who is the victor of this fight?"

The hall was silent.

"There can be no mercy, no forgiveness for betrayal. Do you have any last words traitor?" He was already muttering a last prayer when I caught the word Fenrir. I looked at him in confusion at first, then anger. "What did you say?"

He continued muttering. "What did you say?" I nearly screamed. The sound of that name enraged me. I hit him on the back of the head with the hilt of my sword and he fell to the ground, stunned.

"The prophet of Fenrir will come for you," he whispered.

I stood over him and drove my sword down through his ribs, piercing his heart. He convulsed once and died. What did he mean, the prophet of Fenrir will come for me? The last I had seen of the prophet was his backside riding as fast as he could to escape Freki and his horsemen who raced over the hills to rescue me. I had vowed to find him and exact my revenge for his part in my capture. I intended to kill him for my humiliation and take back the torque that he had stolen from me. When I looked up, the men closest to me had taken a step back at the ferocity of my action. They were accustomed to violent death, that was no surprise. But from their astonished looks, I knew they were staring at the madness that had suddenly overtaken me.

"Are there any more challengers?" I shouted. Somehow, the prophet had infiltrated my camp and persuaded one of my followers to challenge me. This was a new development, and I did not like it. Would there be more?

"Tomorrow, all the Cimbri clans and those others who have been traveling with us, as well as the Aduatuci, will swear their loyalty to me, or they will take what they owned when they joined us and leave."

That night in our room behind the dais, Frida lay with her head on my arm. "Are you sure it is the right thing to do?"

"Dreams don't lie. When I was on my Utiseta, the spirit told me that one day I would be king. Tomorrow is that day."

I rolled toward her and traced my fingertip along the side of her face, from temple to chin, and pulled her mouth to mine. My knee pushed between hers and we lay entwined. "What I know without doubt, is that with you by my side, I can face any challenge, any obstacle."

"No matter what you decide, I will always be there. I love you."

I pulled her close, inhaling the fragrant scent of her hair, and touched my chin softly to the top of her head. I savored the feeling of her closeness, the feel of her breath on my neck, and I felt comfort.

Yule is a time for celebration. A time to honor our ancestors and our gods. A time to feast, to drink, to laugh, and to love. A time to exchange gifts, tell stories, and renew the oaths of loyalty we give to our leaders. Oaths are a serious matter. We are bound by honor to uphold our oaths. They are a sacred covenant that binds us together as one people. Those that offer their oaths, promise to assemble when called, to follow their leader into battle, and to give their lives to protect that leader if necessary. They swear to provide tribute to the leader, in the form of grain and livestock to store against difficult times. In return, the one who receives those oaths promises to protect the oath-givers. He promises to lead them wisely, and not sacrifice their lives needlessly in battle. He pledges to provide protection for their farms and their families and rewards their loyal service with gold or silver. He is the bread-giver. The gold-giver.

The tribe had never had a single leader. Not in times of peace, anyway. We used to live near the sea, in many villages, farms, and homesteads spread out across the north of the Jutland peninsula. Each clan or village had a headman, a hunno, who held his position through personal reputation, usually through a family line. My father had been hunno, as was his father, and his father before him. But if a son were not fit to be hunno, another could be chosen.

In times of crisis, the hunnos gathered and elected a chieftain who would lead the whole tribe. My father had been elected chieftain when we were struck by a great flood that devastated our homeland. The elders had decided that our only choice was to leave. To seek out a new land, where we could rebuild our houses, raise our children, till our fields, and regain our strength and our pride.

That first winter we had suffered, but we survived with the help of neighboring tribes, the Teutones and the Ambrones, who gave us food, clothing, tools, and other necessities that had been lost.

Our people were defeated. Homeless. We walked with heads bowed and shoulders sagging, wallowing in sorrow, with the knowledge that anywhere else was better than where we had been. We could not stay long in one place because the competition for food and other resources always threatened those that already lived there, and that led to conflict, and during that difficult time we did not want war.

My father led us southward in search of the Scordisci, a tribe that had been allies in the distant past. One day, early in our journey, my sister and my aunt were swept away in a wild river. I was a foolish young man, and though I could not swim well, I tried to save them and nearly drowned myself. My aunt Nilda managed to push Hilgi to shore but lost her life in the effort. When I managed to pull myself out of the river, I coughed up the sickness that had afflicted me since I was a child. From that day I grew stronger. I gained a reputation as a warrior and a war leader. When a plague took the lives of a third of our people, including my parents, I became hunno of my clan, and later, the entire tribe elected me as their chieftain.

Our journey began twelve years ago, and in the years since, we have traveled far. We fought the Boii in the dark northern forests, the Celtic Scordisci on the plains of Pannonia, the Taurisci in the mountains of Noricum, and the tribes of Raetia along the great Danubius River. We pushed the Suebi confederation beyond the Rhenus River back into Germania, and we conquered several different tribes in Gaul. We confronted Rome several times, and under my father's leadership, we defeated them at Siscia and again at Stobi in distant Macedonia. I had led our people against Consul Carbo at Noreia and Consul Silanus in Rome's own province of Gallia Narbonensis, each time defeating them decisively.

The assembly had accepted me as king, though they weren't given much choice. Now I sat again in the great chair, wearing the horned bronze ceremonial helmet that we had taken from Manching. When I first saw the helmet, I fell to my knees, for I recognized it as the helmet worn by the draugar that had appeared in my dreams, and I knew that the spirit's prophecy that I would one day be king was true. As my thoughts returned to those dreams, I remembered that the draugar also possessed flaming red hair, much like my own, and I felt a sliver of apprehension when I considered what that might mean.

I shook off my reverie when Eldric's words intruded on my thoughts.

"In the past, our chieftain was elected each year. Today you will swear an oath of loyalty to the king for life! Today, Borrix, son of Haistulf, chieftain of the Cimbri and leader of the northern alliance, descendant of Wodan the sky god, blessed by Donar the storm god, and known to his enemies as the Red Wolf shall accept your oath, and return his own to you.

"I will recite the oath, and you shall repeat it with me, then each of you will come forward, place your hands upon the sacred bull which represents our wealth and power, and swear to honor this oath."

Eldric surveyed the room, his eyes challenging anyone who might resist.

"I swear by the all-father, my unquestioning loyalty to my king," he began, then paused to allow the gathering to repeat his words. "I vow to support him in peace, and to fight beside him in war. With sword and spear I will defeat his enemies; with shield I shall defend his life. If my king should die in battle, I shall not quit the field until I have avenged him, even unto my own death. I shall honor this oath from this day until my last. I swear this by Wodan, and by everything I hold dear."

However reluctant, every one of my followers lined up to place their hands upon the bull and swear their loyalty. When the last had passed, I rose from my seat and placed my own hands upon the bull.

"Let the gods bear witness that I, Borrix, the Red Wolf, first king of the Cimbri, and leader of the northern alliance, accept these oaths of loyalty. I vow to defend and support these men and their people. They shall always be welcome at my hearth, to partake in meat, bread, and drink. Those that break their oath shall be judged and punished by my hand, as the instrument of the gods. Know by these oaths to each other, that we are forever joined as one people by this sacred covenant."

CHAPTER THREE

Aduatuca

January 108 BC

I had failed my people.

At least, that is what I felt on this day. I still suffered with the guilt that I had not been able to end the curse that forced them to wander endlessly. I knew that they wanted a land to call their own, still, many had grown to love the life of the wanderer. We had become good at it. We had become strong. Other nations feared us, many hated us, but everyone respected our power. Even the arrogant Romans whispered in dread of the Cimbri, wondering when we would press our advantage and cross into Italy to ravage their soft and fertile lands.

There was a time that I thought Italy was the answer. But now I was not sure. The curse prevented us from crossing the Alps and entering Italy uninvited. I had tried several times to enter an alliance with Rome, offering our strength in return for land, but each time they had refused. Not only had they refused, but then they betrayed us. Attacked us after agreeing to go our separate ways. I had learned that Romans were not to be trusted.

Only Vallus, my friend who had been my father's friend, was a Roman who had proven that his word was his honor. An Etruscan by birth, he had served in Rome's armies and witnessed the corruption that rotted the Republic from the inside out. He traveled between our two worlds and brought us word of what transpired within the marbled walls of the eternal city. I knew of course that he also shared news of us with the others that he spoke to, but that served to my advantage. His tales of our ways and our wars brought fear into their homes, and I wanted the people of Rome to fear us, because I believed if they feared us, perhaps their leaders would one day see the folly in resisting us. Perhaps the people would convince their senate to offer us the land we requested in return for peace.

But in the meantime, we must continue to move every summer to avoid Njoror's deadly curse that still hangs above our heads like a boulder at the edge of a cliff, waiting to tumble down and crush what lay below.

Those that had been left behind to build Aduatuca seemed to have escaped the gaze of that vengeful god, for now. They had prospered, growing our cattle herd, and for the most part had gotten along with their Belgae neighbors, but I had a notion that was due to those neighbors' fear of our return. There were those among us that saw this, and there was talk of more people staying behind. Many were tired of their life of wandering, and they wanted to put down roots. But I worried that if we tempted fate, we would be risking another disaster even worse than the ones we had already faced.

I had been out walking alone under a clear sky, the sun warm upon my back, when I found myself before the grove where lived the priestesses that communed with the gods and spoke their words to us. My wandering thoughts led me to realize I needed guidance. I needed to visit Hilgi, my sister who had become a seer. The priestesses were special. They had never lain with a man, for that would steal their power. The only men they tolerated were gods; Wodan, king of the gods, and Donar, his son, the god of storm, who came to them in visions and offered their wisdom.

The sisters were all old and ugly, but Skyld, the head priestess, seemed older than the gods themselves. I remembered my fear of her as a boy, and she was old then. Her wrinkled skin was like boiled leather, with deep creases across her forehead. The cracked lines around her eyes looked like a spider's web and deep folds on her cheeks ran down to lips that were sunken inward over empty gums. Her veiled eyes were hard, even cruel, but they contained a wisdom that added authority to her words. "What is it you seek?" she asked in her knowing way, followed by a cackling laugh that grated my ears like that of a sharpening stone rasping down the length of my sword.

"I wish to speak with my sister," I said. My father had taught me to control my emotions, but I could never conceal my revulsion in her presence.

Her dirty white shift hung in tatters off her skeletal frame and the odor of her body crossed the distance between us.

"You have not come to us for some time," she said in her croaking voice. "I had assumed you knew all that you needed to know," she chided me.

"My apologies priestess," I said, inclining my head. "My responsibilities leave little time for anything else."

"No time for the gods, eh? Perhaps if you thought more of them and less of your own concerns your troubles might lessen. You only come to us when you doubt yourself. The gods don't bother with solving the problems of men, they only watch us for their amusement. If you want their help, they require sacrifice. They have granted you strength, and you have acquired much wealth and power. When was the last time you honored the gods with a sacrifice? They don't require your love, only your respect, and they certainly don't abide by weakness. The prayers you send to them are only words. They watch your deeds. They are pleased with the enemies you have sent to the underworld, but they require more from you," she sneered. "Go to your sister," she pointed toward the familiar tent that Hilgi occupied.

As I pushed the flap aside, I paused, remembering the overpowering smell from the last time I was here. Like before, Hilgi sat cross legged before a small fire, rocking back and forth, and mumbling to herself. She hadn't changed. Her hair was a tangled mess, soot smudged her face and arms, and grime was caked under her long fingernails. I sat before her and waited quietly.

"You are troubled, my brother?" she asked, continuing the swaying motion.

It always unnerved me how my blind sister could know that it was me who sat before her, as if I was expected. I had not even known that I was coming here until I arrived. "I have prayed to the gods for guidance, and they have not answered me," I told her. "I believe they are angry with me. Skyld told me that a sacrifice is due, and I will make that happen, but still, what does the future hold for us? Surely our people are not meant to wander the world forever?"

"Skyld is correct, but it is not our gods you have angered. We live now in the land of the Belgae. Many of your followers are Gauls. You have offended their god, Lugos, the three-faced god. It is he that troubles you."

"I follow our gods," I said defensively. "What do I care for a god who cannot protect his own people."

"The three-faced god is powerful," Hilgi said. "Have you grown so arrogant that you can anger a god, even one that is not yours, without fear of consequence? You of all people should want to avoid that. He has watched you kill many of his people, destroy their altars to him, and steal their gold. He is torn because many of his followers now follow you. This is why you are troubled, why you cannot sleep. Lugos requires a sacrifice to make things right. There is a temple to Lugos high atop a mountain a day's ride west of Lugudunon, near where you defeated Silanus. You must go there and offer a sacrifice to Lugos."

How she knew where I defeated Silanus, I did not know. She was blind and had stayed with the caravan while the warriors pursued the Romans south into Gallia Narbonensis last summer.

"What kind of sacrifice?" I asked.

"That is for you to determine," she replied. "But know this, Lugos is a god of three; he has three faces, three penises, and he was born one of three brothers. Three is a sacred number for him. Do well and you shall have his blessing. Do not, and more suffering will befall our people."

I was silent for a moment. "When must this be done?"

"The ceremony must take place during the three days prior to the third new moon of the year. One sacrifice each day, and on the third day of the new moon, you will receive your sign. Take only Eldric the priest and Aldric the bard with you, to form a party of three. Do this, then seek his guidance, and a way shall be revealed."

CHAPTER FOUR

February 108 BC

The sky cleared sometime during the night and the howling blizzard that blanketed the roads with new snow finally blew itself out. The temperature had dropped sharply, and each breath exploded into a white cloud. This weather was not fit for men or beast to be traveling, but to fulfill Hilgi's vision we must get to the mountain by the end of *Hrethmonath*, and I must make the sacrifice by the light of the third full moon of the year.

I threw a thick sheepskin across my horse's back to protect his skin and keep my arse warm. Frida handed me a burlap sack stuffed full of bread, cheese, and dried meat. I tied it to a bundle of bedding and extra furs with a thick leather strap and slung them across his withers.

Eldric the priest and my friend Aldric walked up leading their horses. Aldric had saved my life once. He was a wanderer, and a bard, who recited poems and sang songs of mighty warriors and great battles. He had taken it upon himself to accompany us and to record our story. Frida looked up at me, her eyes liquid in the early morning light. We had talked late into the night, made love, and talked more. There was nothing left to be said. We had parted ways many times, and we knew the dangers of the coming journey. She took a quick step forward and buried her face in my chest, her arms circling my waist. I enveloped her in my heavy bear cloak. I stroked her chestnut hair and chuckled as I plucked a single silver hair that had appeared.

She yelped and slapped my chest and pulled back. "That's because of you, you know. I'll be as white-haired as Skyld soon."

"And I will love you the same," I promised.

Our seven-year-old son, Lingulf, bolted from the doorway and forced his way between us. "Take me with you father? Please?"

I remembered the words of my father when we left our home at Borremose, and I had wished to ride with his scouts. "You cannot come."

Lingulf's face fell.

"I need you to stay here and take care of your mother. I will be gone for several months, and you are the man of our family until I return. Soon, your uncle Hrolf will begin your warrior training. I expect that you will make me proud."

He beamed. "I will father!" He hugged my leg and ran back into our home.

Frida smiled and stood on her toes to give me a kiss. "Come back to me," she whispered, then added, "without any new scars."

I lifted a shoulder, and a wry smile played at the corner of my lips. "I'll be back before it's time to move on."

I vaulted onto my horse and took up the reins. Nodding at my companions, we mounted and turned our faces south.

"I don't know why you need me to accompany you," Eldric whined, shrunken so far down into his furs it looked like his head was missing. "It's none of our gods you are praying to, and I'm certainly no warrior."

"Cheer up, priest," Aldric said with a chuckle. "We're heading south, it'll be warmer down there."

Eldric's further complaints were lost in the folds of his clothes.

"How long do you expect?" Aldric asked me, his long gray braids swaying on his chest with the rhythm of his horse's steps.

"A month there, maybe a bit more. We must be there in time for the full moon."

Aldric whistled. "Well, a bit of adventure is never a bad thing, especially in the dead of winter. I was getting bored. At least sensible folks will be sitting beside a warm fire and not out looking for the barbarian king that has conquered many of them."

"We'll travel mostly at night to avoid any people, and we won't be going near any settlements, so we'll have to live off the land and use what we brought with us sparingly."

The two laughed at more muffled complaints from the high priest.

For the first week our journey was uneventful. We kept to the hills, away from the waterways where the villages lay, traveling through wooded valleys where we were less exposed. Several times we came uncomfortably close to a hilltop fortress, but the weather had turned nasty again and no one was willing to venture forth to investigate three wanderers in the frigid darkness.

We paused to rest on the morning of the ninth day, building a small fire on the lee side of a rocky hill. Eldric sat by the fire, miserably poking it with a twig and trying to coax more heat out of the feeble flames.

"Don't make it too big," I warned. "We're nearing more populated areas, and we don't want the attention."

"I'm tired of being cold," Eldric whined.

"We all are," snapped Aldric. "If we are found, you'll never be cold again."

"The bread is gone," the priest continued.

"We need a rest," I said. "This is as good a place as any. We'll stay here today and leave tomorrow at dark. You two get a shelter set up and collect some firewood. Take care of the horses. I'll look around and see if I can come up with something fresh to eat."

The snow here was not as deep as when we left home, and the wind had scoured the rocks clean in some places, but it wasn't long before I crossed the trail of a wild boar. It seemed to be wandering aimlessly and from time to time I found a spot of blood. After tracking the animal for a while, I topped a rise, carefully edging over the crest. Below me the boar laid in a patch of snow, panting, its chest moving rapidly up and down. It barely had the strength to hold up its head; an old boar that had seen better years. Perhaps it had found its match and been bested by a younger male fighting over a potential mate. Whatever the reason, this boar was weak and would be an easy kill.

I began to circle toward a better position from which to reach the boar when I heard a snarl. I whipped around to face an unseen danger and just a few yards away I saw a large red wolf, crouched down, it's bared fangs warning off whoever might think to take his prize.

"Hello brother," I whispered, thinking of Skoll, the wolf I had raised from a pup. "Let's not fight today, there's enough meat here for both of us." The wolf continued to growl. There was no mistaking its warning, yet it did not attack.

It was then that I noticed a red patch on its flank and realized that the wolf and the boar had injured each other in their own desperate fight for survival. The wolf moved, favoring its side, and I could see a long gash in its belly. "So, you are dying as well," I said. "You have killed each other. Very well then, I can wait." I made myself comfortable and after a time, the wolf relaxed and laid down, watching me warily. The boar's head now laid on the snow and only a very slight movement of his chest signaled that he still lived.

The wolf had circled several times to pack down its bed, gingerly lying down on its side. He was quiet now. After a few more moments, I heard the boar give its final breath, and when I looked back at the wolf, it lay fully down on the snow, its head lolled in death's repose. The two mortal enemies had died within moments of each other and in doing so had provided meat for me and my companions. I took the wolf's hide and butchered the boar, taking what I could carry back to our camp.

"Meat," I said, walking up to the fire and lowering my burden.

Eldric's eyes went wide. "Praise the gods."

Aldric immediately prepared three large cuts, spitted them on a branch and hung the bloody meat over the fire. The smell of meat roasting set our stomachs to growling loudly and I retold the story of the wolf and the boar.

"It is a sign," Eldric said.

"But of what?"

"You are the Red Wolf. The boar is a symbol of the Celts. It means that if we continue to fight each other, we will kill each other off."

Aldric frowned. "Isn't the wolf also the symbol of Rome? What if it means that Rome and the Celts will destroy each other and leave the spoils for Borrix to pick up like he picked up the hide and the meat?"

Unhappy with the challenge to his interpretation, Eldric fixed Aldric with an angry stare. "You are a Celt, are you not? Perhaps you want to confuse the issue."

"He is a Celt, but not a Gaulish Celt," I interjected. "Aldric comes from east of the Rhenus River. The Gauls are Celts that settled west of the river. You know very well he has been beside us for years while we have fought German, Gaul, and Roman. He saved my life when he could have left me to die and has fought beside me ever since."

Eldric's sullen expression relaxed.

"German, Gaul, Celt; we all come from the same people through the mists of time," I continued. "My father told of how our ancestors fought under Brennus as Celts. When Brennus died, the great alliance that invaded Grecia broke up and went in many different directions. Vallus says some went back to the east and founded a land called Galatia. Others, like us, went north and settled in Germania, and still more continued west and eventually crossed the Rhenus and now live in what we call Gaul."

"Then why do we fight each other," Aldric asked.

"Why does anyone fight? To survive."

I pondered the meaning of the wolf and the boar and in the end decided that if it was a sign, it wasn't a very clear one. The next night we continued our journey under a bright half-moon, avoiding the settlements and steadings. We ate well on the boar for several days, and when I began to recognize landmarks that told me we were nearing our destination we paused again. This time we left at daylight, the better to recognize where we were. Late in the day we came across an isolated steading with a stout fence. Smoke rose from the thatch roof of a longhouse and a cow bellowed from somewhere inside the wall. The sound of an axe splitting wood carried to us on a slight breeze.

"Perhaps they have some bread we can purchase," suggested Eldric.

"Do you think it's safe to approach them?" Aldric asked.

"There can't be more than a few men here. I think we'll be fine. Hail the house!" I announced our presence.

After a moment, a man appeared at the open gate. He peered at us suspiciously for a few moments, an axe in his hand. "Who's there?" he called.

"Three pilgrims. We travel to the temple of Lugos to offer a sacrifice. We can pay and we have some boar meat to share if you can spare a warm bed for the night."

The man paused for a few more seconds before replying. "Come. You can eat at my table and sleep in the barn. I put down clean straw just today."

"Our thanks," I told him.

He nodded. "Put your horses in the barn and come inside when you are ready," he said, accepting the remaining haunch of boar meat. He took note of our weapons and clothing, and I could see his doubt, but he said nothing.

When we entered the house, the man sat at the head of a table set for eight people and a woman busied herself at the hearth behind him. Three young men stood along the far wall, large strapping boys who each held a weapon; the axe we saw before, a sickle, and a vicious looking club. They each carried the blonde hair and sharp features of the man at the table.

"Leave your weapons beside the door," the man instructed us.

This was the custom when entering another man's home and we did as we were asked. The boys visibly relaxed and at a signal from their father came forward and sat at the table. A woman who I assumed was his wife appeared with a mug of ale for each of us.

"My name is Aidan. This is my wife, Briana, and my sons Eppo, Atesus, and Catu. Who might you be?"

"As I said earlier, we are pilgrims from the north, on our way to the temple of Lugos. I am Hrolf and these are my friends Eldric and Aldric." I didn't offer my real name. "We wish to make an offering and to ask for his blessings in the coming year."

"Hmmph. You'll need it," he said. He was staring at my eye patch and the scar on my forehead and red hair. I could see the light of recognition behind his eyes. "What with the wars that have been ravaging the land lately. Between the Suebi crossing the Rhenus, the Romans, and the migrating tribes there hasn't been a moment of peace for years. I'm just a poor farmer trying to keep my family alive and my farm from being burned to the ground amidst all this chaos.

"Just last year the Romans made an incursion that was stopped by a northern tribe; the Cimbri, I believe. Word is that they have been wandering for years. I heard that they were the ones that pushed the Suebi back across the Rhenus a couple of years ago. I've no use for Romans, and even less for Suebi invaders, so as long as they leave me alone, I've got no fight with the Cimbri," he said, lifting an eyebrow toward me. He popped a chunk of still hot bread slathered in butter into his mouth.

His wife set a platter of vegetables on the table before us and went back for the boar that she had roasted. Elbows started flying as the boys dove for the meat and bowls of vegetables.

"Stop!" Aidan shouted. The boys froze. "Our guests will eat first."

I nodded my thanks and my companions and I filled our trenchers.

"Your wife is a fine cook," Aldric said, sitting back and patting his stomach.

"You mentioned payment?" Aiden reminded me.

"Yes, of course," I pushed a few gold coins across the table, and he picked them up. He looked at them curiously.

"Roman," I said. He pocketed them and said no more.

"For this you'll have some bread and apples to take with you. I have some dried beef as well. Come in when its light and there will be something for breakfast."

"My thanks," I replied. "I would also appreciate your discretion."

"No one will hear from us of your passing."

"Can you tell me how far to the temple?"

"Four more days south."

Eldric groaned audibly which brought a smile from everyone.

"Ah, then we'll be off to bed. Again, my thanks."

Before long, the crest of a large conical hill appeared on the horizon, and we adjusted our course toward it. The sun shone brightly in a clear sky and the weather had warmed enough that my bearskin cloak rested behind me across my horse's flanks. I was comfortable in a light tunic. Even Eldric wore only one layer of clothing to better feel the warmth of the sun.

As we neared, we could see tall poles with tattered flags fluttering in the wind at the top of the hill. The track we followed turned into a well-used path, and then a road as more and more paths converged toward the temple. Small roadside altars appeared here and there piled high with offerings from pilgrims. We passed several small groups of people who had come to give thanks for the end of another long winter. We had arrived in time, and we camped at the foot of the hill to prepare.

Eldric scrunched up his face, his eyes smarting from the campfire's smoke that had drifted toward him. "Why does it always seem that the smoke is in my face?"

Aldric smiled and shook his head, choosing not to reply.

Eldric held his breath, puffing out his cheeks and waiting for the smoke to change direction. "Cursed smoke," he choked out when he could wait no longer. He moved to another spot. "Ah," he said, "that's better, at least I can breathe now. Borrix, why do you think I am here?" Eldric wondered.

"I honestly don't know," I answered. "Hilgi said to take the priest and the bard and said I must make three sacrifices over three days to receive a sign. She didn't say why. Maybe that is for you to determine."

Aldric sat on the ground with his hands clasped around his knees. "Perhaps it is to bless the sacrifices and show cooperation between your gods and Lugos," he offered. "As for me, I assume it is to record what happens like I have done since I began travelling with you. Over the years, you've all given me much to work with," Aldric said with a sideways look at Eldric, who coughed and wiped his weeping eyes from the smoke which had made its way back to him.

"Damn it!" the priest exclaimed, standing up sharply and backing away from the fire.

Borrix glanced at him without expression. "In four days, it will be *Hrethmonath*. Tomorrow, we begin the sacrifices. One sacrifice to Lugos each day, and on the third day of the new moon, we are to seek his guidance, 'and a way shall be revealed,' she said."

The next morning, we ascended the heights and approached the makeshift temple. Aldric and Eldric stayed back as I walked gingerly to the outer edge of the caldera. The ground dropped away steeply for hundreds of feet into the valley below me. A series of domed hills stretched into the distance forming a curved line. I turned back to the shrine and my companions.

The flags flapped noisily atop long, skinny poles that bobbed with the wind gusts. Several small wooden structures held votives and offerings to Lugos and many were blown over or scattered on the ground. A large wooden image of Lugos stood near the edge of the crater.

Eldric had prepared a small ceremony to bless today's sacrifice and when it was complete Aldric passed me the three burlap pouches.

I had learned that the three faces of Lugos represented the past, present, and future. I chose one of them, hoping I was correct, and addressed the god directly. "Great Lugos, I am here to give you honor and ask for your forgiveness for the harm I have caused your people. Know that it was only done to help my own people and hear my oath. From this day forward, I will do my best to avoid conflict with the Gauls. I will only defend my people and fight the Romans who are our common enemy. To secure my oath, I give you these three bags of gold." I threw each bag into the caldera of the dormant volcano, and then we descended to camp.

We returned to the mount the next two mornings and repeated my oath each time, substituting the gold for "three bags of sling stones with which to slay your enemies" and "three pouches of poppy leaves with which to quench the bloodthirst of your flaming spear, Slaughterer."

When all was completed as I had been instructed by Hilgi, we waited. My mind was preoccupied during the following days, and I slept restlessly as we waited for a sign. Finally, Eldric prepared a drink to help me sleep. That night I fell into a deep sleep and into my slumber came a vision of Lugos, the three faced god. He appeared as a tall, fair haired young man, athletic and strong.

"Why have you disturbed me, chieftain of the Cimbri?" The three-faced god demanded.

"I fear that I have offended you," I said. "It is my hope to appease you and ask for your guidance."

"You have caused much heartache amongst the Gauls," the disembodied voice accused angrily. "You have invaded their lands and killed my people." The head turned suddenly, revealing a second face that I believe represented the present. The voice sounded more reasonable. "But every god respects strength, and though it has been used against my people, you have shown the strength of the gods. At times, the Gauls have benefited from your strength, and at others they have suffered. I accept your sacrifice, and your oath, and I charge you with a task." The head spun again, to the third face, which somehow I knew spoke of the future. "Join my people in their effort to rid themselves of these Romans, and your transgressions will be forgiven."

CHAPTER FIVE

Gaul

April 108 BC

Frida woke with a start. In the darkness, the panic constricted her chest so that she could hardly breathe. "Borr!" she cried out, waking Lingulf who slept beside her.

"What is it, Mama?" the boy asked, fear tinting his own voice.

Frida gasped for air and her rapidly beating heart slowly returned to normal. "It's alright," she reassured him. "Just a bad dream. Go back to sleep." She stroked his hair and lay back down with her arm around her son. She wiped her sweating brow with the sleeve of her shift as she lay sleepless, waiting until Lingulf's breathing indicated he was asleep again. Carefully she removed her arm, rose from the sleeping pallet, and walked to the door.

"Where are you?" she whispered, looking up at the stars.

I stood at the edge of our camp; my cloak settled warmly on my shoulders. I had awakened in the night with a strange foreboding and could not stop thinking about my family. The sliver of a crescent moon shone brightly in the abyssal sky high above while the first hints of color lightened the eastern horizon, turning it from an unfathomable black, to a dark blue, to a lighter gray. The coming light revealed indigo clouds stretched in a thin line just above the treetops. Scattered thunderheads floated in the distance.

"Wake up," I nudged Aldric and Eldric with my foot. "We need to get moving."

Aldric was instantly awake, coming from his bedding with a swirl, while Eldric burrowed deeper into his, covering his face and muttering something unintelligible.

"Get up," Aldric repeated, whipping Eldric's coverings, and dumping the poor priest onto the cold ground.

Everyone ate some of the dried meat while we packed, and we were soon ready to depart. The sun now climbed above the treetops, shooting its warming rays across the small valley where we camped.

When it did, I caught the shine of metal at the base of the tree line across the valley. "Stop moving," I said, pointing. We were on the east side of the valley, still in the shadow of the trees behind us, and as we watched more pinpoints of light indicated a small force of armored men moving about. Then a flash of bright red when a cloak was slung about a shoulder.

"Romans," I whispered urgently. "Slowly now, walk the horses into the trees behind us, quietly." Our supper fire had burned out and if we had rekindled it, we would have been discovered. I sent a quick prayer of thanks to Donar and asked for his protection while I fingered the necklace of boar tusks I now wore around my neck.

We faded into the trees without notice and once safely away from the clearing we mounted and hurried away, circling around to the north.

Throughout the day we nearly ran into several more Roman patrols. "We've got to gain some distance away from the border. For some reason, the Romans are more active than normal."

"Why are there so many patrols?" Aldric wondered aloud.

"I don't know. That farmer mentioned the Romans and Suebi were on the move again, or perhaps he decided to betray us after all and sent word to the garrison in Lugudunon. He obviously recognized me. But it doesn't matter right now. We just need to get through these patrols unseen and be on our way."

A sudden shout interrupted our conversation, when a pair of Roman scouts burst from the trees behind Aldric, urging their horses forward into the attack. One of them drove a short spear through Aldric's back and continued on. He drew his spatha and charged at Eldric. The priest panicked and tried to turn his horse to run, which caused his attacker to miss and his horse to stumble, throwing its rider clear and head-first into a tree. The fall stunned him and broke his shoulder with a loud crack. The second attacker came for me, but I was ready. I knocked his sword aside and chopped into his lower back when he passed, causing him to lose his seat. I dismounted and hurried over to finish the job, driving my sword down through the hollow in his throat, then dispatched the one that had wounded Aldric.

My chest heaved from the sudden exertion. I looked about and saw that the battle was over, then hurried to Aldric who still sat on his horse. "It's bad," he said weakly, trying to stem the flow of blood that spilled around the iron head of the spear that protruded from his belly.

I reached to grasp him around the waist and help him to the ground, but he waved me off. "I'm not going to make it, Borrix. There's nothing you can do. If you pull it out, I'll bleed out within minutes. Get your horses and let's get away from here as quickly as possible, they will be on our trail when they find these two."

We traveled the rest of the day to make distance from the ambush. Eldric prayed over Aldric at every opportunity, and I tried to keep a pace that he could manage, but he weakened with every mile. Just before dusk I heard a thump behind me and looked back to find Aldric lying on the ground. I rushed to his side to find him dead. "I'm sorry old friend. We don't have the time to properly mourn you," I said, and closed his eyes. Eldric said a quick prayer over his body, and we continued into the night.

"Lingulf, go and get some firewood, will you?" Frida asked.

"Yes, mother," the boy answered.

"I'll help," offered Vallus. The old man had wintered over in the Alpes Mountains with Divico, king of the Helvetii, and had arrived shortly after the snows had melted.

Frida smiled, watching them walk out the door. Vallus had been a family friend since Borr was Lingulf's age, and the boy thought of him as a grandfather. Vallus wandered about in the guise of a trader, but his real trade was information. He didn't work for anyone in particular, and he freely told what he had learned to any who asked and fed him a good meal. Vallus was granted safe travel in most lands as everyone had a thirst for news, and Vallus gave away no great secrets.

This spring he had brought the news that Divico and his people were becoming restless again. They had taken much gold and plunder during their first campaign with the Cimbri and planned another move westward that would cross the whole of Gaul, all the way to the Oceanus Atlanticus. Roman incursions had become more frequent, and they felt the need to push them back south of the border of Gallia Narbonensis.

"Divico will take his people, along with any others that wish to join him to attack the frontiers. Teutobod has not decided yet, but it is my opinion that he will join them," he had told Hrolf. "Do you think that Borr, pardon me, Borrix, will join them?"

"He has not discussed where we will journey this summer. He

has been gone for more than a month on a personal journey. We expect him home soon, and then we will begin planning our next move."

Vallus passed the time enjoying Frida's hospitality and teaching Lingulf the lessons that he had taught Borrix. How to read and write Latin, some Greek, geography, history, and some philosophy. Like Borrix, Lingulf took to the lessons. He had a curious mind, and he grasped the unfamiliar concepts quickly, though his friends were constantly trying to pull him away to play.

Hrolf had begun Lingulf's warrior training and had a wooden sword made for him, as well as a child's spear and shield. Hrolf taught him the ways of his people and how they fought, while Vallus showed him the ways of the Romans.

We had left the Roman patrols behind, but now the countryside fairly crawled with Gauls. We had taken back to traveling at night to avoid them and only lit a small fire when necessary and put it out when it had served its purpose.

"Will we make it back alive?" Eldric asked, worry etched deeply in the lines of his face.

"I'll let you know when we get there," I growled. "I don't know what's got the country on edge. But if we make it back, I've decided we'll be going west this summer to avoid this hornet's nest someone has kicked up. We've seen Romans, Gauls, Celts, and Germans moving about. It's a wonder that we've only run into the two that killed Aldric."

The further north we went, the quieter things became as we entered friendly territory. We cut the young green shoots of the bulrushes and collected the tender new plantain and dandelion leaves to eat. Our dried meat had run out and we avoided hunting or making fires. Eldric proved particularly useful with his extensive knowledge of the spring mushrooms and finally, after weeks of eating little and avoiding contact with roving patrols and war parties, we spotted the smoke from Aduatuca rising into the gray sky of an overcast day.

When I walked into my hall, Frida looked up unconcernedly, then back to the hearth where she was tending a pot of stew. With sudden realization, she jumped up and ran to me. The wooden spoon she was using to stir the stew clattered into the fire and was forgotten. "Borr!" she called, weeping into my shoulder. "I was so worried. Are you well?"

I sniffed the stew with anticipation. "Yes, just hungry," I said.

Lingulf ran in the entrance to tell his mother something and stopped abruptly when he saw me. He ran forward and hugged my leg. "Father!"

"Let me see you, boy," I held him back so I could look at him. "I go away for a couple of months, and you've grown like a spring weed. Run and get your uncle Hrolf, we must talk."

Frida handed me a steaming bowl of stew with a large piece of course bread. "Mmmph," I moaned, taking in the wonderful smell. I began shoveling it in and sucking air around the hot stew as it burned my tongue. I savored the flavors of stewed meat, spring garlic and onion, and freshly dug roots.

"Slow down," she giggled. "There's plenty."

When Hrolf arrived, Vallus and Ansgar trailed behind. I told them all of our journey home and of Aldric's death, and I called for an assembly in three days.

CHAPTER SIX

June 108 BC

The sea wind whipped my hair while I stood gazing at the white cliffs of Britannia that rose from the water in the distance like the walls of a huge fortress that defended the island. Gray clouds hovered above the far-off cliffs and streaks of rain reached to the ground farther inland, yet the cliffs shone brightly, reflecting the midday sun.

The sky was clear and blue above my head. I closed my eyes and let the smell of saltwater and rotting seaweed take me back to my boyhood home in Jutland. There we lived in our fortress of Borremose, near the sandy reaches of the Limsfjord and the ever-changing barrier islands that defended our western coast from the sea's relentless waves. Where we plucked amber from the sand to exchange with the traders that came north, boiled the seawater to make salt, and smoked endless racks of herring and cod.

My life was good there. I was happy. The only son of the local hunno, I held a certain amount of privilege, even though our people set more stock in ability than position. When I was a boy, I was limited in my physical ability, and I never expected to take my father's place. I had nearly drowned in the sea as a child and from that day on I was sickly and weak. But my weakness of body was compensated by a curious mind, and my father encouraged my learning.

But I could never have dreamed what we were to endure at the hands of a jealous god. The day came that Njoror, god of the sea, sent the storm that destroyed our people. Homes were obliterated, food stores ruined. Thousands were killed. Our elders decided that our future lay elsewhere, and my father led us away as we turned our backs forever on our homeland. Since then, we had trekked countless leagues across the raging rivers and towering mountains of an untamed wilderness.

We fought many battles along our journey; against other Germanic tribes, Celts, Gauls, and Romans. We defeated them all. Yet, the curse of Njoror kept us from taking advantage of those victories. Until the curse was lifted, we could not remain in any land. We must always continue our quest; always move on, no matter how tempted we were to settle. It seemed that some of our alliance had succeeded in establishing a colony by adopting a new name and separating from our tribe. Time would tell if they would continue to avoid the curse.

Riding on the rolling swells a puffin dove, and after a few moments surfaced with three sand lances clutched in its mouth. It beat the water with its powerful wings, moving forward and gaining momentum until it was able to lift its feet and run on top of the water. After a few more strokes it was airborne. Without warning, a large brown skua streaked after the puffin. The skua were pirates of the sky, pursuing the smaller birds and battering them with their wings until they dropped their meal to be scooped up by the attacker.

The puffin swooped and dove in a dance of survival, trying to shake off its pursuer. In a last desperate burst of speed, it reached the safety of the nesting cliffs as the skua climbed sharply away and returned to the fishing grounds to find another target. A clacking noise arose when the puffin and its mate knocked their short, bright-orange beaks together in greeting.

A cormorant flew by, exposing the white breeding plumage on its neck and thighs when it tipped its wings and turned away, gliding out over the open water. Sandpipers scurried on the beach, ebbing, and flowing with the waves that broke on the shore, then curiously hopping around on one foot. In the distance, a crowd of oystercatchers searched the beach and shallows for cockles and mussels with their long orange bill.

Several squawking seagulls floated nearly motionless as they flew into the wind until one broke away to steal a mussel from another bird on the beach. The thief flew toward a cluster of rocks where it dropped the shellfish and followed it down to pull the meat from the cracked shell.

All these things were happening right before me, yet I noted none of it. My mind was far away. A new thought had occurred to me. I longed to take my people beyond the long reach of Rome, beyond the reach of Njoror. Stories of Britannia had crossed the sea with sailors who claimed they had reached those far shores and were lucky enough to return with a cargo of fish and a tale they would tell for the rest of their lives. All the tribes along the northern coast knew of it, and many of the Gauls had traded with them regularly, sailing across the treacherous channel that separated us. Whole tribes had left the mainland to settle there, and many had relatives on both sides of the water, but still it remained mysterious.

But how could I do that? We had no boats. Even the boats my people had made back in Jutland were small, and never left the sight of land for fear of being lost. How could I ever hope to move the many thousands of my people and all their belongings across the sea? I couldn't. It was only a dream. Njoror had proven he could find us anywhere. Sadly, I turned around and walked back to the fire whose flames were being battered by the aggressive gusts of wind. Ansgar and Hrolf waited patiently for me, like they always did when something heavy weighed on my mind.

"So?" Hrolf questioned.

I looked at him for a moment. Hrolf had been my childhood

friend and now was my trusted deputy. "I was thinking of crossing the sea. Of perhaps escaping the curse."

"I figured as much, and what decision did you come to?"

"It cannot be done. Not with the vast numbers of our people. Many would die in the crossing, and we would be at a disadvantage landing on a strange shore defended by a hostile people defending their homes. Best to just let it go."

"There is plenty of room in Gaul for all of us," offered Ansgar. "And the Gauls are weak. We've been beating them for two years now; they cannot stand against us."

"They aren't weak, they just haven't banded together. We are too many for them to resist one tribe at a time. If they ever make an alliance with each other, it would be much more difficult – besides, I made an oath. We have a new purpose; to ally with the Gauls and push out the Romans." I paused, sighing deeply. "Best that we get moving. We've much land to cover. Let's get them moving again in the morning." I turned away, glancing a final time at those white cliffs.

On the twentieth day of our march along the northern coast we left the land of the Belgae and entered Aremorica. On the western horizon, a great stone monolith slowly appeared, seeming to rise from the very ground as we neared. It towered higher than five men standing atop each other's shoulders, and in its presence, one could feel the power emanating from its rough surface. This type of stone was out of place here, but I could not imagine how men could ever have moved such a heavy object. It could only have been placed here by the gods.

"It is slowly sinking into the ground, Lord," a local man told me. "And when it finally disappears, the world will come to an end."

"What wonders we have seen on this journey," Hrolf said, staring at the great stone.

I had sent out emissaries and wherever we went, ambassadors appeared with carts of tribute, gold and food offered in return for peace. We encountered no resistance, and I had instructed my warriors to refrain from raiding. While on the march we had taken to slaughtering steers each day to cook on several large fires, rather than try to scrounge enough wood for thousands of cooking fires.

Turning south, the caravan crossed the peninsula and after another ten days of easy travel, entered the lands of the Veneti.

The Veneti were a powerful seafaring tribe that lived on a large peninsula in northwest Gaul. Even as a boy, I knew of the Veneti, who traveled the entire northern coastline to Jutland and beyond in their magnificent seagoing ships. Their merchants called at friendly trading ports from frigid Scandia to the western-most points of Hispania, and then east to the pillars of Hercules where the Roman blockade controlled their access to the warm inland waters of the Mare Nostrum. They crossed the channel to Britannia to trade coins, wine, oil, iron ingots, and luxury goods for cargoes of tin, copper, lead, and slaves with those Britons and Gauls who had emigrated from the mainland to establish a busy trading port on the southern coast of the large island. They bought amber and salt from the Cimbri when we still lived in Jutland, and carried it to Gades to trade for wine, olives, olive oil, silver, and gold. They visited the wilder tribes in the north of Britannia and on the windswept northern islands where they traded for wool, seal and otter skins, fish, and eels. The Veneti had controlled a vast trade and communication network along the northern coasts for centuries.

I remembered how we ran along the sand dunes, racing the huge oak ships that sailed along our shores, their broad leather sails bellied out to the gusting winds. With high stems and prows, they stood out of the water much taller than any other ships we knew, towering over our small fishing vessels. Sometimes one of the flat-bottomed ships would beach itself to trade and take on fresh water before the tide floated it again and they left. I remember thinking how wonderful it must be to sail beyond the horizon and look upon strange new lands. Sometimes my father would come home with iron ingots from Britannia or Hispania, the most valuable commodity that we could get to make the better-quality weapons and tools that we needed. Much better than the brittle bog-iron that we found nearby. I often went with my father. Sometimes a trader would throw in an orange or lemon or other exotic fruit that came from somewhere in the east, and I would savor the strange new flavors on the walk home.

I left the tribes encamped on a plain nearby and took a small band of warriors with me to meet the Veneti. Now, we descended from the inland hills toward their bustling capital city near the head of the Blavezh River. I could see beyond the impressive buildings to the busy port where several ships were under construction. Thousands of sea birds swirled and squawked among the towering masts of the trade vessels and larger warships.

A group of armed men walked up the hard packed road from the city to meet us, led by a middle-aged and slightly paunchy man in fine clothing. His robe sparkled in the sun with jewels and golden thread that were woven into the cloth and his hands were hidden inside the large sleeves.

"Welcome Borrix, king of the Cimbri," he stated grandly. He was sweating heavily and produced a snowy white cloth to wipe his brow. "You are approaching the city of Uenet, capital of the Veneti. Your coming has been foretold by your ambassadors, and you are most welcome in our lands."

I walked my horse forward to greet him. "The reputation of the Veneti reaches far, and we are merely curious. My people are camped at a respectful distance, and we only wish to pass by your city on our way southward. I was hoping that I could get a closer look at the famous ships of the Veneti that I have known from a distance since I was a boy."

His appearance and demeanor amused me, and he was obviously pleased at the compliments. "Of course! We are honored by your visit," he said with an odd tilt to his head. "My name is Zenobios Isidorus. I am head of our merchant council, and I speak for our chieftain of this grand city. If it is curiosity you suffer from, we have enough wonderful things to show you. If it pleases you, I will escort you and your men into the city and I will act as your personal guide." Zenobios bowed his bald pate in deference and turned back toward the city.

I answered with a nod and a smile and gestured for my men to dismount. Zenobios was an inquisitive type. "Everyone has heard of the Cimbri and their journey across our world, but we only hear rumor and legend. The opportunity to hear the truth from your very lips is a rarity indeed. Your people lived in Jutland some time ago, did they not, Lord?"

"We did. Twelve years ago, we suffered a great sea flood that killed many and wiped out our homes and our crops. We were forced to leave the land we had known for centuries and embark on a journey that continues to this day."

"But why not settle down?" Zenobios asked. "Certainly, you have the power to take the land that suits you, why have you not stopped wandering?"

"We did not know it at the time, but we had been cursed by Njoror, god of the sea. We can never remain in any place for more than a winter, or he rains death and destruction upon us. He has proven several times that he watches us carefully."

"So, you must forever roam," he said sadly. "Yet that is much like our own people who roam the endless waves."

"But you have a home to return to," I replied. "When we tried to return to Jutland, we found that there were other tribes that had moved into our land, and in any case, we could not stay or risk the wrath of Njoror. We have but one chance, and that is to convince Rome to invite us into their lands. If they will willingly give us a place to settle, we may be able to break the curse. But each time I have made the request, they refused, then attacked us."

"Yes, word has reached us of Rome's defeats at your hands. In fact, many of the Gauls speak of starting their own rebellions against Rome's incursions."

"There is unrest in the Gaulish tribes?" I asked, intrigued.

"Oh, yes. Not so much in the far north where we haven't seen much of them . . . yet. But anywhere Rome has its tentacles, there are those that are glad for their presence, and just as many who resent it. Trade is being monopolized by Romans and the freemen chafe under their masters. They resent the tribute that must be paid to the Roman governors, and the rules that come along with the occupation of their soldiers. Our own profit has suffered due to the Romans expansion into Gaul. Now they have access to the trade goods that we once controlled, and they block the entrance to the Mare Nostrum so that we cannot access their trading ports, yet their ships trade up the coast of Gaul as far as Burdigala. The coast from the pillars of Hercules to Burdigala is regularly patrolled by triremes and several of our ships have been confronted and run off. We are capable of staving off a motley crew of pirates, but we cannot defeat Roman warships. We are being confined to trading to the north and across to Britannia and its isles. We are not fools. It is only a matter of time before Rome comes farther north. Each new year brings a new consul, hungry for gold and power, eager to prove himself by conquering new lands. Even now we see the occasional ship pass our city probing to the north."

We passed through the city gates and entered the fortified compound where we were welcomed with a feast, music, and dancing. Zenobios introduced me to the Veneti chieftain, Advorix, and we talked more about their concerns with the Romans. We stayed for several days, feasting each evening, and talking into the long hours of the night. Advorix invited us to stay where we were now camped and offered to send us grain, fruit, mead, and ale, to supplement our diet of meat, and we agreed to provide them with five hundred head of cattle.

Zenobios escorted me to the docks where I observed the activity with interest. Large counter-weight cranes lifted heavy cargos from the bellies of the great flat-bottomed ships and deposited them on the docks. Then, workers loaded them into ox-drawn carts and wagons that made a steady stream from the docks to the warehouses that lined the wharf. Workers shouldered smaller loads and formed a line that paralleled the carts. Like an anthill, there was movement in every direction, but all was with purpose.

"Would you like to see a ship?" he asked.

"Very much," I replied.

"Have you been on one before?

"Only a fishing boat, nothing of this size."

"Come," Zenobios beckoned, and strode up the gangplank of a ship that had been unloaded.

It was a marvel that such a massive thing could float. The thick timbers, masts, and leather sails seemed too heavy. "How can they carry so much weight?" I asked, referring to the additional cargo that the ships carried.

Zenobios smiled. "Our ships have been sailing the seas for centuries, we have learned much. The oak timbers can weather the strongest storms and can even resist a battering from a warship. The flat bottoms allow us to beach them on the islands and shores where we trade and float them again with the tide."

"You've given me much to consider," I said. "I thank you for your hospitality and I accept your lord's invitation to stay in your lands for the winter."

CHAPTER SEVEN

Spring 107 BC

Over the winter, I returned to talk with the Veneti chieftain, Advorix, many times. We were often joined by Zenobios Isidorus, who asked an endless amount of questions. They both wanted to know of our journey, and I sorely missed Aldric who had composed so many poems and tales about us. It occurred to me that very little would survive my own lifetime when the memory faded, and no one was there to tell our story.

I brought Lingulf with me to listen and I tried to pass that knowledge on to him as best I could. He was a bright boy, and it was time now to begin his training to take my place one day. I made him sit in the shadows for hours and endure council meetings and less important discussions. Frida came too and became good friends with Advorix' wife. Always, our conversations turned to the incursions of the Romans. I shared what I had learned in more than ten years of fighting them, and the Veneti king and his nobles welcomed my thoughts. Like so many others in Gaul, the Veneti feared the Romans' power, but had had enough of their heavy-handed "friendship".

When we needed a change of topic, I told him of my dream of crossing the channel and taking my people away from all the war and the never-ending quest that we had endured for so long. Advorix brightened. "Would you like to sail to Britannia on one of my ships?"

I was somewhat shocked. The thought of traveling to the isle excited me, but I had never been on the ocean and my old fear of water came back with a rush. Seeing my doubt Advorix sought to reassure me. "Have no fear, our ship captains know the waters well and our ships are capable of withstanding any storm. We rarely lose a ship. In fact there is less danger in a trip like this than your wandering around Gaul," he said with a chuckle.

Still, the thought of entering Njoror's realm concerned me. "Can we father?" Lingulf pleaded. My curiosity won out, and to Lingulf's delight, I agreed. We came back in a few days and Zenobios escorted us aboard one of their impressive ships. The boarding plank was withdrawn and the ship moved gracefully away from the wharf as the practiced oarsmen turned it out into the open sea.

As the city grew smaller in the distance, we hugged the coastline, staying far enough out to avoid the treacherous shoals that guarded the tribal lands to the west. After two hours we could see the headlands of the Armorican peninsula. The horizon before us opened into a vast expanse of blue above and below. We turned northward and the wind picked up, and we watched with excitement when the ship's officers shouted their orders. The crew responded automatically to the routine of hoisting the sail, and the rowers shipped their oars. The vessel leaped forward before the wind. My long, unrestrained hair flew behind me when our forward motion overtook the wind that filled the sails. The flat-bottomed ship shivered at first when each wave slapped against its hull, but as we picked up speed it seemed to lift and skim over the waves.

Lingulf shouted for joy from the bow, waiving his arms at the dolphins that raced us just below the surface, breaking free of the water with a sudden leap and then diving effortlessly beneath the waves. The calloused sailors grinned at the boy's excitement as he ran back and forth along the rail, pointing at each one.

At mid-day of our second day of the voyage we could see Britannia in the distance. "First we will pass the headlands of the Cornovii," Zenobios told me. "They do not welcome anyone to their shores. Ships that have landed there have been captured and their goods stolen, their ships burned, and their crews murdered or enslaved. We are sailing for the land of Cymru farther north. They are savage warriors, and they don't welcome casual visitors, but trade is important to them, so our ships are welcome."

On the third day, the ship beached itself on a sandy shelf below steep cliffs, atop which sat a wooden hillfort. We were met by a contingent of fierce looking warriors, clad in animal skins, leather, and rough woolen cloaks. The poorer of them carried crude clubs and iron farm implements, while several who appeared to be a sort of nobility possessed swords, daggers, and the occasional spear. One man wore a bronze circlet on his brow, indicating he was their leader. "Who is this that accompanies you?" the leader asked Zenobios in his strange language, looking at me. Through his interpreter, Zenobios replied. "Great King Dewydd, he is a king in his own country and is merely curious to meet the leader of the mighty Cymru who he has heard so much about. His name is Borrix, king of the Cimbri."

I noticed a spark of recognition at the name. *Even here at the ends of the earth they have heard of us*, I thought.

"You are Borrix," he said matter-of-factly, nodding at his own words. "Word of your exploits has reached us from time to time," Dewydd said. "We have contacts with Gaul through the Veneti and others."

"It is my honor to meet the great King Dewydd," I said, using Zenobios' words. I held out my hand in friendship and he grasped my forearm in the way of warriors.

"Come Borrix! Let us eat and drink and tell stories while the merchants make their trades."

I beckoned Lingulf to walk beside me. I bumped him with my

elbow to remind him to close his mouth and act dignified. We sat late into the night while Dewydd regaled us with his own tales of prowess, bragging about his kingdom and its riches. But when we climbed the cliffs to the fortress, I had only witnessed a sorry thing of weathered logs, many rotted where they stuck out of the ground and repaired by rolling large rocks against their base to keep them from falling over. Inside the walls, the ancient buildings were of turf and the people who came out to stare at us with vacant eyes were dirty and disheveled.

The "Great King" it turned out was only king of a muddy patch of earth, but that patch of earth commanded the beach below which was the only place in the area that afforded a safe harbor, and thus he commanded the trade for the entire region. His people amounted to the twenty or so warriors and an equal amount of women and children that lived within the fortress, and a similar number who lived outside its walls. Zenobios told me later that every village chieftain in Cymru called himself a king.

When dawn came and the ship floated on the tide, we bade farewell to King Dewydd and continued on our way. We made several more stops with similar experiences, and when the cargo hold was filled with wool, salt, tin, slaves, and a few hunting hounds, the ship turned around and headed south. On the return trip we sailed further from the coast to make better time.

"What is that green smudge on the horizon?" Lingulf asked Zenobios, shading his eyes against the afternoon sun.

"That, dear boy, is Eire, or Hibernia as the Romans call it. It is a mostly unexplored place that is beset by wild men and even wilder beasts. One dares not approach the isle too closely for the sea serpent known as Oillipheist is known to drag whole ships beneath the waves. Some say our own ancestors travelled there centuries ago and became the inhabitants of that mysterious place, but no one goes there now."

Lingulf's eyes grew large, and he stared at the distant island.

The voyage had given me time to think. I had decided that although we could easily conquer the scattered tribes that lived in Britannia, we could never stay because of the curse. It simply wasn't a solution. Instead, I made different plans.

"I'm not sure about fighting their ships," Advorix said. "My people are not prepared for war. We are sailors and merchants. Of course we have our warriors, but all-out war?"

"I will provide all the warriors you need; you need only bring your ships. I have received word that our allies, the Tigurini, will be keeping the Romans busy this summer along the frontier. This is the perfect time to push them back from your ports."

In the spring a fleet of Veneti ships sailed south along the Armorican coast with five thousand Cimbri warriors aboard. It wasn't long before we encountered a sail on the horizon. "Roman galley!" the lookout cried, pointing toward the open sea. The Veneti's oaken ships were big and strong, their sails much larger than the smaller galley's. The fleet turned like a pack of wolves chasing a deer, and the Roman ship rapidly reversed course. He had seen us and was making an attempt to escape. It took several hours but we gradually closed on the ship. I was amazed at the speed the crews had coaxed out of the enormous vessels. The sloped bow and flat bottom of our ship struck the galley on the rear quarter as it tried to veer away. Roman faces looked on in helpless panic when their oars were shattered and their boat tipped sharply toward us, tumbling many of them into the water. Those wearing armor sank immediately beneath the waves, while many others struggled to get away from the collision.

My warriors lined the rail high above the deck of the Roman ship and cast their spears onto those below. Ropes with metal hooks were cast into the rigging of the smaller ship and men began to board. Hrolf and I were the first to put boots on the enemy deck and led the slaughter while both ships listed dangerously. The stern of the Roman ship had been pushed below the waves and was taking on water. The moans of the men whose ribs and arms had been broken from the impact of their oars when the ships collided mixed with the terrified screams of the shackled slaves who were slowly being dragged down into the water.

The battle was over in minutes and the galley sank beneath the waves, taking the dead and wounded with it. Several captives had been hoisted back to our ship as my men hastily withdrew. Our boat settled back into the water and the Veneti carpenters checked for damage. We had taken the first step in what I hoped was a new campaign that would bring the fight to Rome on the open seas.

"There can't be more than four gallies guarding the pillars of Hercules," I said.

"You don't know that for sure." Bricius was the captain of our ship and the commander of the fleet.

"We've sunk ten gallies since we began and only lost fifty men and two ships," I said.

"And the rest have flown back toward the pillars, but we don't know where they are. There could be dozens there waiting for us." He was a cautious man and was not accustomed to taking risks. He only sailed when the weather was fair and only attacked when we outnumbered the enemy by at least three to one. "It's too late in the day now to go further. We'll anchor offshore for the night and move on in the morning."

His tactics had served us well, but I was more audacious, and I wanted to follow up our success. We had rounded the northern tip of Hispania and paused to discuss our plans just offshore of the Roman settlement of Portus Cale. In the end, he agreed to sail as far as Gades to see what we found. If we ran into more than we could handle, I agreed that we would withdraw.

An orange sun settled down in the west, and bands of dark clouds seemed to rise before it. "I don't like it," Bricius said, sniffing the air. He glanced up at the pennant on top of the single mast. It had been hanging straight down in the still air and now was flapping gently toward shore. "A westerly wind. We're in for a storm." Bricius sent orders out to prepare the fleet, and our crew was immediately bustling to make the ship ready.

Several hours after dark the wind picked up abruptly. Gusts snapped the pennant out sharply and pushed waves against our hull. The ships swayed and tugged on their anchor ropes and the whitecaps grew larger and began rolling one upon the other. A jagged flash of lightning reached down from the sky and seemed to touch the water miles away.

"Njoror," I whispered to myself uneasily. My men were huddled in a cluster at the back of the deck. They lived their lives outdoors and could not bear the confining interior of the ship's hold. They, like me, were praying to Donar to be saved from the wickedness of the storm. Three flashes in quick succession this time and thunder rolled over us. It was coming closer. The light reflected the fear in the men's eyes.

A drop of rain splattered. Then two; twenty; a hundred. A sudden torrent forced by the wind drenched us and lightning flashed again, lighting up the night. Thunder crashed, vibrating in my chest. The temperature dropped suddenly, and we shivered in our wet clothes. From the darkness came the sound of splintering wood; a mast had snapped on another ship from the force of the waves and wind rocking the ship. Our ship suddenly lurched. The anchor ropes had broken, and we were being driven toward shore.

Another crash came from the night accompanied by men's screams as ships were blown into each other. We could see nothing in the blackness. When the ship came to an abrupt stop, the force threw our own mast forward and back again, tearing it from its step and ripping up decking, throwing large splinters in a deadly rain. Men were thrown overboard and into the violent surf. The ship had torn out its belly on a rocky shoal, but it was finally still. The storm blew itself out in the nights darkest hours and when the day dawned clear and bright, it seemed almost an apology for the disastrous night.

We had been stranded half a mile from shore. There were hundreds of men in the water, making their way toward land and clutching to any flotsam that passed nearby. The water was choked with sails, floating debris, and bodies. A ship limped toward us with less than half its oars in the water. Its mast lay half broken over one side trailing rigging behind that kept dragging the ship off its intended course. A man in the bow hailed us and they came as close as they dared. I watched my men jump into the water and get pulled aboard the broken ship. When they were all safe, I joined them. Others in the water swam toward it and were rescued as well.

Hundreds made it to shore, but none had weapons or armor. They were spread out along the narrow beach and sandy spit that protected the mouth of the Durius River. We had chased all their ships away, but as we watched, a column of Romans marched down from the fortress and attacked them, killing the unarmed men mercilessly.

We continued to pick up survivors in the water and before long several more ships joined us. Two were so damaged they would soon sink, so we transferred the men to the seaworthy ships. Of the fleet, only four still floated. The decks and cargo holds were crammed with injured men, the rest supplied the crews and rowing benches. We scavenged enough oars to refit the remaining ships, but the masts and sails were beyond repair, so we cut them loose and after one last search for survivors we turned our bows northward and limped back to Uenet, hoping that we would outpace any enemy ships that might follow.

PART II

THE NEW MAN

109 – 105 BC

JEFF HEIN

CHAPTER EIGHT

Utica, Roman Africa

May 109 BC

The ancient city of Utica was the bustling capital of the Roman province of Africa. Located on the northeast coast, it was founded by the Phoenicians a thousand years ago, taken over by the Carthaginians, and ultimately went to the Romans at the end of the Third Punic War. Roman cornu trumpets announced the arrival of Metellus' legions as the galley's were expertly rowed into their wharfs to discharge their cargo. In a short time, the clump of Roman sandals accompanied by more from the trumpets and shouts of their centurions followed the marching legionaries as they disembarked and marched inland to establish their castra. Mobs of men crowded the docks to help unload the tons of supplies that accompanied the army, hoping to be paid for their labor. Row upon row of two wheeled carts pulled by oxen stood by to be loaded, their drovers gathering and discussing the coming of the new army as they waited.

Seabirds squawked and shrieked as they lit upon the masts and rigging. A pair of curious seals surfaced and blew air, then dove again, conducting an inspection of the newcomers. More ships waited in the harbor for those that arrived first to move out of the way. The strange sights, sounds, and smells of the port overwhelmed the senses of the young legionaries, many of whom were away from home for the first time in their lives. Soon after they marched away from the sound of the waves and the sea breeze, they began to feel the oppressive heat. Their heads began to bake in their metal helmets, and under the chain mail they wore, they could feel the heat on their shoulders. It was still spring, and the sun was already giving them a taste of life in Africa.

The terrain changed as soon as they were out of the city. The palms and grass of the coast were replaced with the rocks and sand of the African desert and the young men began to question their excitement at the prospect of war and adventure.

October 109 BC

The Numidian king Jugurtha had been a thorn in Rome's side for years. An ongoing war between the king and his brothers had resulted in unrest and instability in a country that provided Rome with much of its grain, and the Roman senate could not allow this to continue. They had sent envoys to negotiate, called the brothers to Rome to mediate their disagreement, and eventually sent two Roman consuls to end the conflict with military force, but both had been bribed or defeated and returned home in disgrace. Now, Consul Quintus Caecilius Metellus had been tasked with bringing peace to Numidia and he had arrived with two new citizen legions and two auxiliary legions to enforce the will of the senate.

Since their arrival in Utica, Metellus' senior legate, Gaius Marius, had been busy retraining the legions who had already been in Africa for two years. Consul Lucius Calpurnius Bestia had recruited them, brought them to Africa, and left them behind to enforce a peace that didn't exist. When his successor Consul Spurius Postumius Albinus had returned to Rome in shame after his failed attempt, he had left a defeated and disheartened army behind. When Metellus arrived, he found an all but useless army. Metellus immediately assigned Marius to whip the African legions back into shape, and Marius leaned into the job with enthusiasm. Marius used his experience under Scipio Aemilianus to create an effective training regimen. Scipio had been faced with much the same situation when he had taken over command of the Numantine war twenty-five years ago and had created the fighting force that eventually won a war that had been going on for more than twenty years. In the months since they had arrived in Africa, Marius had used Scipio's example to restore the pride and warfighting ability of the African legions. During the process, Marius added to his legendary reputation of a soldier's general. He marched with his men, carried his own pack, and required his officers to do the same. He ate with them and sat around their fires listening to their stories and jokes. He dug trenches, cut trees, and pitched tents. But most of all he listened, and he was visible to his men. They came to know that their general cared about them, that he was one of them, not some aristocrat who had done little to earn his position; this was an officer who had seen it all. Marius had grown up on a modest farm in Arpinum, a backwater country town, and joined the army at seventeen as a young cavalryman. He had drawn his first blood under Scipio Aemilianus in Numantia and had seldom slept in his own bed ever since; preferring the soldier's life over the stuffy confines of a city whose rich aristocrats gorged themselves at feasts and orgies while the poor begged for coins and starved in the streets.

Marius was a true believer in omens and soothsayers, and while at Utica, he visited an *augur*. "Stay true to your gods to realize your dreams. You are destined for many great and wonderful things. Your many trials are the tests of your worthiness," the old man told him. Marius was reminded of the prophecy made so many years ago that promised he would rise to the pinnacle of power seven times, but as yet, the consulship had evaded him. Nevertheless, he was encouraged by what he heard and his faith in himself was renewed.

While Marius trained the African legions, his friend Publius Rutilius Rufus continued training the fresh legions that Metellus had brought to Africa. Rufus had also cut his teeth under Scipio and he and Marius had crossed paths many times over their careers. Metellus spent his time developing a strategy and gathering intelligence on Jugurtha. Seemingly the supplicant and returning to his old tricks, the Numidian king sent envoys to beg for only the lives of himself and his children and offered all else to the Romans. Instead of entertaining Jugurtha's bribes, Metellus took each of the envoys aside and persuaded them to betray Jugurtha, then returned them to the king. But this effort was unsuccessful. When the legions were ready, Metellus marched them into Numidia, their first mission to capture the ancient city of Vaga, Numidia's capital, and the seat of Jugurtha's power.

When Jugurtha's spies reported Metellus was on the march, he withdrew from Vaga, taking all his treasure with him, making sure that everyone in the country knew what he was doing. The king hoped that when Metellus heard of this, that the Roman army would follow him into the wilds of Numidia, onto the ground that suited Jugurtha's strengths, but Metellus refused to fall into Jugurtha's trap. Instead, the consul methodically captured the small villages on the way and when he reached Vaga, he took it without bloodshed, fortified the city, and stayed put.

Now firmly under the control of Metellus, some stability returned to the countryside and trade increased, the country returned to prosperity, while Jugurtha remained in the wilderness, plotting his return. Eventually, Metellus ordered his army into the desert to flush out Jugurtha, leaving the city in the charge of his Chief of Engineers, Prefect Titus Turpilius Silanus.

Numidia

November 109 BC

Consul Metellus stood with his subordinate commanders, his dark hair and eyebrows tinged a sandy brown by the dust of the

Numidian desert that clung to each of them. The Numidian king Jugurtha had attempted to bribe, coerce, and deceive Metellus, as he had the previous Roman dignitaries sent to stop him from taking over the African kingdom. The handsome Numidian king was accustomed to getting his way through his underhanded dealings and judicious use of his looks and personality. But this time Jugurtha's overtures had achieved nothing. Metellus had proven incorruptible, and he was pursuing a successful campaign to deny Jugurtha the support of his own people. Each time Jugurtha sent emissaries to negotiate, Metellus refused their offers, and used the talks as a diversion to maneuver his troops into position to occupy more land. Metellus adopted the same tactics used by Jugurtha to keep the king off balance.

Finally, Jugurtha realized that his usual strategy of trickery and inducements were not going to work. He was not about to surrender to Metellus, so his only recourse was to meet the Romans on the battlefield. However, Jugurtha was no novice at warfare. In fact, as the commander of the Numidian cavalry auxiliary attachment, he had learned much of what he knew from Scipio Aemilianus, the same general under which Metellus, Marius, and Rufus had begun their military service during the Numantine war, and he knew those officers and their tactics well.

Jugurtha knew he could not match the Romans in a static battle, one-on-one. His strength lay in the mobility of his Numidian horsemen and his knowledge of the terrain. He used ambushes, guerrilla tactics, and superior military intelligence to his advantage.

Once Jugurtha abandoned his attempts to avoid conflict, he began his resistance in earnest. He mobilized a large army and used his kingdom's terrain to bypass the Roman legions while they marched about, then attacked their supply lines and other soft targets with lightning-fast cavalry raids, and then withdrew swiftly back into the interior.

Knowing that he must defeat the Romans on a larger scale to end the war, he selected a site that favored his own strengths while negating that of the Romans. Along the Muthul River, in the south-western desert of Numidia, he concealed his troops on a large hill overlooking the wide river plain.

"Sir," blurted the dust covered scout that had just ridden in to report to Metellus. "We have found a large force of Numidians just to the east of the river." Sweat trickled down the man's face and dripped on the map when he bent to indicate where he had seen the enemy.

"How strong?" questioned Metellus.

"Hard to tell sir, they are well camouflaged and isolated. The area was difficult to approach unseen, but we estimate at least four thousand horse. Maybe ten thousand infantry. We also heard elephants, sir, at least a dozen."

Metellus thought for a few moments. "Alright, you are dismissed. Get some food and water, then get back out there and keep an eye on them." Metellus looked at Marius, his eyebrows questioning. "What are you thinking?" he asked.

"He thinks he has us trapped," Marius said. "He's found a spot with enough room for the legions to march between the river and that range of hills," he tapped the map. "I think we must augment the right flank nearest his forces. The left flank must keep contact with the river as our only source of water. Place the slingers and archers amongst the maniples on the right, prepared to receive the attack."

"He will not face you man to man," Gauda stated. "He will use the hit and run tactics that are familiar to our people. He knows he can't beat you in a set-piece battle, so he will continue to sting you and wear you down. Even the infantry fight in this manner. They are not armored warriors like yours, they are farmers and craftsmen, and they can move faster than your soldiers. They won't stand and be slaughtered in a battle line, they will strike and fall back to regroup, then strike again." Tall and handsome, with dark skin like his half-brother, Gauda was a rival for Jugurtha's throne. Metellus had not recognized his claim, leaving that to the senate, but had agreed to let him join them on this expedition along with a contingent of Numidian cavalry that supported him.

"What of the elephants?" asked Rutilius Rufus.

"Indeed, they are a fearsome beast, but they are easily routed," Gauda said. "They fear fire. I suggest that you have several ox-drawn carts laden with straw and pitch. When you see where the elephants will be used, light the fires and drive the carts at the beasts. Once they are panicked, they will cause havoc in their own lines."

"Alright, we will continue in march formation and allow him to think we don't know he's there. Marius, I want you to stay with the infantry. When Jugurtha attacks from our right, turn and meet him, along with Gauda's cavalry. I will command the cavalry on the left flank and meet his, wherever he deploys it. Rufus, when the ambush begins, I want you to take a cohort of infantry and an ala of cavalry and establish a fortified campsite near the river to secure a water source. If they see you break off you may be attacked, so stay ready."

The legions marched north, keeping the Muthul River to their left and the range of wooded hills where Jugurtha lay in wait on their right. Dust swirled about the feet of the men and animals that plodded along the river plain, waiting for the enemy to show themselves. When the rear of the Roman formation entered Jugurtha's killing zone, two thousand Numidian infantrymen charged forth from their hiding place and cut off any retreat, trapping the Romans in front of the bulk of the Numidian army.

At Jugurtha's signal the main body of Numidians swept down from the hills and attacked the center of the Roman formation. The Romans were accustomed to a close-order fight within arm's reach of each other, but the Numidians never closed with the armored troops. Instead, as Gauda predicted, they stopped a distance away and launched their spears, arrows, and sling stones then quickly retreated to the tree line and regrouped. The Romans in turn launched their missiles, but their disciplined lines did not break formation and pursue them. Instead, they pulled back their wounded and refreshed the lines, waiting for another attack.

"Hold!" shouted Marius. "Do not break ranks!" Again, the Numidians surged forward on the flanks while those that had cut off the Roman rear renewed their attack.

Jugurtha's cavalry burst from the hillside and rounded the Roman's flank, attempting to get behind them. Gauda's cavalry was greatly outnumbered and when they charged, Jugurtha's horsemen simply dispersed, not giving Gauda any type of formation to mass their strength against. When Gauda's cavalry stopped in temporary confusion, Jugurtha enclosed them and attacked. Gauda was separated from the infantry and fighting for his life when from a great cloud of dust, Metellus and his Roman cavalry came charging from the north. They slammed into Jugurtha's cavalry, who turned and raced back for the safety of the hills with Gauda and Metellus in pursuit.

Marius was under attack again from the elusive Numidian infantry, and casualties were mounting, but when he saw Metellus breaking Jugurtha's cavalry he seized the opportunity. "In ranks, quick step, forward, march!" he shouted. His officers repeated his order, and the disciplined ranks of the Romans stepped forward before the Numidians had time to pull back. The Numidians broke up and dispersed, taking only minor casualties, but the back of Jugurtha's force was broken and Marius allowed his men to pursue and kill as many as they could.

Meanwhile, Rutilius Rufus had secured the camp and now stood near the river, watching the dust of the battle to his south. "Sir!" one of his men cried out, pointing toward another cloud of dust rising in the distance.

"To arms!" cried Rufus, mounting his horse. "Battle formation, facing north!"

The dust came closer, and his horse began to stutter-step nervously as the rumble of forty-four charging elephants reached its ears.

"Gods!" Rufus cursed. "The fire carts are with the main body. Steady men, steady," he tried to reassure them while they stood waiting behind their shields. Their faces drained of color when the strident sound of the elephants trumpeting reached their ears, and they felt the ground trembling beneath their feet.

One man threw down his shield and began backing away, his eyes wide with fear. "Stop that man!" Rufus shouted. A legionary stepped in front of the panicked man and jabbed him with the point of his gladius. "Get back in line," he growled, giving the gladius a push so that the needle-sharp tip pierced the other man's skin and drew blood. The deserter's eyes were wild with fear, then it passed suddenly, and determination returned. He picked up his gear and took his position back in the line just as a centurion walked up. "We're ready here, sir," said Lucius Aurelius, standing behind the man who had chosen not to desert.

Then slowly, something changed. The cloud of dust seemed to envelop the enemy from behind. The elephants with their towers that held the bowmen and spearmen high above the ground disappeared as the cloud moved past them. They had slowed, or stopped, for some reason. The trembling lessened, then stopped completely.

As the cloud of dust reached the Romans it dissipated, and they could see that the elephants had slowed to a snail's pace. Something had entangled them, and they lost their momentum. Their accompanying infantry was mingling about the great beasts. Rutilius recognized his opportunity and ordered his men forward. The legions stepped out, their confidence returning as they could see that the foundering elephants were starting to panic. The men on their backs tried to hang on but were thrown to the ground with the wild swaying and trampled beneath the great feet.

The Numidians had miscalculated and ran the elephants straight into a wide stream that ran from the hills down into the river. Many had become mired in the silty mud, and several had fallen to their knees, unable to stand up in the soft earth. Rufus sent his cavalry crashing into the Numidian infantry and slaughtered those who could not run fast enough to the beckoning hills. When the Roman infantry arrived, they continued the killing until the entire Numidian force was routed and only four of the elephants remained alive.

Lucius found himself fighting beside the man he had returned to the ranks. Together, they joined several others who attacked one of the elephants and its riders. It took many wounds to kill the great beast, but finally, Lucius was able to put it out of its misery.

"Had that stream not been there, I doubt we would have survived that," Rufus thought to himself. As the sun was setting on the western horizon, he shouted to his second in command, "Clean this up and return to the camp. I'm taking the cavalry to see how Marius and Metellus are faring."

In the gathering twilight the two forces nearly attacked each other when they neared. Metellus and Marius had rejoined forces and were marching toward the river when Rufus found them.

"We routed the bastards," Marius said.

"But we didn't crush them." Metellus sounded frustrated.

"The army will disband now," Gauda offered. "Those men are not professional soldiers. They will head for their homes and for the hills to avoid another encounter with you. You have defeated Jugurtha for now, but make no mistake, he will raise another army, and he will come again."

Marius rode his horse straight backed and solemn. "But not this year."

"No, not this year, and that will have to be good enough for now," said Metellus.

CHAPTER NINE

Numidia

December 109 BC

Gaius Marius waved a scroll before his friend Publius Rutilius Rufus. "I have received more information on Silanus' battle with the Cimbri this last summer if it can be called a battle. There was an inquiry of the survivors, like the one I conducted after Noreia. Incredible, another consular army wiped out."

"Jupiter's thunderbolt! How could this have happened again? Did they learn nothing from Carbo's defeat?" Rutilius Rufus replied.

Marius sat down and unrolled the scroll. As legate, he was entitled to a large tent which included his sleeping quarters and a sitting area where business was conducted. Several chairs and a high legged table that was covered with maps and missives dominated the room. "There's not much detail here, but apparently Silanus has returned to Rome in disgrace, and he's been arrested. Survivors said that the Germans hit them while in the march formation when Silanus turned the legions and ran. It was a disaster," Marius said flatly. "Carbo and Silanus destroyed by the Cimbri, Albinus by Jugurtha, Cato by the Scordisci. This is what happens when the senate keeps appointing generals based on their ancestor's importance and wealth rather than on merit. But there is more going on here than incompetent generals. We aren't facing phalanxes of Italian armies of similar size and tactics to our own anymore. The enemy has changed. After two hundred years the manipular army has run its course. The barbarians fight in mass formations and great numbers that are overwhelming our legions. We've taken too many losses. Even when we win, it's too costly in manpower. We can't sustain the losses we have seen over the past century. Already it is difficult to recruit enough men to fill the ranks of any new legions."

"That's true," Rutilius Rufus agreed. "We had difficulty getting enough men to fill Metellus' legions to come to Africa. The propertied classes have been depleted by military losses and by extended campaigns, biting into our available manpower for the dilectus. But I know you well enough to know that you wouldn't be talking aloud if you hadn't already been thinking of a solution."

Marius leaned forward, his elbows on his knees, warming to the subject. He had always loved the challenge of a problem that needed fixing. He also had no problem taking other people's good ideas and improving upon them and making them his own. "I've studied these military losses at great length, including interviewing many of the soldiers and officers who took part. The greatest defeats come when inept officers are leading the legions. That's not likely to change anytime soon, the senate is always beholden to those of a certain class with the riches to buy influence. But I think with some changes, the army can adapt to this new type of fighting, even with generals that are more politician than soldier. I've an idea for the manpower problem as well. We've discussed it before, you and I, but altering the requirements for service in the military will have to wait until one of us becomes consul.

"In the meantime, I've some ideas. I intend to be ready when the opportunity presents itself. In the maniples, we've always separated the ranks by class and age. This creates weaker units because they don't all have the money for proper armor or weapons. The younger men are not tested in battle, and the men to their left and right are the same. The Velites are the youngest and poorest of all and have little to no protection, but after they have launched their javelins, they are at least allowed to move behind the Hastati before clashing with the enemy. The Hastati are the least armored and least experienced of the heavy infantry, yet we put them in the front and expect them to absorb the most punishment before bringing in the Principes who are better equipped and trained. We save the Triarii, our best troops, until the Principes need relief, or until the battle is already won or in danger of being lost before they are employed. They are the strongest, best equipped, and most experienced of our soldiers, why should they be behind the lines, all in one group? The boys in front could benefit from that experience.

"I've never liked the idea that the senior veterans, those with experience in battle are placed in the rear, leaving the younger and inexperienced men in the front ranks to learn the hard way, if they survive. I am still working this out, but I believe if we take the concept of the cohort that has been experimented with already, and we took away the separation by age, creating a mix of men of all ages, the experience and knowledge of past battles would be shared among the men. This would bolster the confidence of the younger soldiers that they are not just placed up front to be killed first. Perhaps we would see less panic among our armies when the situation gets dire if the newer recruits stood beside a veteran."

"Hmmm, interesting," Rutilius mumbled, rubbing his chin thoughtfully. "Metellus used cohorts at Muthul, but with the old rank structures. You are talking about dismantling and completely restructuring the basic units of the army. It would not be an easy transition. Though, it's been done before when the maniples first replaced the larger Greek style phalanx. It's an intriguing idea and I can see where it might address some of the manipular legion's weaknesses. Have you thought about how it could be implemented?"

Marius traced his ideas into the sand at their feet. "The current legion is made up of ten maniples of Hastati and ten Principes. Each maniple is broken down into two centuries of sixty men each. The Triarii are half that, and the Velites are a mass of twelve hundred skirmishers to the front of the legion for a total of four-thousand two-hundred men per full-strength legion. First, I propose to do away with the triplex acies battle formation that we've used for centuries.

"The new legion will be made up of ten cohorts of six hundred heavy infantry, all dressed, armored and armed identically by the state.

Rutilius snorted, "You think you can get the senate to approve that kind of cost?"

Marius grinned. "That's the beauty of it. The Gracchi already passed the law that provides for this twenty years ago, but the greedy bastards in the senate have allowed that to fade away and the men have returned to paying for their own kit, with the result that many soldiers go to war with inferior equipment. That means more injuries and deaths that could have been prevented if they were properly equipped," Marius went on.

"Each legion would consist of ten cohorts. Each cohort is subdivided into six centuries of one hundred men. In turn each century would break down to ten contubernia of ten-man tent groups, like what we do now. This new legion would number a total of six thousand heavy infantrymen, significantly larger and stronger than the manipular legion with larger subunits that are integrated with men of all ages and experience, all trained the same way and armed and armored with the same quality of weapons and equipment."

"That would make a cohort a complete unit, each with the same capability. I like it," said Rutilius. "With the manipular legions, we have to take two maniples of Hastati, two Principes, and two Triarii plus some Velites to get a full makeup for special missions."

"Whew," Rutilius whistled slowly. "You really have been thinking this through."

Marius grinned like a cat with a mouse. "I've been thinking about tactical employment as well, but that can wait for now. First, I want to create an experimental unit with enough men to make up one cohort, then train and equip them according to the new standard. I'll pay for it myself. When they are ready, we'll put them into the fight to test it. What I don't know yet is who I should put in charge of it. I need someone I can trust, someone smart who can grasp what we're trying to do."

"What about that young Lucius you seem to favor? I heard he fought well at Muthul, and I understand he was at Noreia. He's young, not too old or entrenched to favor the old system over something new."

Marius pondered his friend's suggestion. "Yes. Yes, you're right. He's a bright boy, and he's performed well on the battlefield. He can read and write well; he'll make an excellent staff officer for this. I'll have him help me with the details, but I'll have to put more experienced men in charge of the unit itself."

"Lucius Aurelius, I have an assignment for you."

The young soldier stood at attention before the legate, his mind racing and wondering what was in store. Lucius had signed up four years earlier in response to the Cimbri invasion of Noricum, where he had been severely wounded and distinguished himself at the battle of Noreia. Gaius Marius himself had awarded Lucius with the gold *armilla*, armbands that signified his bravery in battle. After recovering from his wounds, he had been assigned to the garrison in Rome that provided special services to the senate, like crowd control and personal security. Marius had recognized him there and had him assigned to his personal staff. When they arrived in Africa he was sent back down to the centuries, where he distinguished himself again at the battle of Muthul until Marius called him to his staff once more.

"You are going to help me reorganize and reform the entire army."

Confused, Lucius tried to be silent. He sucked in a nervous breath and failed. His brow knit and his dark eyes looked worried as he tried to comprehend the consul's words.

"Relax," Marius chuckled. Marius was thickly built and of moderate height. He placed a large hand on the younger man's shoulder. "You will work directly for me, report only to me. You will take my ideas and write them down and put them into a comprehensive manual of the organization, equipment, and training for a new unit, then you will assist the centurions of this new unit to learn their new organization and mission, who in turn will train their troops. You will watch over the training and report to me on their progress until they are ready for me to observe them. The centurions will have more experience in leadership and tactics, but you will oversee the development of this new unit. Are you up for the job?"

Lucius was overwhelmed. "Yes, sir!" he managed to utter.

"Good. You'll be paid as a signifier. A substantial raise, as I'm sure you know, with the appropriate rations and privileges. You will carry my authority, but don't forget the centurion placed in charge will carry his own authority. You will have to figure out the balance needed to work together. Any questions?"

In fact, questions bounced all over the inside of Lucius' skull, but he was unable to express them, and he just shook his head.

"Excellent," Marius said. "Don't look so nervous, boy. You'll do fine. Be here tomorrow morning when the duty horns sound and we'll begin."

Lucius saluted smartly, turned about, and marched out of the legate's tent.

For several weeks, Lucius reported to Marius to discuss and document the new military structure. Occasionally, Rutilius Rufus would sit in and offer his perspective. One morning Lucius reported to find a centurion standing in the legate's tent, in what sounded like an argument. When he entered, Lucius heard his name mentioned and the pair abruptly cut off their conversation and turned toward him.

"Lucius, this is Centurion Quintus Cassius Scaeva. He will be the centurion in charge of the new cohort. Cassius, this is the young man I was telling you about."

The centurion was a wiry man, taller than the general. He scowled at Lucius and the menacing glare that shot forth from under the brim of his centurion's helmet could have melted steel. He gripped his vitis so tightly his knuckles were white. He was obviously not pleased with what Marius had just told him.

"General, you cannot be serious. You expect me to subordinate myself to this boy? He's barely started shaving."

"I am serious, Quintus. But you will not be subordinate to him. I expect you to work together to create the cohort that will form the basis of the new legions. Lucius has been at my side developing these plans and he is charged with helping you achieve my goals. You have the tactical experience to take it from a written concept to a battlefield success. Lucius has proven himself as a soldier, but he is bright as well. You will treat him with respect. Don't let your pride set this up for failure."

The centurion turned toward the general with a glare that would have gotten any other soldier disciplined, his lips tightly pressed together to prevent himself from objecting further.

"I will forever be in your debt for saving my life in Gaul, but never forget that I am your general, and you will do as you are told," Marius warned, coldly.

Scaeva looked at the general, the expression on his face unchanged. Suddenly, the centurion straightened to attention and saluted, his face a mask of indifferent obedience. "As you command, General."

Marius frowned at the tone but chose to ignore it. "Both of you report back to me in one week. I expect to see some progress. You are both dismissed."

Scaeva turned and stalked out of the tent fuming and mumbling under his breath, closely followed by an embarrassed Lucius.

Rutilius, who had been sitting behind a partition chuckled when he stepped around the curtain and said, "I don't think Quintus Cassius is very happy with you."

"Do you think?" Marius scoffed.

"Young Lucius has his work cut out for him," Rutilius observed.

"I want two men who will go to the ground with each other to make this project work. I don't want men that will just nod their heads and go with my opinions alone. These two will take what I have given them and produce the best army unit Rome has ever seen. Quintus Cassius will learn there is steel behind that boyish face soon enough. Quintus will be the brawn; Lucius will be the brains. This will work."

Once out of earshot of the tent, Quintus Cassius Scaeva turned on Lucius. "Don't follow me boy. We are not equals. You will give me the details of what the general wants, and then you will make yourself scarce. I don't need some snot nosed brat to help me make a fighting unit."

CHAPTER TEN

Numidia

January 108 BC

Quintus Cassius Scaeva softened his attitude toward Lucius as he learned more about the young soldier who had received an *armilla* from Marius himself for his actions at Noreia and had fought well at Muthul under a centurion that Scaeva new and respected. The boy did show some intelligence and aptitude for what they had been tasked with and it left Scaeva the time to apply the hands-on training he preferred, while Lucius handled the administrative burden of organizing a new unit.

Each maniple of Marius' retrained African legions had given up fifteen Velites, five Hastati, five Principes, and five Triarii to fill the ranks of the experimental cohort. Six hundred men that Marius had hand-picked. The new unit was highly motivated and eager to show their general what they were made of. Scaeva was a veteran of many battles and a respected leader, and the men listened intently to his words.

Lucius had called a meeting of the experimental cohort staff and was facing a horseshoe shaped formation of thirty-five officers of various ages and experience. Scaeva had selected a training area some distance from the castrum to keep away from prying eyes, and this group was the first to see it. The men realized that this officer's boyish face was misleading when they heard the steel in his voice. He was no longer an untested recruit but had seen two major battles and carried the scars to prove it. He also carried the authority of their general, but he wore it lightly, and the men respected him for that.

"Good morning. I am Lucius Aurelius. I am the direct representative of General Marius, and I am here to inform you that you have all been selected to be part of a new evolution of the Roman army. We are going to transform the current organization of the manipular legion to one that is better suited to the enemies that we face today. The manipular army was developed more than two hundred years ago to fight an enemy who fought much the same as we did. Since the expansion of the Republic beyond the Alpes, we have faced a much different enemy. One that fights as individual warriors within a compact mass that takes advantage of surprise and exploits the intentional gaps in the manipular legion. Here in Africa we face a mobile cavalry that appears suddenly, strikes quickly, then disappears.

"This new legion organization calls for ten cohorts to a legion, each cohort made up of six centuries of one hundred men. Each century will be commanded by a centurion and an optio, along with a signifer, cornicen, and tesserarius. The main tactical unit will be the cohort, a solid mass of six hundred legionaries, all armed and armored the same. This is a much larger and stronger formation that can be broken down further into centuries, or even down to the ten contubernium that make up each century, whenever the need arises."

Somebody whistled softly. "A six-thousand-man legion," he whispered.

"You have been selected to be the leaders of this new cohort that will prove the effectiveness of this organization. Eventually, when the new legion is formed, you will become the first cohort.

"Centurion Quintus Cassius Scaeva is the cohort commander, the pilus prior. He will train you on the battle drills associated with the cohort, and I will manage the administration and logistics."

Lucius paused and scanned the faces. "Are there any questions?" Seeing there were none, Lucius stepped back. "Remember, General Marius is watching, and we only have a few months of training before we are expected to show how it will perform. Centurion . . ." he said in deference, turning the formation over to Scaeva. While Scaeva took over the session, Lucius returned to his quarters.

One man in the group of officers followed Lucius with his eyes, watching until he disappeared in the distance, and then returned his attention to his new centurion.

CHAPTER ELEVEN

Vaga, Numidia

February 108 BC

For the past several months, the Numidian city of Vaga had flourished under Roman control. Stability had returned to the region and under the control of Prefect Titus Turpilius Silanus, trade and profits had grown.

Metellus had left a strong garrison under Turpilius Silanus and Metellus' chief of engineers greatly strengthened the city's defenses. But Vaga was Jugurtha's capital city, and he sorely wished to retake it. The Numidian king, though, soon determined that it was nearly impossible to take the city militarily, at least not without a great loss of life on both sides. Jugurtha could not afford to have his army appear to be killing his own people, so true to his nature, he came up with a devious plan and gathered together the nobles who remained loyal to him.

Festival of Ba'al Hammon

Titus Turpilius Silanus, along with his officers and commanders raised their cups to a toast along with the Numidian nobles, merchants, and other important citizens in honor of *Ba'al Hammon*. The palace of Naravas, Vaga's chief magistrate and high priest of Ba'al Hammon, was sumptuous. Beautiful woven tapestries hung from the walls and vividly colored tiles created large frescoes on the floors. Carved wood furniture made from the trees of the African interior adorned each room. Every space of the large central table was filled with exotic foods that many of the Romans had not seen before. A beautiful girl, her face half covered with a transparent veil danced to the music of a light drum and a flute, the metal disks attached to her garment jingling softly. Naravas clapped his hands, and the music stopped. He spoke loudly so that all could hear.

"This feast is to honor the horned god *Ba'al Hammon*, the giver of life, the bringer of rain and sun, he who ensures our harvest by bringing the insects and the birds to pollinate our crops." A man entered the room leading a ram to where Naravas stood. The magistrate picked up a beautiful jewel-encrusted dagger and continued. "Lord *Ba'al Hammon*, accept this sacrifice from your humble servant." He nodded to a slave standing at his side who pulled a rope that led to the bell tower high above them. In the tower, another slave holding a staff with a brass ball attached to one end, turned and struck a large bell three times. Its sound echoed out across the city. Upon the third strike, Naravas turned toward Silanus and plunged the dagger down. Silanus, startled by the action managed to push himself back. His chair fell over backwards and tumbled him in a heap. Meanwhile, each of the Numidians who had been seated between the Roman officers produced a dagger or hand axe and killed the Roman closest to them. In an orgy of blood, the leaders of the Roman garrison were dispatched without mercy, save for Silanus, who in the chaos of spurting blood and screams somehow managed to escape with a deep cut to the side of his face.

"Find him!" Naravas shouted.

Silanus ran out into the street where he was greeted with more screams. Everywhere he turned was death, the streets ran red with Roman blood. Mobs of angry Numidians roamed the city, searching for survivors. Women and children dropped rocks from second story windows upon his men trying to get back to the citadel, only to find Jugurtha's troops waiting for them. Silanus did not know it yet, but nearly the entire garrison had been killed. Somehow, he managed to reach the outskirts of the city and escaped into the desert.

Metellus, who had been taking in the coastal air at Hippo Diarrhytus heard the news and marched his legions to Vaga. His troops were led by a contingent of Numidian cavalry, and when the city guard saw the horsemen, they mistook them for more of Jugurtha's troops and opened the gates welcomingly as hundreds of townspeople came outside the walls to greet them. On Metellus' order the troops surrounded and killed them. Alarmed by what they now realized was an attack on the city, the gates were quickly closed, and the citizens manned the walls.

"They will pay dearly for this treachery," Metellus vowed. "They must be made an example that no other city will follow. Bring up the onagers, we will reduce their wall to rubble and take the city."

Vaga held out for three days, by which time another legion had arrived. When the wall fell, they surged through the gap. Men of military age were slaughtered outright, and the rest were captured and sold into slavery. The city was razed and burned to the ground.

"Silanus must be tried and put to death," Marius insisted. He knew that Metellus was conflicted on the matter. Titus Turpilius Silanus, like Marius, was a client of Metellus. "He was the city commander and somehow escaped the carnage unharmed, while his entire garrison was slaughtered in the streets. Doesn't that strike you as odd? He's either a coward or a traitor."

"Very well, a concilium will be assembled," Metellus sighed. "You will lead it. If he is found guilty, he will be punished accordingly." Metellus had the right to assign punishment as he saw fit based on the verdict of the concilium.

"Titus Turpilius Silanus, chief of engineers of the army of Africa and prefect of the city of Vaga, you are charged with cowardice, conspiring with the enemy, and treason," announced Gaius Marius. "What do you have to say for yourself."

"The prefect maintains his innocence of all charges," replied Publius Rutilius Rufus, who was acting as the defense.

The concilium was held in the open air outside Metellus' camp. A large rostrum had been built and a shade cover had been drawn above to protect the participants from the scorching sun. The men who had come to watch were allowed to leave their armor at the camp.

For his part, Silanus sat miserably looking down at his hands. He had heard the rumors that traveled the camp, and he knew that the trial was a pretense. He was the commander of Vaga's garrison when it was wiped out by a Numidian uprising led by the man they had come to Africa to defeat.

Marius nodded. "Present your cases."

The tribune chosen as prosecutor stood and addressed the court. "Prefect Titus Turpilius Silanus was assigned by Consul Metellus to oversee the city of Vaga when it was captured from Jugurtha last year. His time in the city was spent fraternizing with the city's leaders. He fortified the cities outer defenses but failed to recognize the threat from within. While attending the parties thrown on his behalf, those same leaders conspired with Jugurtha and his followers to attack the garrison right under his nose.

"On the night of the massacre, the Roman garrison of Vaga were told to leave their weapons and armor at the citadel, that they were in no danger during the Festival of *Ba'al Hammon*, and that they should enjoy themselves and join with the citizens of the city in their celebration. The entire garrison was furloughed to enjoy this feast, there was no reaction force assigned. Was this because Titus Turpilius Silanus was so incompetent that he put his men at such great risk, or was he in league with the murderers? All the garrison's senior officers attended the feast with the city's chief magistrate, leaving them conveniently vulnerable to be butchered like cattle. Mysteriously, the only survivor of that fatal banquet was Silanus himself, who somehow managed to get away during the confusion, nearly unharmed.

"His men were slaughtered in the houses where they were invited to enjoy a meal away from the soldier's fare, in the taverns where they drank and sang together, and in the streets as they wandered about the city, oblivious to the danger. Women and children dropped rocks at them from rooftops and windows as they tried to make their way back to the citadel where their arms were kept. This all occurred within minutes of the midnight bell of *Ba'al Hammon*. How is it that this uprising was so expertly executed, that so many people knew of the uprising and exactly when it was to happen? How is it that Titus Turpilius Silanus did not learn of this, and how, or why, did he leave his men to pay the price?

"I ask you, is it the usual practice of an occupying force of an enemy city to lock up their weapons and saunter about as if they were in the streets of Rome? No, of course it is not, most especially on a night that the Carthaginians, Numidians, and Vagans worship a demon that they believe makes the grass green and the grain to grow. This *Ba'al Hammon*, the horned god that demands the sacrifice of children for his favors.

"In that, Silanus violated a core principle. We must ask ourselves, why would a man who has seen battle, who has risen to the rank of chief engineer and assigned as prefect, do such an obviously abnormal and unsafe thing?

"Titus Turpilius Silanus must be held accountable for his actions on that horrendous day, and I intend to show you the proof of his guilt."

Marius, head of the military court sat with his wide chin on his hand, revealing no emotion. The prosecutor had done well, and Marius was confident that Metellus would be placed in the uncomfortable situation of assigning punishment when Silanus was found guilty. Silanus' case would not be able to withstand the anger and resentment by the entire army at his failure.

The trial went on for several days, and in the end, Silanus was found guilty of gross negligence, falling short of treason. The most damning evidence was his survival, and the order to store their weapons at the citadel.

As Marius predicted, Metellus was reluctant to sentence Silanus to death, but had no way out. Titus Turpilius Silanus was scourged and beheaded in a public execution that satisfied the ranks of legionaries and seemingly put the matter to rest.

CHAPTER TWELVE

April 108 BC

Roman Africa

Gaius Marius and Publius Rutilius Rufus stood watching the new cohort maneuver through their battle drills. The well-trained unit responded immediately to the commands blared by the cornu trumpet, or by the gravelly voice of Centurion Scaeva. They moved smoothly from march formation, to battle formation. They extended and shortened the line, threw pila, created a shield wall and testudo. They demonstrated attacking, defending, and removing wounded soldiers from the front line. They split from a solid block of six hundred men to six centuries of one hundred men, then to sixty contubernia of ten men each.

The soldiers all wore new mail armor, the lorica hamata, that was usually only worn by the Triarii or senior officers because of its cost. Marius himself had paid for those, as well as new tunics and cloaks. Their pila, gladius, scutum, and other items were from their existing kit. The soldiers seemed to be exact copies of each other. The only noticeable difference was in the grizzled faces of the veterans compared to the smooth skin of the younger legionaries, but all wore the confident expressions of men who knew their business and shared in their pride for a top-notch unit.

The optios and centurions were resplendent in their plumed helmets and new red cloaks. Every bit of metal shined blindingly in the North African sun. The new cohort was truly a sight to behold as Scaeva marched them up to the senior officers and came to a synchronized halt. With the last step, a shout echoed across the sands, "Marius!"

Gaius Marius struggled to keep from smiling from ear to ear. "You men are the first of a great transformation that is to come. You and your leaders have done an excellent job, you have made me proud to be your commander."

He turned to Lucius who stood several steps behind. "You and Scaeva have done an outstanding job. See that they receive an extra month's pay and some time off. That goes for the officers and yourself, as well. The next time we go into the field, they will be placed in the line."

July 108 BC

"I wish to return to Rome in time to stand for consul." Gaius Marius stood before his commander, Quintus Caecilius Metellus. The Praetorium was the military headquarters of the camp as well as Metellus' living quarters.

Metellus, whose patrician family had long been a patron for Marius' equestrian family, studied his senior legate. "Why?" he asked. "Aren't you a little too old to run for consul?"

Marius, now forty-nine and well past the age that most were elected to the highest political position in Rome, glared at Metellus.

"I don't see how my age has anything to do with it," he spat, close to insubordination. "There is no restriction for being too old."

Metellus felt a small flutter of victory in the pit of his stomach when he saw Marius' reaction. The two had known each other since they were youths, and they had never liked each other. They did, however, share a grudging respect for one another's abilities, even while they talked each other down. Since Marius had become a wealthy man, he no longer felt the need to grovel for Metellus' money and political support. Now, Marius saw Metellus only as a means to an end, and Marius wanted to become consul. Slandering Metellus had been his pathway to mobilizing the public to vote Metellus out, and Marius in, as commander of the war in Numidia.

Metellus knew that Marius did not respect him, nor even like him. He also knew that Marius had aspirations for consul, but despite everything, the man was a valuable soldier. He knew his business, and Metellus did not wish to lose him for the better part of a year while trying to win the war against Jugurtha. He was tempted to send Marius back to Rome just to be rid of his frustrating attitude. But he knew that it was better to keep him close, rather than send him back to Rome where Marius could cause more trouble behind his back.

"I need you here. You signed on to pursue this war with me and I expect you to stay here and do that. Perhaps you should wait until my son is ready to run for consul and run with him," Metellus added. He could not resist another barb.

Furious, Marius stood. "It will take that long for you to win this war!" He stormed out of the consul's tent.

Metellus couldn't help indulging in a self-satisfied smile.

Rome

August 108 BC

In a dark corner of a taberna off the forum in Rome, sat Marcus Marius, younger brother of Gaius Marius. Across from him sat the Tribune of the Plebs Titus Manlius Mancinus. Both were dressed well below their station so as not to bring unwanted attention to themselves, but the handsome Marcus stood out in a crowd. His stylized haircut and impeccably clean nails marked him as someone of wealth. Tall, and confident, no one would mistake him for a common man. Manlius on the other hand looked like a rat that had just crawled in from the street. His shifting eyes took in the room and settling on Marcus, waited for him to speak. "My brother is going to run for consul this year," said Marcus. "But Metellus has refused to allow him to return to Rome to campaign in time for the election. He has asked me to help him begin his campaign for him. That is why I have asked you here, to listen to his proposal."

"I'm listening," replied Manlius, his hooked nose obscuring the scar on his upper lip.

Marcus sat straight backed, his head held high. "Since Gaius' voice is being suppressed, we need someone to spread the word of his intentions. The truthful word, not the false information that defames him and acclaims others. My brother's enemies control the flow of information in the city. They hold back news of certain people's success and replace the absence of information with the things that will push forward their own agendas. If one controls the information, one controls the populace. Their manipulation of the news that reaches the citizens, allows them to control the vote. If the people don't know what is happening, how can they know who truly represents their interests?

"The nobilitas continue to be voted into office simply because the people do not know they have other choices. We cannot gain control of the Acta. It is controlled by the state and influenced by those same patricians who wish to manipulate the news to their own purpose. When it is posted every day in the public places and read from the rostrum in the forum, the information it contains has been scrubbed to remove anything they don't want to reach the ears of the people."

"This is something most of us already know, it's a fact of life,"

Manlius sneered.

"What we need is a whisper campaign that will inform the citizens. Something that challenges the status quo on what information they receive. Gaius will send me his words, and I will provide you with the message that he wants to present to the people. If he can't be here in person to speak for himself, we will speak for him. He will also need representation in the senate. I will work on that. What I need you to do is work in the trenches where the common people are. Places like this," he gestured at the room. "Places where people gather and talk. Recruit more associates. Men who can be trusted. Create a network that can pass along these messages quickly and efficiently. We won't need to rely on just the false narrative of the elites. We will have a network of information that flows freely down to the most common man and presents them with the truth. People need to hear what he has done, and what he plans to do. This is a perfect job for a Tribune of the People. Are you up to it?"

"That depends. What am I to gain for my trouble? If someone were to learn of my involvement it could put my position at risk. He's not a very well-liked man among the upper class." Manlius shrugged with his palms outstretched, as if waiting for Marcus to put a coin in them.

"You will be compensated of course. And you will receive a stipend to be used as you see fit to accomplish this goal. If Gaius is successful, you can count on his support in whatever your next endeavor may be."

Manlius considered for a few moments, then simply nodded.

"Good. Your first payment will be delivered to your home. You can begin immediately."

There had always been an underground network of information that flowed throughout Rome and the Republic, aside from the more formal sources. Manlius only needed to tap into them and provide the information that Marcus Marius gave him.

Within weeks, the network was full of news of the war in Numidia. The words were having an effect on the citizens' perception of the war. Once thought impervious to scrutiny, Quintus Caecilius Metellus was now being doubted, and the gossip even wondered if he were not accepting bribes to avoid defeating Jugurtha as the previous consuls had been accused of. Word of the uprising in Vaga and the murder of its garrison, and Metellus' subsequent death sentence of Titus Turpilius Silanus was being twisted to damage Metellus' reputation.

Marius' roles were being exaggerated to make him look even more brilliant and successful. It was a very successful information campaign, and just like the Acta that delivered the news approved by the elites, this new network delivered the news in Marius' favor. Also like the Acta, it was light on actual truth, and heavy on half-truths, omissions, and outright lies. The people ate it up and Marius came to be looked upon as the only man that could defeat Jugurtha and bring the legions home.

Over the summer, Marius developed his network of agents both in Rome and in Africa. His leadership style, battlefield successes, and quite genuine actions endeared him to his soldiers who saw him as one of them, a general willing to withstand and suffer the same hardships as they did. When they learned of his intention to run for consul, they naturally wanted to support their general. Of course, word circulated that the elites, the patricians and nobilitas, wanted to prevent him from running and that made the soldiers even more committed to his cause. They wrote letters home to their families and friends to support their general and his popularity rose dramatically.

News of the uprising in Vaga and the subsequent execution of Titus Turpilius Silanus was subtly changed to implicate Metellus as another patrician commander who had placed the poor, unqualified Silanus in a position above his ability to deal with, and then when he was found inadequate for the job, executed him to keep it quiet. Metellus' defeat at the battle of Zama was made to look as though it were his fault for making poor decisions that Marius tried to tell him not to do, and Marius' role in the battle of Muthul was played up, making him solely responsible for the victory. Metellus was portrayed as being hesitant, not taking the initiative against Jugurtha, and hiding safely in the villages instead of campaigning against the elusive Numidian king. There were even whispers that Metellus accepted bribes from Jugurtha to avoid direct battle.

Marius' liberal use of embellishments of his own successes as well as the dark lies that circulated in the alleys of Rome, were quite successful. The new man who had always despised the way of dirty politics, had learned his lessons well.

CHAPTER THIRTEEN

Marcellus had been astounded to find Lucius in Africa. He had been present when Lucius briefed the officers that first day and watched as Lucius returned to his quarters. Later, Marcellus managed to reunite with his old friend. The two had joined the army just as the Cimbri had appeared on the northeast horizon. After the battle of Noreia he had been part of the decimation that Gaius Marius had served on the surviving troops. Like Vulca, he was lucky enough not to be the one in his rank selected to die as punishment for their commander's failure and their unit's cowardice. When the horrible punishment was over, they were immediately marched away to be dispersed among other units, and Marcellus never knew the fate of any of his friends. When Lucius Calpurnius Bestia had been elected consul, Marcellus had been among the volunteers who joined Bestia's consular army, which was headed to Numidia.

Marcellus had taken part in several indecisive skirmishes under Bestia before that consul returned to Rome and left his bewildered army in Numidia. Soon after, a new consul arrived, Spurius Postumius Albinus. Under this new commander, the army literally did nothing but sit around in the North African heat and while away their time. Boredom was the rule and discipline became lax. The men became surly, the leadership lost control, and they turned into no better than a gang who robbed and abused the local citizenry.

When Spurius left for Rome, he left his brother Aulus in charge of the army. A man with little experience, and less respect, he motivated the army to attack Jugurtha's treasury city of Suthul with promises of loot. That attack turned into an embarrassing defeat and the army was forced to walk under the yoke before returning to Roman Africa where again their commander returned to Rome and left them in the desert to rot.

It was the beginning of Marcellus' third year in Africa when word arrived that a new commander would be arriving soon. Quintus Caecilius Metellus was the new consul, and he was known throughout the army as a no-nonsense commander. But the news fell on deaf ears. The army who had been so poorly led and then betrayed by their commanders was no longer in the mood to play soldier.

When Metellus assigned Marius to kick the African legions back into shape, Marcellus recognized him and was fearful of another decimation. Instead, he found that Marius was focused on returning the pride and military discipline of the legions, and Marcellus in his gratitude for avoiding another horrible punishment responded well. He threw off the apathy and sloth that had taken hold of those left behind and applied himself. His enthusiasm was infectious and soon those around him began to respond. Marcellus stood out as a leader and was recognized as such.

When word got out that a special new unit was forming, Marcellus volunteered and found himself looking into the eyes of his old friend Lucius.

"I still can't believe you're alive," Marcellus marveled, tapping the rim of his cup against Lucius' again. Lucius remembered him as the youth he had met on the road to Piacenza where they both took their basic training for the army. Marcellus was always boasting of how he was going to kill barbarians by the hundreds. "I thought everyone in our contubernium was dead. When the barbarians charged us out of the trees at Noreia, I lost track of anyone in our unit, and when the storm came, all I could do was run to get away from the falling trees and the Germans. I wound up back at Aquileia and after the decimation they shipped me out immediately. I never saw anyone again."

"I saw Decius and Porcius dead on the battlefield. Vulca helped me back to the hospital and may still be alive," Lucius said. "He visited me at the hospital later, but I don't know if he got through the decimation. The rest I have no idea."

"Well, you've obviously done well," Marcellus offered. "Working for a big man like Gaius Marius. You were fortunate."

"Lucky, yes. They gave me an *armilla* for Noreia. I still don't know why. I think it was just a political thing. I sure as Jupiter didn't earn it." He sat shaking his head, his haunted eyes staring into his cup. "The memory of that day at Noreia still haunts me. The loss of so many, just for the vanity of one man. And then the decimation." He shuddered.

"Well," Marcellus clapped a huge hand to his shoulder. "That's behind us now, isn't it? Things are looking up. A toast," he said, raising his cup. "To those friends we may see again . . ."

"And to those who shall rise no more," Lucius finished.

CHAPTER FOURTEEN

Roman Africa

September 108 BC

The summer campaign season was nearly gone and Metellus was no closer to defeating Jugurtha than he had ever been. His army had marched the length of Numidia without success, in pursuit of the more mobile cavalry forces Jugurtha commanded. He was never able to pin the Numidian king down to a decisive battle.

Despite their tactical cooperation during the war, Marius and Metellus battled behind the political scenes as Metellus sent reports of success back to Rome, while Marius countered with messages of disappointing failure to resolve the war. In the end, the political sparring went in Marius' favor. Both men had deeply entrenched camps of believers who supported them and few of those minds were changed by the rhetoric, but there were always new voters, and those who were undecided. And that's who Marius courted the strongest.

The new cohort had performed well in several engagements, proving its viability, while Marius made adjustments here and there to perfect his vision. He encouraged the members of the new cohort to contribute their thoughts, something that was unheard of in any command. Marius, ever the soldier's general, wanted to hear from the troops on the ground and what they thought. He regularly held listening sessions not only for the officers, but for the enlisted men as well. He encouraged them to learn their new unit well, and to observe everything. The effects of their weapons and tactics on the enemy. The effectiveness of their own armor and shields. He considered their comments, and threw most of them out of course, but they adored him for listening to them. One excellent suggestion resulted in an evolutionary change to one of the Roman army's most successful weapons.

The pilum had been a staple in the Roman army for centuries. It was a six-and-a-half-foot long javelin, with an iron fore-shank and a pyramidal shaped tip that was attached to a wooden shaft by a flat tang. Marcellus had noted something that everyone knew to be true, but did not see an opportunity for improvement. But Marcellus was more than the muscle-bound boaster that he had been in his youth. He noticed that when the pila were thrown, many of them would become stuck in the enemy's shields. The weight and awkwardness of the javelin sticking out from a shield made it unwieldy and resulted in the enemy casting their shield aside and making them vulnerable to the swords of the Roman legionaries.

Often, an enemy was able to wrench a pilum out from their shield and cast the undamaged weapon back into the Roman ranks. Some pila though, bent on impact, probably due to faulty production or softer iron. Though unintentional, this made the pila useless to the enemy as a weapon. Marcellus knew he was onto an idea but wasn't quite sure how to put it into words, so he visited his friend Lucius to discuss it.

"What if all the pila were made purposely so that the tips would bend?"

Lucius frowned and rubbed his chin. "Wouldn't that lessen the penetrating power? The pila often punch through the shield and into the warrior behind, wounding or killing him. If the tip is softer, it would bend on impact and lose much of its power before it broke through."

"Hmmm." Marcellus was looking closely at the pilum that he held, examining it thoughtfully from tip to tip. He paused as his gaze passed over the tang where the iron fore-shank attached to the wooden shaft. He was staring intently, instinctively knowing the secret he was looking for lay right in front of him.

The iron tang at the back end of the fore-shaft was seated between two projections of the wooden shaft and fastened together with two iron pins. With the sudden shock of a lightning bolt from a midnight sky, the answer came to him. "It's the pins!" he shouted, startling Lucius who had turned away for a moment.

"The pins!" he shouted again, thrusting the pilum toward Lucius with both hands.

"Yes?" Lucius said, not understanding.

"The pins are iron," Marcellus said excitedly. "There's two of them. If one were to break, it would create a pivot point."

"Yes," Lucius said, understanding beginning to dawn.

"One could be designed to break on impact. Perhaps a wooden peg would work. It would keep it fastened until the impact broke it, then the wooden shaft would pivot with the same effect as when the soft fore-shafts bend. And the iron could still be made strong to ensure the penetration."

"You're really onto something Marcellus. That's a genius idea. I'll make some sketches, and we will take your suggestion to General Marius tomorrow."

"Brilliant!" Marius said. "What's your name, son?"

"Marcellus, sir."

"Marcellus what?" Marius asked.

"Just Marcellus, sir. I have no cognomen. My mother died when I was a child, and I never knew my father. I grew up on the streets of Rome by myself."

"Well, *just Marcellus*, you've earned yourself a bonus. And if this works out the way I think, perhaps a promotion."

Marcellus, uncomfortable as he was to be in the personal presence of such a great man, didn't know how to react. Lucius bumped him with his elbow. "Say thank you."

"Th . . . thank you, sir."

Marius' face cracked into what could be mistaken for a smile. "Lucius, have the armorer make this change to the new cohort's pila. I want them to begin testing it immediately."

"Yes, sir," Lucius said. He and Marcellus saluted and left the tent.

"A promotion," Marcellus said dreamily.

"If it works out," Lucius reminded him.

"And a bonus."

Lucius chuckled, "Come on, let's go see the *actuarius* and get you that bonus."

"Lucius Aurelius," called the messenger as he entered Lucius' tent the next day. "You have a letter." Lucius looked up curiously at the sound of his name and took a leather pouch from the messenger. He had received several letters before and assumed that his mother had written him with news about life back home. But when he looked at the writing on the leather case, he saw that it was from his old friend Vulca. Surprised and pleased, he gingerly removed the pages of thin birch wood from the leather case that held them, a leather thong tied through two holes drilled in each page bound them together into a small book. It was written about a year ago in Gaul and had somehow found its way to his hands in faraway Africa. The wood had dried and shrunk, and the edges were chipped and splintered from many miles of travel. The ink was smudged and almost illegible in some spots, but he could make out the words well enough.

"My good friend Lucius Aurelius. I hope that this letter finds you whole and healthy. I write to inform you of what I have learned of our friends. As you know, poor Decius and Porcius were killed in the battle with the Cimbri at Noreia, and Foligio has never been heard from again, may their souls rest well in Elysium. I witnessed Titus Romanus killed during the decimation and through the grace of Jupiter, I survived. I saw you on the rostrum beside General Marius and was pleased to see him award you the armilla and to know that you would be spared the punishment and humiliation. Of all of us, you were always the wisest and the bravest.

When our legion disbanded, I was assigned to the legions of Gaul, and this is where I still am today. I have worked hard to overcome the stigma of our loss at Noreia, and I have recently been rewarded with a promotion to centurion. With this position I have gained some small influence and used that to try and track down any of our old unit that may still be alive. That is how I found out that you had sailed to Africa and that Aulus had marched north with Silanus to fight the Cimbri. As you may know, Silanus, like Carbo, marched to his doom with most of his troops. I am sorry to report to you that Aulus was killed in the fighting. I cannot seem to find any word about that oaf Marcellus, but if he's alive, I'm sure he's making a nuisance of himself to everyone around, and we'll be sure to hear from him in the future.

In any event, I am well and have taken over my new command of the castrum that guards the trade road from Narbo to Burdigala on the northern coast. It is a small fort near Tolosa, which is about halfway between the two larger cities. The duty suits me, as it is relatively quiet, and my boys have little to do but keep watch, patrol, train, and clean their gear. The Germans disappeared after they ripped apart Silanus' legions and killed poor Aulus and haven't been heard from since.

You will be happy to hear that I have taken a Gaulish wife that follows me everywhere and I now have a fat baby boy that keeps me smiling every moment that I spend with him. Well, my friend, I hope you are enjoying the African desert while I freeze my mentula off in the mountains of Gaul. Be well, and take care of that upstart Jugurtha for me, will you?

Your friend, Vulca."

Lucius was deeply moved. He and Vulca had grown close during their recruit training and Vulca had helped him from the battlefield of Noreia to the hospital at Aquileia. They had not seen each other since the decimation and until now Lucius was not even sure if Vulca had survived.

He was sad to learn that Foligio's sweet voice would never again be heard drifting into the night as he sung the songs of the soldier's homelands while the flames of the cooking fires burned low. And poor Aulus, thought Lucius. The quiet one of our contubernium who never troubled anyone, now gone with the others. He shuddered at the thought of Titus being beaten to death by his comrades as punishment for the poor leadership of his general, what a cruel way to die. Vulca did not know that Marcellus lived and had risen in the ranks also.

"I must tell Vulca," he said to himself, and prepared his reply.

CHAPTER FIFTEEN

Mid-November 108 BC

Marius pestered Metellus for months to return for the election, and Metellus finally grew exhausted of his subordinate's complaining. Metellus for his part had become aware of Marius' attempts to undermine him back in Rome and with his own troops. He was not without his own network of informants of course.

Finally, with only twelve days before the election, Metellus allowed Marius to return to Rome to participate in the election for consul, confident that he had delayed his old opponent sufficiently enough to ruin his chance at being elected. But he underestimated the energetic Marius.

Not to be deterred, Marius made the trip from Metellus' camp to Utica in two days. While his ship prepared to sail, he took the time to make a sacrifice. The soothsayer that he consulted assured him that great good fortune beyond belief and expectation was in his future. Buoyed by the prophecy, he set sail and arrived in Rome three days later, where throngs of excited people greeted him. "You've done well," he said to his brother Marcus, waving at the adoring crowds. "It's not a triumph, but it's certainly an enthusiastic welcome home."

"They love you," Marcus replied. "They think you are one of them, risen to the highest pinnacle of success."

Marius glanced sideways at his brother. "They're right," he said with a nod.

Marius didn't waste any time visiting the senate or any of the nobilitas. Instead, he gave speeches in the forum, and in the marketplaces. He visited taverns and walked the streets of the city. The plebians far exceeded the numbers of the patricians. He knew that the vote he needed was the plebians and he drew enormous crowds. He even visited villages and cities outside Rome where the sentiment against the aristocracy was strong and for the new man was even stronger.

With great fanfare, Marius was introduced to the assembly by Titus Manlius Mancinus, the tribune of the people that his brother Marcus had enlisted months ago. Marius made damaging attacks against Metellus in particular and how he pursued the war, and the wealthy aristocracy of Rome, blaming all the problems of the poor on them, which of course was mostly true. He promised to kill Jugurtha or bring him in alive. He promised to change the property requirements for military service, which gave thousands of disaffected farmers and urban poor hope to climb out from their poverty and filth ridden lives. Soldiers ate regularly, had the best medical service, and were paid a salary, as well as promised a share of any booty at the end of a war, and everyone knew Jugurtha was filthy rich.

"If I need to make an impression upon the people, I will show them the wounds upon my own body, earned while fighting their enemies, not a vestibulum in a grand house filled with busts and portraits of long dead forefathers. I am not high born like Bestia, or Albinus, or even Metellus. I am Marius, the new man. The man who will march Jugurtha through the streets of Rome in chains!"

The people were delighted by the man who seemed to have no fear in renouncing the upper class. He called them names, recounted their faults, and blamed them for everyone's troubles. The crowds chanted his name, and it echoed throughout the city. Marius soaked it up. His name was written on the walls of the city, graffiti that let everyone know who Gaius Marius was. With only six days to campaign, Marius won a huge victory, and immediately moved to make good on his promises.

However, Marius had made many enemies, and the patricians were still a very powerful force within the senate. They prorogued Metellus's command in Numidia, seemingly blocking Marius from assuming command of the war. Marius immediately instructed Titus Manlius Mancinus to convince the concilium plebis, the assembly of the people, to negate the senate's decision and award him the command instead. It worked, and Marius was named commander of the war in Numidia. Metellus was to return home.

CHAPTER SIXTEEN

Rome

November 108 BC

Vallus had returned to Rome in search of relief for the constant pain he suffered from his last few remaining teeth. They had become abscessed, and his gums were swollen and painful. He had decided it was time to do something about them and sought out a dentist with a reputation of not killing his patients.

He had tried all the usual remedies to drive away the tooth worm, such as cutting his gums with the sharpened bone of a hare and gargling the ashes of a deer horn. He had even tried spitting into the mouth of a frog he had caught under a full moon and commanded it to carry away the pain. Nothing had worked.

Now he found himself lying on an uncomfortable table staring at the ceiling of a non-descript parlor in the home of a man he did not know. Aristides was a Greek freedman who had chosen to remain in Rome to ply his trade. Hunched over Vallus, he was using a probe to inspect Vallus' teeth, mumbling as he looked, "Mmmm. Mmmhmm. Tsk, tsk, tsk." Vallus nearly leaped off the table when he touched a particularly sensitive spot. "Well," said Aristides, "you're in terrible shape. The good news is I can help, but it's going to cost you." He placed his tools down on a small table.

"The cost is not a problem." Vallus rubbed his irritated jaw. "Can you take away the pain?"

Aristides helped him to a sitting position. "Oh, yes. The pain will be gone when you wake up."

"Wake up? What do you mean?"

"Well, my assistant here will mix you a potion. You will drink that potion and then, while you are asleep, I will remove your teeth. When you wake up, you will be swollen and sore, but the pain will be less."

"Less? Not gone?" His face fell in disappointment.

"Yes, you'll need a few weeks to heal and for the swelling to go down. I'll be cutting your gums to get those broken and rotted teeth out you know. I'll clean them out with vinegar and pack them with cloves and garlic to get the infection out. You'll bleed for a day or two, but if you rinse with salt water and keep those poultices fresh, you'll feel better quickly."

"I don't know how long it's been since I've eaten anything besides mush or liquids," Vallus complained. "My ass burns because I only shit a stream of water."

"Well, you'll still be eating mush and shitting water until the swelling is gone and your gums heal, but you'll be able to move on to soft foods. Stew, soup, bread soaked in vinegar or wine, things like that. Eventually your gums will harden enough to bite into an apple."

Aristides looked thoughtful. "Ordinarily, I wouldn't offer this you see, most people are satisfied to have the pain gone. But if what you say about cost not being a concern is true, perhaps you would be interested in more."

Vallus squinted one eye. "What do you mean?"

"All of your teeth will be gone," Aristides said. "But I can replace them with a set of false teeth if you've the coin for it. Here, let me show you."

The dentist went to a nearby cupboard and produced a set of ivory dentures. "You see, the ivory fits on top of your gums and the teeth that are set in the top of the ivory act like your real teeth." He clapped them together several times, making a clacking sound.

"Those look like real teeth," Vallus said.

"Oh, they are real teeth, I assure you."

"From other people?"

"Oh, yes," the dentist nodded. "We only take the best, and only after the patient is dead. They don't have any more use for them," he said with a chuckle.

Vallus wrinkled up his nose.

"They'll be thoroughly cleaned, don't worry. Completely safe. We can start right away if you like."

It didn't take Vallus long to come to a decision.

"Excellent!" Aristides called for his assistant.

It was dark when Vallus awoke. He felt heavy, groggy. It was an effort to open his eyes, and his mind slowly cleared from the fog that enveloped him. He tried to raise a hand to touch his face but could not move his arm.

"Easy," Aristides' servant said. "You're strapped to the table so you couldn't fall off. Let me loosen the straps."

Vallus sat up slowly with the assistant's help. "Here, drink this," the man offered him a cup and Vallus drank greedily.

"Slowly," he said

"What did you give me?" Vallus asked, slurring his words. "I feel like I'm so heavy yet floating at the same time." A wave of nausea hit him and seeing his expression the assistant handed him a bucket. He dry heaved several times and spit into the bucket.

"It will wear off quickly. It's from the poppy tar. It induces sleep and takes away pain."

Pain, Vallus thought. He had forgotten. He rolled his tongue around his mouth, feeling for the jagged edges of the broken teeth. His tongue was numb, and his face felt swollen. I rubbed some of it on your gums to ease your pain. It will take a while for the feeling to come back."

"You will sleep here tonight and in the morning you can go home." He helped Vallus to a sleeping couch and placed the bucket nearby.

Two months later Vallus was back to see the dentist. "Good, good, the swelling is gone and there's no sign of infection. You've healed nicely. We can start fitting you for your new teeth."

After a few more visits to allow the dentist to fit the teeth to his gums, Vallus was a new person. He went straight to a taberna and ordered a meal to try them out. He no longer had any pain. The feeling of the teeth was strange, but in a good way. He had to learn not to pull too hard on anything or the teeth popped out, but as long as he bit down hard and cut off whatever he was eating, he could chew it.

Vallus had spent more time than usual in Rome on this visit. He was getting old, he told himself. Not much time left to enjoy myself so I might as well live it up a bit. Vallus' friend Felix and his wife Sofija now lived in and cared for Vallus' house in Rome.

The sounds of children's squeals and bare feet slapping against the tile floor as they chased each other about brought a smile to Vallus' lips. He had always enjoyed the presence of children, but never had his own. "How much time has passed," he said wistfully, shaking his head.

"Aye," replied Felix. "We have been married six years now. And three children to show for it."

"You need to stay off of her," Vallus joked. "I'll have to get a bigger house."

Felix looked down sheepishly. "I can never repay you for your generosity, my friend."

Vallus waved him off. "There is no need for any repayment. Having you here to care for my property is enough. You are a good friend, Felix. And it comforts me to know that this house shelters your family."

"So tell me," he went on. "Now that I am no longer in pain and can think clearly, what is the news in Rome these days?"

"The elections are near, and the senate is in an uproar. They don't want Gaius Marius to win, but he has been campaigning non-stop since he arrived back in the city. Word is, Metellus tried to keep him in Numidia, but he managed to get back in time to run for consul and it looks like he's going to win."

"Marius, eh? I know of him."

"Who doesn't?" Felix laughed. "The *proletarii* love him. He has no filter, and he has no problem insulting the aristocrats and calling them out for the city's problems. He has a nickname for every one of them. It's refreshing really to have some truth in the campaigning. Trouble is, he'll be like any other politician and once he's in office, the promises will just fade away."

"What's he saying?"

"He's promising the *capite censi* that he will lift the requirements for property ownership and enroll them in the army so they can earn a living. He's also promising to win the war in Numidia by the end of the year. Ending that war will stabilize the grain flow that feeds the poor. He's promising the soldiers land of their own in Numidia when the war is won. Those are big promises, I think."

"Well, don't be too sure. This Gaius Marius is an extraordinary man. He's quite capable of doing what he says."

"We'll see," said Felix, unconvinced.

CHAPTER SEVENTEEN

Rome

107 – 105 BC

The city was abuzz with talk concerning the new consul Gaius Marius. The excitement was palpable. He had won with a strong showing at the ballot boxes and word was spreading about his promises to defeat Jugurtha.

Marius lost no time in beginning the recruitment for his supplemental legions. Notices were posted throughout the city and Italian countryside. *Praecones*, or public criers, announced the information for the benefit of those who could not read.

Consul Gaius Marius has decreed the emergency removal of the requirement for property ownership as a stipulation for military service. Men of military age that are fit and willing to volunteer for service in the legions, regardless of their status as a landowner, should report to the Campus Martius at dawn, between the Nones and Ides of Ianuarius. This includes men of the capite censi. Veterans are preferred. Arms and armor will be supplied.

The *capite censi* were known as "the head count" because they were counted in the census simply by counting heads. They were the people who owned little or no property, considered to be the lowest class of citizens, and normally were ineligible to serve in the military.

In recent years, the *capite censi* had grown. The result of wealthy land speculators buying up rural estates and farms that went bankrupt because their owners were away at war. These were citizens who had once owned enough land to qualify for service in the legions and now were poor and destitute, with no means of earning a living. They were citizens who had no hope of climbing out of their poverty and often turned to crime to survive.

Caught in the depths of despair, sudden hope had presented itself for many. Marius had thrown them a lifeline. There were many of course who could not qualify; women, children, the old and infirm. But for those who did, their life now had a purpose, and they had Marius to thank for that. The euphoria that was felt when a citizen was chosen to join the ranks of legionaries was infectious.

In their eyes, the aristocrats were the state, and the aristocrats had stolen their land and livelihood, even as they were serving the state. Marius had restored their pride and self-respect, and they loved him for it. There was a new ideology forming. That of loyalty to their general, rather than loyalty to the state.

"I want you to continue recruiting to fill the supplementary legions, then get them trained and on the ground in Africa by the *Ides of Aprilis*," Marius instructed his senior legate Aulus Manlius. "My quaestor is recruiting the cavalry, and he will report directly to me. When we arrive in Africa, I want to get moving immediately."

"How do you want them trained and equipped?"

"The same. There will be no changes yet, we are still testing the new concepts. And I have not had time to change the law yet, so they will pay for their own equipment out of their wages for six years."

Manlius nodded. "Men are pouring out of the city to the Campus Martius to sign up by the thousands. We'll wind up having to turn most of them away, but there are many veterans and men of adequate health and fitness. We'll have no problem finding enough to fill the legions. The problem will be the cavalry."

"Don't worry about the cavalry," Marius said testily. "The recruitment contracts will promise land at the end of their service as well as a share of any spoils. There'll be no lack of it when we finally defeat Jugurtha. And we'll secure the peace with Roman colonies across Numidia."

Since arriving back in Rome, Marius had spent some time visiting his wife and son. He was a stiff and uncompromising man. He did not know how to act around children, or for that matter around his wife. They talked at some length, but inevitably the conversation turned toward his military life and Julia could only listen. When she talked of home life, Marius immediately became bored. Theirs was a marriage of convenience, not love. Though they had become somewhat close during their courtship, it was never comfortable; and while Marius had been in Africa, the years apart had done them no favors.

Julia was a beautiful woman and a gentle soul. She was a widower who brought two sons to the marriage: Quintus and Gnaeus Granius. Quintus, now seven years old and Gnaeus, six, kept their distance from their stepfather, though when called they came forward. No longer babies, Marius felt more comfortable speaking to them, however he spoke as a general, not as a father, and they never built a bond.

Gaius Marius the younger was two years old now, and his father was a stranger to him. The consul's stern visage frightened the boy and when Marius made a half-hearted attempt to play with him, he ran for his mother's arms.

"Oh, Gaius," Julia intoned. "Don't be upset. He doesn't know you. This is the first time he's seen you since he was born."

"I'm not upset," Marius said. "He will grow to know me with time. They all will. But this nonsense in Africa has to be finished first."

"I know. I will talk to them of you. They will know of your feats. And when they are older, you will have more in common."

"I'll be leaving soon. The legions are almost ready."

"I'll be sad to see you go again," Julia said. "I will write." She knew that he would not.

"Good," he said simply.

Lucius Cornelius Sulla's thirty years of life had been tumultuous at best. Born into a modest patrician family, his mother had died when he was a child, and his father died just as he achieved manhood. His stepmother loved him dearly and indulged his every whim, spoiling him beyond repair. A long-dead ancestor had ruined the family's fortunes when he was expelled from the senate for possessing more than ten pounds of silver plate, against the law at that time. He was the last of Sulla's forebears to serve as consul.

Though the Cornelius line faced a decline in their prosperity over the past decades and his father had nothing left to leave the boy, Sulla's stepmother was considerably wealthy in her own right. Sulla was given a modest stipend which allowed him to pursue a carefree lifestyle, and no one was more carefree than Lucius Cornelius Sulla. As a youth, he indulged himself without concern. Sunlight was unfamiliar to him as he usually slept through the day and spent most of his waking hours in the dark of night. He was a frequent visitor to the city's brothels where he tested every version of sexual pleasure that interested him. Every form of entertainment, drink, and sex were his pastimes. He was particularly fond of attending plays and of the garish makeup and costumes the actors wore, often trying them himself. But the after parties sponsored by the theater owners and acting companies were where Sulla spent most of his time.

Wild orgies of masked and painted men and women, writhing in ecstasy, pleasing each other with no constraint, no taboo, no shame. Sulla was a perfectly formed young man especially popular with the ladies. Though his piercing blue eyes and chiseled face were handsome, he also suffered from a condition that left bright red splotches on his skin. This only served to intrigue others as they became an indicator of when he was aroused.

During this time he became enamored with a young actor by the name of Metrobius who became a companion throughout his life, both friend and consort. Metrobius introduced him to a former slave turned high priced call girl who became his patroness and lover. Nicopolis, being somewhat older and taking a motherly fondness of Sulla, left him her considerable fortune when she died. His stepmother died soon after, also bequeathing him her fortune, leaving Sulla flush with wealth. Suddenly, he was presented with the possibility of a life that held more promise than the physical pleasures and debauchery that had become his daily experience. At the age of thirty, with no military experience, he decided to run for quaestor.

His good looks and easy manner made him popular, and he won easily. He was assigned by lot to the army of Gaius Marius who had won the consulship in the same year.

Marius took an instant liking to the young Sulla. A stern military man who stood by the iron discipline necessary for the legions, it was unusual for Marius to take such an interest in a man like Sulla, who possessed such an opposite personality. Marius, like everyone else was drawn to Sulla's easy smile. Sulla was accustomed to a comfortable life and continued that when his duties allowed, but he was extremely focused and driven when it came to his military duties.

"So, are you married?" Marius asked Sulla.

"No sir, no longer. I've been married, twice, they are both dead now."

"Children?"

"A daughter from my first wife, Julia. The girl is being raised by her mother's family."

"Julia? My wife's name is Julia. We are probably related through our wives and the gens Julia. Well, don't think you'll get any special treatment if we are. I expect you to work hard and learn the business. Ordinarily a quaestor would come with ten years of experience with the military. You have none. You've got a lot of proving to do."

"Yes, sir," I understand.

Sulla saluted and left the consul's tent. He was determined to make good on this opportunity and fell immediately to his tasks.

While others were busy recruiting the *capite censi*, Sulla was ordered to fill the ranks of cavalrymen. This was no easy task as many of the citizens wealthy enough to own horses and have experience riding them had been depleted in recent decades. Citizen cavalry was becoming scarce.

Sulla was determined to prove himself to his new commander. Even he had heard the name Marius and was aware of the man's reputation for winning. He knew that Marius' support could be the springboard he needed to rise up the *cursus honorum*, and conversely, Marius' disfavor could completely put an end to his career before it started. Sulla's new determination to succeed drove him, and he threw himself into his work, tirelessly seeking out enough horsemen to equip the legions.

CHAPTER EIGHTEEN

April 107 BC

Gaius Marius stood at the bow of the lead ship in the fleet that transported his consular army to Utica. The brisk cross wind caused the ships to buck and dip as they crashed into the waves crossing their path. The snap of the sails as they bellied out with the wind meant that the slaves that rowed the ships got a welcome rest. The saltwater spray created by the motion blew back into his upraised face as he reminisced of his time spent fighting against the Balearic pirates nearly twenty years ago. He remembered how sick he was on that first voyage and how Quintus Caecilius Metellus Balearicus had stood in the same spot he did now, looking toward the horizon and the fight to come. Back then, he was ill from the voyage, now, he relished the motion of the boat and taste of the saltwater as it trickled down his face and dampened his tunic.

His commander then bore the same name as the man Marius now sailed to replace as commanding general of the war in Numidia. They were probably cousins, but who really knew outside their own family. The Metelli were numerous, and the family boasted many generals and consuls in the last hundred years. He relished the thought that he had come full circle, and now, the new man was consul, while a member of the powerful Metellus family withdrew.

Upon Marius' return to Utica he found that Metellus had already left for Rome, refusing to meet with him to turn over the army, leaving it to Rutilius Rufus.

"Why don't you stay," Marius offered. "We've worked together for many years; you know me as well as I know myself."

Rufus looked at his friend. "No," he paused. "No. I have considered it, and I am grateful for the offer. But I have other plans that I must attend to."

"Like preparing for your own run for consul?" Marius quipped.

"Perhaps." Rufus tipped his head. "Honestly, I'm not sure yet. I do know I'm going to spend some time not thinking about war or politics. Perhaps spend some time with my family."

"Hmmph," Marius grunted, thinking of his own time spent with family.

After the formal ceremony to change out commanders was complete, Marius immediately ordered the legions out into the desert. The new legions and the veterans established camps and began training while they awaited the arrival of Sulla and the cavalry. Marius built up his stores of supplies and prepared for his approaching campaign against Jugurtha.

May 107 BC

A horn bugled the approach of a mass of horsemen from the east. At the head of the column rode Lucius Cornelius Sulla, resplendent in his shining helmet and cuirass, red cloak flowing in the light breeze. The entire formation reflected brightly as the African sun shone down upon them, thousands of pin pricks of light shooting off into the dry air as if the entire force were electrified by Jupiter's bolts.

The troops halted outside the camp, while Sulla walked his tall white stallion through the gates before dismounting and proudly strode up to the praetorium where Marius waited in the shade. "Quaestor Lucius Cornelius Sulla reports," he said, executing a crisp salute to his consul. "Your cavalry, sir," he said, turning and gesturing out the open gate at the assembled horsemen.

The corner of Marius' eye twitched. Just when he had begun to think that Sulla would not succeed in his mission, he showed up with some of the best-looking troops he had ever seen.

After a week to acclimate the cavalry and include them in some training, Marius implemented his plan to invade the interior of Numidia. Units of the newly arrived cavalry were sent out to reconnoiter and make contact with Jugurtha's forces. The infantry legions marched out into the desert; the veterans fresh from their winter break but knowing what was in store. The new legions overly enthusiastic and oblivious of what war in Numidia was like.

"These men are some of the roughest I've seen." Aulus Manlius, Marius' senior legate pulled his horse up next to the consul. He had just conducted a horseback inspection of the column of men marching behind them.

"They may not have the polish of the legions yet, but they are loyal, and eager to prove themselves," Marius said.

Unfortunately for Marius, Jugurtha continued his campaign of guerrilla ambushes and never offered a target for Marius to focus on that would allow him to employ the Romans' superior infantry forces and tactics.

Jugurtha had allied with the Mauretanian king Bocchus, the father of one of Jugurtha's wives, and they now attacked Marius' troops on multiple fronts.

Frustrated, Marius took a tactical pause near the end of summer to determine a new approach. *How can I bring Jugurtha to ground,* thought Marius. *I must find a way to corner him. These pin prick ambushes and disruption of my supply lines are causing havoc with morale.*

Marius finally determined that chasing Jugurtha around the desert only served to wear out his own troops while they suffered from thirst and the inability to close with their enemy. Returning to Metellus' previous strategy, he decided to focus on capturing or destroying the cities and strongholds of Numidia, thus depriving Jugurtha of his refuges. The first city in the new plan was Capsa.

Marius sent his legate Aulus Manlius toward the city of Laris as a diversion, and pretended to move in the same direction, but once out in the desert his main body turned south and circled around to approach the city of Capsa undetected. While out of sight of the city, Marius ordered his cavalry to race ahead and seize the gates while the bulk of his forces moved up as quickly as they could. The city was taken unawares and rather than capture it and leave a garrison, Marius burned it and killed everyone in it. "I don't have the manpower to garrison every city," Marius said. "And I won't leave any more strongholds behind me for Jugurtha to make use of."

Sulla, meanwhile, was back at Marius' main camp. As an administrator, he had learned the power of delegation and while his subordinates kept the supply lines running, he had created quite a comfortable life for himself. Through the labor of slaves and soldiers he had a bath constructed, a necessity in such a hot and dirty place. *How did they get along this long without a public bath?* He thought. But Sulla, accustomed to luxury, not only built the public bath, but included a private bath for himself where he brought in men and women from across North Africa to join him in parties that wound up as days-long orgies of food and sex, all while Marius and his men were slogging across the desert.

One day, while Marius was searching for a way to bring Jugurtha to ground, the thought occurred to him to use Sulla's natural abilities to seek out an alternative solution. Marius was the straightforward soldier. He could use tactical deception to make the enemy think that he was going to do something, then surprise him with a different strategy. He had learned to navigate the world of politics and it's webs of lies and deceit. But he was not the wily chin-wagger that Sulla was. He did not understand the intricacies of diplomacy and intrigue that came so naturally to Sulla. Marius instructed Sulla to make contact with Jugurtha's ally, King Bocchus of Mauretania.

However misguided, Sulla's irresponsible behavior resulted in an opportunity, when he discovered that one of his guests had contact with servants of King Bocchus.

"I want to get a message through to Bocchus," Sulla told her one evening while they sat in the steaming water with his arm about her shoulders.

She laced her fingers through his, the hot water gently lapping against her breasts and buoying them seductively. "This can be done," she assured him.

"Good. Tell him . . . tell him that I wish to meet. Quietly. No one else is to know."

She nodded her head and began to rise.

"Tomorrow will be good enough," he said, pulling her down to him. "Tonight you have another task."

But Sulla's attempts went unanswered. While Marius continued his campaign throughout the next year, Sulla continued his attempts to speak with Jugurtha's father-in-law. Marius had Jugurtha on the run. His strategy of destroying or conquering and garrisoning Numidia's major cities had driven a wedge between the Numidian king and his people. They were turning against him, and he was forced to flee to Mauretania to beg for assistance to continue the war.

For some time now, Bocchus had begun to regret his association with his son-in-law. Jugurtha's actions had caused Bocchus to fear the repercussions that would come if they were to lose the war with Rome, and he was looking for a way out.

When Marius invaded Mauretania in pursuit of Jugurtha, Bocchus saw that his reign was now at risk. Sulla, who had joined Marius in the field, was proving to be a respectable troop commander as well as logistician and diplomat. One day his troops came across a delegation of ambassadors from Bocchus who were being attacked by a group of bandits. The Romans rescued the delegation, and Sulla sent them on their way with gifts and an escort back to their king. Bocchus finally saw an opening, hoping that Sulla was a more reasonable alternative to Marius. He finally agreed to a parley.

"There is no greater friendship to be had, than that of the Roman Republic," Sulla began. "If only you had made this decision from the start, you might have enjoyed many favors rather than suffered so much misfortune."

"Please understand that I only took up arms to defend my kingdom," Bocchus pleaded. "I could not have allowed the invasion of my lands without making the attempt to defend it. Unfortunately, Consul Marius is much more the general than I."

Through months of further negotiations with Sulla, and trips to Rome and back by his delegations who bargained with the senate, Bocchus finally agreed to turn over Jugurtha. He asked Marius for the favor of Sulla accepting the Numidian king into his custody as they had built such a rapport. Marius agreed.

On an evening deep in the desert, on the pretense of an agreed upon meeting, Bocchus arranged an ambush. All of Jugurtha's companions were killed and the Numidian king placed into chains. Jugurtha was turned over to Sulla, who presented the king to Gaius Marius, thus ending the Numidian war.

JEFF HEIN

PART III

REBELLION

107-106 BC

JEFF HEIN

CHAPTER NINETEEN

Gaul

107 BC

Spring brought the news that the Tigurini were on the move toward Roman territory in southern Gaul. The border had been quiet since Consul Silanus was defeated nearly two years ago but the tense peace in Gaul had been shattered like the first blinding flash and deafening roar of thunder announces the arrival of a furious storm.

Junior Consul Lucius Cassius Longinus rode at the front of his consular army when they marched north to intercept the Tigurini. The sub-tribe of the Helvetii had ventured forth from their mountain strongholds in the western Alps to run rampant in southern Gaul. Now, Longinus' spies reported that the Tigurini had joined with the local Volcae Tectosages and incited them to rebellion. The Volcae's capital was the oppidum at Tolosa, just inside the border of Gallia Narbonensis on the river Garumna. Rome could not afford for the unrest to spread, and Longinus was sent to quell the rebellion.

Longinus was yet another consul that came from a family with a long line of political men with moderate military skills. Like other men of his time, he had received the usual education that included the histories of Rome's battles, and training in tactics and individual battle skills, but his climb up the *cursus honorum* had been mostly political appointments. Longinus had been sent to Numidia four years ago to assure Jugurtha's safe travels so that the king could return to Rome to testify in the corruption trials that the tribune Gaius Memmius had forced upon the unwilling senate. As propraetor the following year, he had served a quiet and successful term as governor of Gallia Narbonensis. Just as he was about to hand over control of his position to the new governor, Quintus Servilius Caepio, he had received a petition from the Cimbri leader who had been pillaging Gaul. The barbarian king requested land for his people in return for military service and a promise of peace. Longinus returned to Rome with the letter and the senate promptly denied that request and sent the newly elected Consul Marcus Junius Silanus north with their reply, along with Longinus as his junior legate.

Unfortunately, Silanus had not been up to the task, and when Caepio went behind his back and captured the Cimbri king, he unleashed a storm beyond his control. Silanus was defeated and most of his army killed. Longinus narrowly escaped with his senior officers and some of the men. A year later, mostly due to his years in Gaul, Longinus won his election to consul and was given imperium to defeat the Germanic tribes and bring stability and prosperity back to Gallia Narbonensis.

Accepting the Senate's decree, Longinus felt a bit of unsurety. He knew he did not have a great deal of experience in waging war, and consequently, Longinus wisely hand-picked two very good men to be his legates. Lucius Calpurnius Piso Caesoninus who had been consul five years previously and Gaius Popillius Laenus, whose family boasted consuls and generals going back two hundred years. Longinus commanded two legions of citizens and two of auxiliary with their attached cavalry: more than twenty thousand fighting men, plus non-combatants, and camp followers. He had every confidence this would be enough to deal with these troublesome peasants.

Near Tolosa, Gallia Narbonensis

May 107 BC

Divico, the chieftain of the Tigurini, presided over a large outdoor council beside his counterpart, Copillus, chieftain of the Volcae Tectosages. The day had begun overcast, but the sun broke through the clouds shortly after dawn and the day was comfortably warm. Copillus and other minor tribal headmen saluted Divico in a toast and the mood was light. The Tigurini had recently arrived from the east, following their ambassadors who had offered an alliance with the Volcae to resist Rome. The Volcae had chafed under Rome's heavy-handed friendship for more than a decade while the Roman soldiers pushed ever farther north. The Volcae were a proud people, and when Rome included much of their tribal lands in the newly established province of Gallia-Narbonensis, the Volcae were angry. Tribal legend told that the Volcae were part of the same Gallic invasion of Greece that the Cimbri had participated in centuries ago. That invasion was abruptly defeated, seemingly at the hands of angry gods who sent a terrible storm, freezing weather, and shook the earth in anger, swallowing up many of the invaders in landslides and gaping fissures that suddenly appeared in the mountainous terrain. Their leader, Brennus, was severely wounded, and the leaderless Gallic army succumbed to infighting. Suffering terribly from his wounds and in despair over the total defeat, Brennus later committed suicide. Without their charismatic chieftain to hold them together, the great alliance of tribes broke up and the Volcae retreated westward, eventually settling in middle Germania near the Danubius River. Later, they were pushed further west and finally settled in Gaul, establishing their new homeland centered on Tolosa.

The past misfortunes of the Volcae were blamed on that invasion and the sacred treasures they had looted from the temple of Delphi. Upon the Volcae's arrival in Gaul their priests determined that in order to regain the gods' favor, they must offer those cursed treasures as sacrifice. The surrounding lakes and rivers became the offering sites for tons of silver and gold, weapons and armor, jewels and gems. The Volcae grew strong again, and over the following centuries established themselves as a major power in Gaul. Many smaller tribes paid them tribute each year and their temples and treasuries now overflowed with the riches they had accumulated. Divico saw this strength and knew that they would make good allies to bring the fight to Rome.

"I appreciate that you are here honoring our alliance," Copillus said to Divico. "But what of the Cimbri and the Ambrones? Or Teutones? We would be far more likely to win with their strength behind us."

"Borrix does not answer to me. Nor does Teutobod or Amalric. The Tigurini have traveled far to join you in your fight against these invaders. We have engaged them across the frontier. The other tribes that are here with us are just as angry about the constant encroachment on our lands. Your entire tribe is here, fighting on your land, for your homes and fields. We will have no difficulty defeating these armies. If anything, Borrix has shown us how easily they are defeated."

"I'm not sure easily is the right word," Copillus said. "These Romans should never be underestimated. I would much rather have the numbers of the northern tribes behind me."

"Well, they are not here, and we are. We will take this fight to the Romans, and we will push them back to the Mare Nostrum."

Longinus drew his legions up on a field several miles east of Tolosa while a misty drizzle fell on the ranks of miserable legionaries who shivered in their soaked linen undergarments and mail armor.

Fifty thousand Tigurini and Volcae warriors, their bronze helmets adorned with creatures of all sorts, shook their brightly colored shields in front of them as they shouted their war cries. The clangor of swords and spears banging on the metal boss of their shields carried across the battlefield to the Roman legionaries.

"What a racket these savages make," Gaius Popillius Laenus complained. The junior legate sat his horse beside Consul Longinus.

Longinus did not reply immediately. He sat tall in his saddle and stared at the wild warriors with a grudging respect. "These savages have beaten every army that has faced them recently," he finally replied. "It is foolish to blame it all on the incompetence of our generals. If nothing else, these barbarians can fight."

"These are Gauls," Senior Legate Lucius Calpurnius Piso snorted in derision. "We've beaten them many times before, we'll beat them again."

"They're not all Gauls," Longinus noted. "That group on the left? Those are warriors from farther east. Look at the difference in dress and hair styles."

"They're all barbarians," Piso said. "They're from north of the border, whether they tie their hair up in knots or wear it long. Look at them, screaming like madmen."

"Yes, they are all related. But this is a clear indication that they are working together. For that tribe to have travelled this far from their homeland just to support the Volcae Tectosages, indicates there is significant communication and cooperation going on. This is going to be a conflagration if we let it build."

While the Roman generals watched, the tribunes ordered the legions into defensive formation. Longinus did not plan to attack, but rather to stand strong and accept the charge of the barbarians that he knew would come. The onrushing charge by overwhelming numbers of screaming warriors was their hallmark. The

Tigurini leader Divico walked his horse across the front of the enemy formation; his white stallion, full of vigor, pranced and hopped in his excitement. The king of the Tigurini was young, and an imposing man. Tall and muscular, Divico was also handsome, violent, and eager for plunder. He saw the Romans as a threat to his own people, but also an opportunity to gain fame and riches. He hated them, hated that they thought they had the right to impose their authority on anyone they chose.

He envied Borrix, who had proven himself time and again against the Romans and whose treasury overflowed with riches. He liked and respected the Cimbri king, very much, but the Cimbri were not here today. This battle would be won by the Tigurini and their allies; warriors of the Volcae Tectosages, and other tribes eager to fight the Roman invaders.

Laenus focused on one of the enemy leaders, stalking on foot before the shouting warriors, encouraging them to their battle frenzy. There was something about him that was strange. He was tall and blonde like the others, but something about his movement was odd. It hit him suddenly that what caught his eye was the subtle difference in the stride, a feminine movement. By Jupiter, the leader of that group appeared to be a woman dressed up in men's clothing, wearing a coat of Gaulish mail and a bronze helmet. But there was no mistaking the slight sway of the hips that distinguished a woman's gait from a man. She appeared just as fierce as the rest, though slightly slimmer of build.

A horrendous noise rose from the Gaulish lines, a pre-arranged signal from the dozens of carnyx and signal horns that launched the huge body of barbarians across the field. Their leaders ran several paces to the front, setting the example of courage and ferocity for their followers. The Roman ranks stood firm, the shields of the first rank interlocked, their iron discipline kept their feet rooted to the ground. But no man enters battle for the first time with confidence. The pungent smell of piss running down the legs of the newer recruits who had heard the fearsome stories of the vicious Gauls, wafted through the formation. These men were raised on the stories of the massive defeats of Carbo and Silanus and the inhuman treatment of the prisoners and survivors. The soldiers could see the fearsome enemy hurtling at them like a stone shot from a catapult; death personified. The veterans might have had more control, but they knew what faced them, and they set their faces into grim masks of determination.

Divico and his sister Errani, the warrior woman, were among the first to reach the shield wall. Laenus watched her lead her followers into the fray, fascinated that a woman led hundreds of savage warriors into battle, and lost sight of her when the sides clashed together. Just before the lines met, the Velites launched their darts in quick succession, targeting the third and fourth ranks of Gauls, separating the front ranks and lightening the impact upon their own front lines. The Velites melted between the ranks of Hastati behind them, and the enemy who fell wounded or dead tripped up the following ranks and slowed their charge. Longinus, wisely acting on the tactical advice of his legates had instructed his artillery to fire into the tightly packed mass of warriors just after the Velites launched their darts. The *ballistae* killed and maimed hundreds with the large stones that careened through the mob while the over-sized arrows impaled two or three men at a time.

Divico was wounded early in the fight when the man opposing him struck over his shield, slicing deeply into the king's shoulder. "The king has fallen!" his men cried out. Hands grasped him and carried him to the rear while his companions fought on. The pressure on the front lines began to lesson as the terrible casualties inflicted on the tribes from the Roman artillery took effect. The two fronts parted, and Longinus ordered his men to stand fast. There would be no pursuit today. He allowed the enemy to withdraw and ordered his men back to the camp to rest and tend their wounds. Though it was a minor battle in terms of numbers, the day was the first victory the Romans had seen over the Germanic tribes in a long time.

"Sir, we should pursue them and finish this," Laenus urged him.

"No, that is enough for the day, they are beaten. Besides, it will be dark soon," Longinus replied. "We will reorganize and pursue them tomorrow, and we will make sure they understand what it means to revolt against Rome. See that our wounded and dead are cared for legate. Let the officers know that we will march at dawn to pursue the barbarians."

Laenus saluted, turning to carry out his orders.

Longinus was pumped full of pride. He was the first Roman commander to decisively defeat a barbarian army in the north since Ahenobarbus defeated the Arverni more than ten years ago. Tomorrow he would finish the job.

Longinus had been governor of Gallia Narbonensis and then had served as legate under Consul Marcus Junius Silanus a year later when the Cimbri massacred the consul's four legions on a hellish march across Gaul while the legions tried to escape the fate their commander had brought upon them. Well, it wasn't entirely fair to blame it all on Silanus. It was the new governor Quintus Servilius Caepio who had set the conditions for defeat by betraying the Cimbri king and kidnapping him during peace negotiations. The fury with which the Germans had fallen upon Silanus' men was terrifying. Caepio's actions had been the catalyst, and he had been recalled to Rome. Silanus was waiting to stand trial for his defeat.

In his tent, Longinus conferred with Senior Legate Lucius Calpurnius Piso.

"A toast, consul," Piso handed Longinus a cup of watered wine. Piso had served as consul five years earlier, just after Gaius Papirius Carbo had lost the first battle with the Cimbri. He was an aristocrat who approached war as if it were a game of *latrunculi*, moving his units around the battlefield without getting his hands dirty. "It's about time we saw a victory over these barbarians. A brilliant strategy."

"Thank you, Lucius," Longinus accepted the compliment. "But it was the advice of Laenus and yourself that won the day."

Longinus was a tall man. Thin and balding, with a stoop in his shoulders that brought his head forward. He looked like a vulture sitting on a branch contemplating his dinner. His eyes were watery, and he had an open face that invited trust and a manner that encouraged conversation, some even thought he was a bit stupid, but he used that to his advantage.

"You're too modest," Piso replied.

"In any case, we will be pursuing them tomorrow morning. What do our scouts tell us?"

"They have withdrawn from the field, leaving their dead and their entire wagon train. They are heading back north with their tail between their legs. It looks like they are heading toward Burdigala. Apparently the Bituriges Vivisci, I'll never get used to these barbarian names and how they twist the tongue, have also risen up in rebellion. Some of their warriors were probably here today. They'll be seeking refuge there."

"Excellent. I want to keep up the pressure. Keep the scouts out and maintain contact. Tomorrow our boys will be rested up and we will follow them. Bring their wagon train along. Strip everything useful from the bodies. We need to send the message that their insolence will not be tolerated. Our men will fight all the harder if they see there is booty to be had."

The next morning the camp was torn down before the sun was fully up in the sky. The wounded had been treated and the worst sent back to Narbo in oxcarts. The scouts reported that the Tigurini and Volcae Tectosages had continued their flight northward. The rhythmic stomp of the Romans hobnailed *caligae* began as the legions moved out.

"Sir, we should put out security on our flanks," Laenus said. "Procedure calls for flank security when we are in enemy territory." Laenus was a senior officer who lived by the book.

"Take care of it," Longinus replied. "But we need to quicken the pace. We're nipping at their heels, and I want to keep them on the run." But the enormous wagon train that now consisted of all the Roman supply wagons as well as all the captured carts and wagons of the Tigurini was slowing the march.

"Sir!" A tribune approached on horseback. "I've sent skirmishers forward to harass their rear elements, but they are ranging too far away from the main body and making themselves vulnerable to ambush. The legions are moving too slowly to keep up."

"We could leave the wagon train to catch up. Maybe leave a couple of maniples of infantry for protection," offered Piso.

Longinus, unwilling to give up the caravan or to split up his forces decided to recall the forward units. "We know where they are going. Pull your men back to the main body and continue the march at pace."

"Yes, sir," the tribune acknowledged and spun his horse about.

For five days the legions tramped along the simple road between Tolosa and Burdigala, beside the Garumna River, over hills and through forestland, and past the occasional farmstead and hamlet. They saw no one. Word had spread of their approach and the Gauls had left the countryside desolate of both people and livestock. With each passing day the retreating Tigurini and their allies gained more distance. With more distance they gained time. Time which they used in their favor while the Romans continued to march forward, deep into unfriendly lands.

Burdigala was the chief town of the Bituriges Vivisci. Roman trade ships docked at Burdigala's wharves, and a detachment of Roman soldiers enforced an uneasy peace in the city, while Roman traders walked the road overland from Narbo through Tolosa. The influx of Roman goods dropped the prices of commodities through the floor, forcing local merchants out of business. Like the Volcae, the Bituriges were ready to stop the steady creep of Roman expansion, and an alliance with the Tigurini and Volcae provided the assurance they needed to resist.

At Burdigala, the word of the invasion of Gaul by a Roman army inflamed the countryside and the revolt had spread in earnest. The Roman garrison inside the city was overwhelmed and chased to the wharves where the survivors fled on any available ship. Warriors were streaming into the city, reinforcing its defenses and preparing to do battle while Longinus approached from the south.

Before noon of the sixth day after the battle at Tolosa, Longinus' legionaries could see a change in the landscape as untamed forest gave way to meadows and tilled fields. They had descended from the mountain range that nestled Tolosa and were nearing the coastal plains where fields of wheat, barley, and oats swayed seductively in the light breeze. Vast orchards of olives, apples, cherries, plums, and pears were in various stages of blossoming. Vineyards of delicate grape vines stretched to the horizon. On the hilltops, patches of carefully managed forests provided firewood, building materials, nuts, and sap. The land was strangely familiar to the young Italians who marched through it, and they were surprised to find this reminder of home in what they thought of as the wilds of Gaul.

Longinus's scouts returned with the news that they were a day's march from Burdigala. There was still no sign of the enemy, but the young decurion had a good eye for terrain. "Sir, there is a large river crossing that we will reach by noon tomorrow. It is fordable but the water is high with spring melt. It will cause the column to pause while the trains navigate the ford. The valley's walls are steep and come close to the crossing point. It looks to be a likely place for an ambush."

Longinus raised his brow and looked to his officers. "Your thoughts?" he questioned.

"We could set up a castrum on this side of the river," offered Laenus. "Then while the forces cross, they can begin the work on a second camp that we occupy for the night after the crossing."

"Too many men will be occupied with building camps," said Piso. "We need to just cross and keep moving. Split the legions and secure both sides while the trains cross."

"I agree with Lucius," Longinus said. "We need to keep moving. I want to keep them on the run."

"They are not on the run anymore," argued Laenus. "By the time we cross, it will be nearly dark. It is unwise to go without a camp for the night in enemy territory."

"Alright, but one camp on the far side. We'll split the legions to give security on both sides. While the legions cross, they can divide their efforts between security and camp construction."

Darkness had settled on the land before the last wagons crossed the river by torchlight. As the exhausted mules and drivers entered the safety of the camp, Longinus was standing near the gate watching them. There had been no enemy contact during the crossing and Longinus was confident that the Tigurini had retreated out of the area. "I've changed my mind. We're going to stay in camp tomorrow. The men are tired and need a day of rest, we've pushed them hard. The animals too." Turning to Piso he said, "Send out the scouts tomorrow morning. I want to know how far it is to Burdigala and what we are facing. Right now, I'm planning to leave the trains here unless something changes."

Then he turned to Laenus, "Gaius, when we move out the morning after tomorrow, you will stay here with one auxiliary legion and defend the camp and the trains. The rest of us will seek battle and bring these barbarians to heel. I don't expect any difficulty with that, but if we run into trouble, we'll fall back to the camp. Any questions?"

CHAPTER TWENTY

Outside Burdigala

May 107 BC

Divico, chieftain of the Tigurini, Copillus of the Volcae Tectosages, and Aeneiran of the Bituriges, sat in a war council surrounded by their lesser chieftains, senior warriors, and advisors. The Cimbri would not be joining in this battle. The Ambrones and Teutones, not plagued by the curse that kept the Cimbri moving every summer and sated for the moment with the riches they had accumulated the previous year, had decided not to participate in this year's campaign. The Ambrones remained in the vicinity of Aduatuca and the Teutones occupied the area of the Donarsberg along the Rhenus River.

"The Romans are a day's march from us," Divico began. "They've been following us since Tolosa, and they are anxious to do battle." Divico shifted to ease his discomfort from the wounds he had taken at Tolosa.

"The Bituriges will hold the city," Aeneiran stated flatly. "The Romans will come from the south and demand our surrender. They will probably assume you are within our walls."

"They will employ the heavy *ballistae* they used at Tolosa and try to force your capitulation," Divico said. "They have divided their force and left one legion behind at a camp a day's march from here, further weakening their already much smaller force. They likely are not aware their garrison in the city has fled. Let them come, I have a plan."

It was a warm spring morning in mid-May when Longinus's legions left their camp, marching down the well-traveled road to Burdigala. The road had widened from the cart path that came down from the mountains around Tolosa and was now a flattened, hard packed earth road that allowed enough room for two carts to pass each other without having to leave the pathway.

The surrounding landscape showed obvious signs of recent human activity yet was eerily absent of life. Longinus assumed it was their approach that had sent all the locals streaming for the protection of the fortified city that came into view in the distance, squatting atop a large hill next to the Garumna River.

As they neared the city, the legions smoothly deployed from their march column into the triplex acies, the battle formation that aligned the maniples of Hastati, Principes, and Triarii into the familiar checkerboard squares that had been so effective for hundreds of years.

Longinus immediately sent his legate Lucius Calpurnius Piso forward to demand the surrender of the city under threat of total destruction. There was no response. After several hours of shouting demands toward the walls, Piso turned away and returned to his commander.

"The barbarians don't even have enough courtesy to reply. They never even came to the gate," complained Piso. "They just stood at the top of their walls and jeered at us."

"Emplace the *ballistae*," said Longinus. "We will give them until dawn to respond. Then we begin battering their walls."

When the morning sun rose above the treetops there still had been no word from the city. A single ballista launched its stone in a great arc toward the palisade. It dropped twenty yards short of the wall and rolled to a stop, leaving a furrow where it traveled before it bumped impotently against the earthen rampart that formed the bottom of the wall. The warriors standing at the top of the wall gave a raucous cheer that could be heard across the fields where the Roman artillerymen grinned knowingly. They now had the range to the wall and spread the information to the rest of the crews. With a shouted order, the entire battery fired a barrage of stones that flew straight and true, slamming into the palisade that sat atop the earthen wall, splintering logs and sending bodies flying.

Inside the wall, Aeneiran ordered his men down from the ramparts when the second volley crashed into the wall. The rows of legionaries stood, watching the artillery soften up the city. All eyes were forward, watching the growing gap in the wall and anticipating the order to move forward. Longinus, secure in his assumption that all of his enemies were inside the wall had neglected to assign security to his rear and flanks. While the legions stared at the city, tens of thousands of warriors appeared behind them, surging through the flaxen fields, in and around the orchard trees and vineyards, like an ocean wave that found its way inland.

With a cry of alarm from one of the Romans who happened to catch movement out of the side of his eye, the rear ranks of the legions turned, man by man to see an overwhelming horde of huge, blonde warriors closing within javelin range. The Tigurini and Volcae Tectosages began their war chants and quickened their pace, screaming their fury as they charged forward, their lead warriors smashing into the side and flanks of the legions with a deafening crash.

Longinus and Piso were among the first to fall alongside their senior staff and subordinate officers. Piso had just enough time to recognize that the sword that killed him was that of the female warrior he had watched at Tolosa. Divico's sister Errani and her followers had been given the honor of finding and killing the Roman generals and their command staff.

Like at Noreia, the tables were turned when the warriors attacked the much smaller maniples of the Triarii first, the most experienced of the Roman fighters, rolling over them with the irresistible shock and overwhelming numbers of the north men before they were able to respond. Within moments it was a free for all when the Tigurini and Volcae Tectosages flowed through the open spaces between the maniples, never allowing the superior tactics of the more disciplined legions to take effect. The individual squares of the triplex acies found themselves surrounded and cutoff from support as the screaming barbarians cut them down. Centurions called for the Hastati to turn and launch pilas, but the masses had become packed together as they shrank away from the violence of the attack. There was little room for them to draw their arm back and throw their missiles. Some of the scorpion operators managed to turn their smaller weapons and fire a bolt off with some effect, but the speed and force of the attack defeated them before they could fire a second time.

When the artillery abruptly stopped, the roar of the attack reached the city and those brave souls who still stood atop the walls called to the men below to open the gates. "The attack has begun!" they cried. Aeneiran urged his men out of the city, venting their anger and lust for battle as they ran forward, attacking first the batteries of *ballistae* that had caused so much damage. The artillery men fled to the ranks of the infantrymen behind them for protection followed closely by the raging tribesmen who exploited the sudden change of initiative.

The Romans found themselves without leadership and as capable as the individual centurions were, the fighting devolved into dozens of small battles, each maniple fighting for its own life unable to support one another, each outnumbered five to one and attacked from all sides so that they were pared down one rank at a time while the men in the center could only wait for their turn, unable to help those in the front ranks.

It was a disaster, and it was over quickly. The legions were destroyed to the last man. There was no opportunity to escape.

When the fighting had ceased and only the tribes remained standing, the leaders met on the battlefield.

"Gather your men," Divico said to the others. "We march immediately to the camp before they realize what has happened."

Without warning, the multitude of warriors descended upon the camp alongside the river. All of the large weapons had gone forward with Longinus to attack Burdigala and the only defenses the camp had left were the pila that each legionary carried. Divico did not want an extended siege, so he sent word to the camp for a parley. He would allow Laenus and his men to live, but only under harsh terms of surrender.

"You will return everything you captured at Tolosa, including any prisoners, and half of your own wagons, oxen, food, and equipment. You will leave behind your weapons and armor, and you will turn over one thousand hostages."

"A thousand hostages?" Laenus stammered. "Half of everything?"

"You would rather we take everything? You will not leave your camp alive if you do not agree. Maybe I should leave your men to starve, surrounded by fifty thousand allied warriors. You have what, maybe ten thousand including the slaves and camp followers? No, you seem to be an unusually bright officer. You will accept my terms to save your men."

Laenus could not look up. He was caught. He was vastly outnumbered and had no hope of escape. The shame of surrendering to the tribes would ruin him. Yet, he could not sentence his men to certain death. At least he would be giving them the chance to fight another day. "I accept your terms," he said miserably.

"And one more thing," Divico said. "You will all pass under the yoke when you leave."

All Laenus could do was hang his head.

The next morning the Romans opened the gate and marched out in their tunics and sandals. Despite the circumstances, Laenus was determined to retain as much pride as he could. The legionaries stood tall, until they approached the framework under which they must pass. Several spear shafts had been sunk into the ground and an ox yoke was suspended between them. Passing under the yoke was a tradition that crossed cultures. It represented a defeated enemy's subjugation and was a sign that they were now subservient to their conquerors. The yoke was chest high so that the Romans had to bend over to pass below, bowing their heads in submission. The Romans had used it against their enemies for centuries, and in turn, their enemies used the tradition against them. The severed heads of Lucius Cassius Longinus and Lucius Calpurnius Piso were stuck on the top of the spear shafts that held the yoke, in order to witness the humiliation.

Before long, the last of the Romans vanished around the bend in the road leading back to Tolosa and then to Narbo. Divico stood in the road, watching as if he could still see them. He finally had his victory.

"I wish that they would all return to their city," he said.

"Mmmmm," Copillus mumbled beside him in agreement. "They will keep coming and we will keep killing them. We have no choice now."

CHAPTER TWENTY-ONE

Near Tolosa

Fall 107 BC

Since the loss of Longinus and his legions at Burdigala, the countryside had been aflame with the rebellion. It seemed that every warrior in every village rose up against the Roman occupiers. Caravans were attacked and raiders crossed into Narbonensis to attack Roman estates.

At his castrum near Tolosa, Vulca climbed the ladder to the sentry's platform an hour before dawn for his routine check on the guards. His tesserarius, or watch commander, greeted him with a salute. "Good morning, Commander. All is quiet."

"Mmmhmm," Vulca acknowledged. The red transverse crest on his centurion's helmet looked black in the pre-morning darkness. The shadow from his visor further shadowed Vulca's dark complexion. "Walk with me," he said to the tesserarius. It was Vulca's custom to visit the guards at least once during the night. It was good for soldiers to see their commander and even better that he spoke to them occasionally.

As they approached the first sentry, the man snapped to attention and saluted. "All quiet, sir."

It was dark and the soldier's face was further shadowed by his helmet brim and cheekpieces. "How old are you, son?"

"I'll be eighteen next month, sir," he said, puffing out his thin chest with pride.

"You came with the replacements that arrived last week?"

"Yes, sir."

"And what do you know about our mission here?"

"Uh, well sir," he began unsurely. "We're here to guard the trade road between Narbo and Burdigala," he said with sudden confidence, remembering his briefing.

"That's what they told you at Narbo. What do you know about what is going on now?"

"We heard about Consul Longinus, sir," he said carefully, unsure if it was wise to speak to a senior officer about the defeat of a Roman army.

"What did you hear?"

"Only that he was defeated by the barbarians, sir, and that his legate Gaius Popillius Laenus surrendered the rest of the army," he added with a tone of disgust.

"Don't be too quick to judge. I've faced these barbarians before, and they have destroyed three consular armies and countless other tribes. They are warriors to be respected, even feared, but they can be beaten. Longinus proved that when he fought them at Tolosa. We have to trust in our superior training. We have to stay alert, prepare, and fight wisely. Above all we have to trust in the men beside us. The Gauls are out there, and they are supported by the Germans. There are tens of thousands of them, we are just an outpost of five-hundred men."

The young man stared at Vulca. "You have nothing to say?" the centurion asked.

"T...t...truly?" he stammered. "How could we ever hold them

off?"

"It's why I have had you and your companions working so hard the past few months to strengthen our position; the ditches and stakes, the additional *ballistae* that has been emplaced. We've reinforced the gates and cleared the brush and trees back two hundred paces and brought in food and water against a siege. Have confidence, we are well established here," he reassured the young man. "In any case, we're to be relieved soon. The garrison at Tolosa is being recalled and we will return to Narbo for duty in the capital."

The man visibly relaxed and Vulca moved to the next sentry. "All is quiet, sir."

"So I've heard," Vulca replied dryly. "Tell me soldier, have you seen anything?"

Confused, the legionary looked to the watch commander, and back to Vulca. He had just reported that all was quiet, and he didn't understand the question.

Seeing his confusion, Vulca went on. "I keep hearing that all is quiet, but have you *seen* anything?"

Both men paused, unsure what to say. It was the darkest time of the night, just before dawn. There was little to see.

Vulca gestured over the wall. "Look out there and tell me what you see."

The man did as he was told. "I can't see anything, sir," he replied nervously.

"That's because you're looking straight forward," said Vulca. "Don't stare directly at something. Use your peripheral vision, the sides of your eyes. Look for the subtle variation in the darkness of the shadows. Some are black, some are dark gray, light gray. Don't try to focus on stationary objects, watch for movement, shadows passing before shadows. Don't look down into the fort where the light is. Allow your eyes to adjust to the darkness. That's it. What do you see now?"

"I can make out the shrubs better," he said. "I can see some branches swaying in the breeze," he said excitedly.

Vulca reached out and squeezed the man's shoulder. "Good man," he said. Turning to the tesserarius, Vulca instructed him to ensure that the other men were trained as well. "There's more to sentry duty at night than listening."

"Yes, sir!" The watch commander turned and went to instruct his men.

Vulca turned and looked over the wall. He was looking east, and the sky was graying above the treetops. The birds were coming awake in the forest, their twitters and whistles and chirps promising a peaceful day. The bright colors of the fall foliage were coming alive in the rising sun. Vulca loved greeting the dawn of a new day. This one promised to be warm and sunny. He closed his eyes and breathed deeply through his nose, enjoying the forest sounds and the feeling of the sun's rays on his face. His reverie was shattered by the incongruous blast of a warning horn.

His eyes popped open at the sound and his blood ran cold. Thousands of warriors had silently materialized from the forest and stood at the edge of the clearing. "Jupiter, Juno, and Minerva," he muttered, staring at the panoply of painted shields that mirrored the many-colored treetops. He did not need to issue orders; he had drilled the men constantly so that each knew his place.

Men spilled from their barracks to form up on the parade ground while others hurried toward the *ballistae*. The archers took their places on the wall and still others stood between them prepared to throw their javelins when the enemy came within range. Vulca had nearly five-hundred men, stout walls, and sharp defenses. He had prepared well, but when he looked out to the trees, he could not help but feel the cold fingers of fear winding up his spine like a creeping vine winds its way up a sapling.

Optio Marcus Decimus, second in command, spotted Vulca on the wall and hurried to join him. "The decani have it, you've trained them well," he said to Vulca, referring to the subordinate leaders of ten-man squads who lived and worked with the men. Normally a tribune would have commanded a detachment this large, but in this case, caravan guard duty at a lonely outpost was below the status of a tribune, so the duty fell to the newest centurion in the legion, Vulca. He had insisted that the decani be trained to act swiftly and with confidence. He had worked hard to prepare them. All the men had been drilled on their duties in the defense of the castrum. Vulca was proud when he looked around at them standing tall and confident within minutes of the warning horn's blast.

The two enemies stood eerily silent. Vulca knew the Gauls would sing the barritus to work themselves up before a battle and instill fear in the enemy. But they just stood there, staring toward the castrum, as if waiting for something. This unexpected silence unnerved the Romans even more than the usual racket that preluded a battle.

The young soldier Vulca had spoken to earlier looked to his left and right, not sure what to think about this change in the behavior he had been told about. He was sweating heavily in the cool morning air, and he shivered nervously when a trickle of sweat ran down his back.

As Vulca and his men watched, the mournful cry of the carnyx arose from amid the mass of warriors; bronze trumpets that rose several feet above their heads, the ends shaped like the heads of various animals sacred to the Gauls. Some of the horns had moving parts that resembled the tongue of the animal and fluttered as the air moved across it and out the mouth, creating an undulating sound.

The result was a cacophony that carried across the field to the Romans. The horns were a signal to the men to begin their barritus. They raised their shields to their mouths and began the low moaning that surged into the tumultuous combination of horns, drums, human voices, and the clash of weapons on shields.

Men on the walls bit their lips in determination, mouths went dry, and knuckles that gripped weapons went white. The decani shouted to them to bolster their courage at the sight of so many warriors but it was ineffective, and the men began fidgeting as they contemplated the possibility of dying in a remote corner of Gaul for a cause that few cared about. Vulca decided that it was time to speak.

"Men of the legion of Gaul!" he shouted. Heads turned in the direction of their stoic commander. They knew him to be a quiet man of few words and were mildly surprised to hear the strength of his voice when he addressed the entire castrum. "You are soldiers of Rome. You are the best trained, the best equipped, and the best led soldiers to ever trod the face of the earth. You are the descendants of the men who fought for Scipio, Brutus, and Ahenobarbus. Your forefathers marched through the shining city in triumph over barbarians just such as these. This was no accident! Rome always has done what is necessary to win. We stand behind stout walls and defenses that will account for many of our enemies. We are prepared to rain death upon their warriors with our *ballistae*, and we have among us some of the most experienced soldiers Rome has ever fielded. Swallow your fear, trust your comrades and your leaders. You are all sons of Rome, and you will be victorious this day. Fight for Rome, fight for your pride, or fight for a woman, I don't care, but above all fight for the man beside you, and show these barbarians what true Romans are made of!"

The men let loose with a cheer and looked back to the enemy with renewed confidence. With an eye for terrain that was equal to those far more experienced than he, Vulca had moved the castrum when he arrived so that it was backed up against the Garumna River and was set into a shallow horseshoe bend that protected the rear and sides of the fort. He had dug ditches and emplaced obstacles that would break up any charge that got nearer to the fort but left a wide-open space within range of his *ballistae* to create a killing field when the Gauls charged. He had done everything he could think of to give his men the advantage of their position and he was confident they could hold out until the expected replacements arrived. Now it was up to them.

At the center of the Gaulish formation a large man wearing a helmet crested with a bronze hawk that made him look even taller, appeared and shouted incomprehensibly toward the Romans. Copillus wore the mail coat and enameled sword belt of a lord and Vulca knew that this must be their chieftain. His suspicion was confirmed when the man swept his arm forward and began to run toward the castrum, followed by his retinue and the thousands of warriors to each side. The Volcae Tectosages lands straddled the border between what the Romans called long-haired Gaul, which was free Gaul to the north, and the Roman province of Gallia Narbonensis in the south. The province had only existed for fourteen years; since the defeat of the Arverni and Allobroges. All of Gaul had since been a mixture of those who resisted Roman incursion and those who desired the luxuries of Rome and were willing to accept the dominance of the Romans. The Tectosages had clung to their ancient traditions and bided their time. With the coming of the Tigurini, they were convinced that now was the time to throw the Romans back south.

Tame Gauls cut their hair short and trimmed their famous mustaches to mimic the Romans and show that they were a partner in trade and willing to submit to Roman governance. But free Gauls still wore their hair long and their mustaches thick and flowing. Their long hair flowed behind them like the banners their men carried to identify the separate clans. Standard bearers carried bronze figures of boars, horses, and birds affixed to tall poles and tried to stay near their clan leaders while the mass of warriors raced forward.

Vulca had emplaced range markers on the field and set orders for his *ballistae* to begin firing when the lead warriors passed the first marker. The artillery commander watched and at the appropriate time unleashed a barrage of boulders the size of a man's head that flew over the walls and into the packed mass of warriors. Dozens of men were broken and killed by the large stones that crashed into the ground and careened through the formation. Alternating with the boulders, they fired a cluster of stones the size of a man's fist that spread out into a wedge of shot that decimated large parts of the mass of warriors. As devastating as the flying stones were to the Gauls who had never experienced this type of weapon, the scorpions that fired iron tipped bolts as long as a man terrified them. Fired at great speed on a level surface these bolts often penetrated several men at the same time, killing them instantly with the kinetic energy built from the torsion weapons engineered by the Romans.

Vulca's defensive plans worked well as the Gauls were forced to pause at the obstacles that channeled them into a smaller area where the killing machines did their best work. The Gauls quickly saw that they were being massacred and the front ranks turned to retreat, only to be pushed forward by the ranks behind. There was no signal for an organized retreat in the Gaulish army and they continued to crush forward until enough men realized what was happening. Then, like the receding wave on a sandy shore, they began to fall back to the tree line until the entire army was once again out of range of the artillery. Hundreds, perhaps thousands of Gauls lay dead on the battlefield. Not a single Roman had engaged directly in the fight. Not a man was lost. Vulca went to each of the artillery crews and congratulated them. "If we live, ensure each of them receives double pay this month," he instructed Marcus Decimus. "They have saved all of us and given us another day to fight."

The Tectosages disappeared into the trees and withdrew to a clearing where they could tend their wounded and regroup. "We can't fight those weapons!" cried one of the Tectosages leaders. "I've lost a dozen men, and we didn't even reach the walls," said another. Copillus was dejected. He had allowed himself to assume the Romans were an easy target walled up in their small fortress. He had lost his impressive helmet in the one-sided battle and his long hair was matted with blood and brain matter that sprayed on him when the man beside him was decapitated by one of the flying stones. "We have committed to the destruction of the fort, and we will see that commitment through!" he said, jumping to his feet. "The Volcae Tectosages will not simply give up and go home! There are only five hundred men in that fort, we command thousands. It is obvious a frontal assault cannot work by itself; we must think of another way."

Copillus sent men back to the edge of the tree line to watch the castrum and assure the Romans knew that the fight was not over.

Within an hour, the Romans had restocked their supply of stone shot and missiles near the *ballistae*. Half the men had been relieved and were sent to eat and rest. Half the garrison would be on watch from this point on, night and day, for however long the siege lasted.

"Marcus, I want you to get scouts out to find the relief column," Vulca told his optio. "They should be on the way here and they need to be warned what they are walking into. Tell them that we can hold out for several days, but we need them to drive off the Gauls. They'll come back but I suspect they won't willingly walk into that trap again."

The next day a steady rain washed the killing field clean of blood while the carrion birds flapped and fluttered. The Gauls refused to recover their dead under the watchful eyes of the Romans who were prepared to fire their fearsome weapons at anyone who came within range. The sun's light was a dismal gray covered by low hanging iron-colored clouds. As the sun set and the day cooled, a misty fog came from the river and blanketed the castrum and the battleground before it, making it impossible to see the tree line from the fort. An occasional voice, clink of metal, or thud of wood let the Romans know that the Gauls were still there, still watching.

Around midnight, a small glow took shape near the tree line and grew to a large fire. The bright light allowed the Romans to catch glimpses of movement around the fire as the Gauls danced to the beat of their drums and chanting of their druids. An occasional scream pierced the darkness and at random times a shrill blast from a carnyx or battle horn nearer the castrum caused the men to nearly jump from their skins. The soldiers on the ramparts watched, fascinated, and fearful at the strange sounds.

The night was suffocatingly black. The rain had stopped, but no light from the moon or stars escaped the thick, dark clouds that remained. The men had difficulty tearing their attention away from the strange ceremonies that were taking place to their front and the bright fire blinded their night-vision when they occasionally looked away into the darkness.

"I don't like this," Vulca muttered to himself.

"Sir?" questioned Marcus Decimus, standing beside him on the rampart.

"I don't like this," he repeated louder. "They are up to something. We whipped them yesterday and today was quiet, but they haven't left. Tell the men they must avoid looking directly at that fire. Keep their eyes looking into the darkness so they won't be blinded by the light. They need to tune in their ears to any unlikely sounds. I can feel something is about to happen."

Copillus slid silently between the rushes at the edge of the river. He led a group of forty warriors along the riverbank toward the rear of the castrum. The party had smeared their bodies with soot from the cooking fires and wrapped anything metal in cloth to avoid any reflection of light from the bonfire and to prevent any unwanted noise. They took advantage of the fog and near total darkness and now neared the rear of the fort. The men each carried ropes with a loop at the end that they would use to ensnare one of the upright logs on the palisade and climb over. While the Roman sentries were focused on the commotion to their front, five men climbed silently to the top of the wall. By a stroke of bad luck, the boy who Vulca had spoken to earlier was on the parapet. His commander's words had taken hold. The young soldier saw movement from the corner of one eye when one of the raiders topped the wall nearby. Before the Gaul could react, the youngster drove his gladius into the Gaul's chest, toppling him back over the wall, as the boy shouted an alarm.

"We are attacked! Gauls are over the wall!"

His warning shouts ended abruptly when one of the Gauls swung a sword down into his neck and shoulder and he fell to the ground inside the compound, his lifeblood draining into the packed earth.

A horn blew. Alerted to the danger, soldiers ran to the wall. A desperate fight began on the narrow walkway. Copillus led the way toward one of the watchtowers with five men following him and killed three more sentries before they reached it. More Gauls topped the wall and immediately leaped down to open the river gate. Soldiers were running from their barracks to find a swarm of enemy dropping over the wall. The inside of the castrum brightened as more torches were lit, the flickering flames further confusing those inside. The Gauls formed a half-circle around the gate while several men lifted the heavy oak bar and swung the doors open. The approaching soldiers stopped in their tracks when they saw hundreds of Gauls streaming through the gate.

Vulca quickly assessed the situation and put the archers and slingers to work but the Gauls were engaged in hand-to-hand combat with his soldiers, and they could not fire without hitting their own men. "To the walls!" he shouted. "Retake the walls and get the archers up there!" Decimus had already made that call and met Copillus as he descended the tower steps. The Gaul had the advantage of gravity and forced his weight onto Decimus, pushing him back. Decimus lost his footing and fell backwards onto the man behind him and Copillus and his men spilled from the tower, killing Decimus and the men with him.

"Stay here and guard this tower," Copillus ordered several men before turning and leading the rest into the castrum. "Find the officers!" he shouted. "Kill the officers!"

Gauls were pouring into the river gate and many of the Romans had fallen. Vulca looked around and realized the battle was lost. Making a quick decision he called to the men around him. "Withdraw to the east gate." The men around him responded immediately and formed a defensive wall around their commander as they backed away from the center of the fort. Once the gate was open, the Romans streamed out, each in their own direction fleeing the battle. Of nearly five hundred men, only thirty made it across the river and into the trees to the east. In twos and threes, they made their way south toward Tolosa. Several hundred men had been killed in the battle. Those who were badly wounded were killed and the rest were chained.

The Gauls, their battle rage sated, did not follow them into the darkness or pursue them the next day. "Let them tell the world of our victory here today." Copillus celebrated with the coming dawn, which brought a warm breeze and bright sun. His men pillaged the barracks and storage rooms, taking bags of grain, weapons, gold coins, and personal belongings. When the fort was empty of anything useful, they tore down the palisade and built funeral pyres for the Tectosages dead.

About midday Vulca spotted the relief column marching toward Tolosa. He brought what men that had followed him to the tribune in command.

"I am Centurion Vulca, commander of the garrison at Tolosa," he reported to the tribune in charge of the relief column.

"Your messenger arrived yesterday, and we doubled our pace. What happened Centurion? Your message said you would be able to hold out until help arrived."

"Sir, we were attacked by a superior force of Gauls, perhaps fifteen thousand against my garrison of five hundred. The first day we killed hundreds of them with artillery without losing a man. But the second night they attacked in force under cover of darkness, and they breached the walls. My men put up a valiant effort, but it was impossible to beat those numbers once they were inside the fort. I am prepared to receive whatever punishment awaits me, sir."

"There will be no punishment, Centurion. From all accounts, your preparation of the battlefield saved the castrum in the first battle, and your courage and leadership in the last ensured the survival of these few men at least. You and your men see our quartermaster and get refitted. We will return to Narbo and let the governor determine the response to this attack."

CHAPTER TWENTY-TWO

Rome

January 106 BC

Quintus Caecilius Metellus had gotten his triumphal parade through the city though the war in Numidia was far from won. The senate, filled with the family members and supporters of the Metelli voted to grant him the cognomen of Numidicus, conqueror of Numidia, even though no such thing had transpired. No one doubted Metellus had done his best, but the nimble and persuasive Jugurtha had once again eluded defeat. Nevertheless, Metellus was treated every bit like the conquering hero, a false title to be sure. After the conclusion of the grand parade and three days of feasting sponsored by Metellus, the senate met to decide the assignments for this year's consuls.

Marcus Aemilius Scaurus, the venerable princeps senatus, stood in the center of the floor and addressed the senate. "Quintus Servilius Caepio as first consul has requested the theatre of Gaul, with his imperium to include the retaking of Tolosa and the punishment of the Volcae Tectosages, as well as other local tribes who are guilty of participating in an uprising that resulted in the loss of two legions under Consul Lucius Cassius Longinus and has caused instability and disrupted trade throughout the region. As Caepio has served honorably and effectively as governor of Gallia Narbonensis, he is most familiar with the land and the tribes, I support his request and call for a vote."

Caepio received a unanimous vote and sat in his *curule* chair smiling smugly. Gaius Atilius Serranus sat beside him awaiting the vote on his own assignment.

"Second Consul Gaius Atilius Serranus has requested the theatre of Numidia with imperium to bring about the conclusion of the ongoing war with Jugurtha. I support his request and call for a vote."

Normally, most of the senators would vote how Scaurus voted. But not this time. Most of the senate knew that Serranus was not a soldier and had little chance of ending the war. A faction of patrician senators was trying to oust Marius from command in Africa and Marius' friends were defending him. Publius Rutilius Rufus was a staunch supporter and close friend to Gaius Marius, who was still in Numidia in winter quarters with his troops.

"No! Marius must be granted proconsul in Africa," shouted Publius Rutilius Rufus above the squabble of arguing senators. "No matter how much he is disliked personally, he is the best general to defeat Jugurtha, and he has him on the run. To strip him of his command at this critical moment would be a grave mistake."

The curia quieted at the commanding voice and dominating presence of the tall and handsome Publius Rutilius Rufus. Rufus was a respected statesman and orator, and an exceptional soldier who had distinguished himself at the battle of Muthul against Jugurtha. As a young man he had learned the art of war from one of Rome's best, Scipio Aemilianus, in Numantia, and as legate to Quintus Metellus in Numidia he had proven himself an extraordinary commander. He had returned to Rome to prepare for the next elections and planned to run for consul for a second time. He was defeated nine years earlier by Marcus Aemilius Scaurus, who was now princeps senatus, and arguably the most powerful and respected man in the senate. After his loss, Rufus instigated a personal feud with Scaurus when he prosecuted the new consul for influencing the outcome of the election, accusing him of bribing the electorate. Scaurus reciprocated and charged Rufus with the same, but both trials were unsuccessful.

The two had been rivals since their earliest days when they both served on the staff of Scipio Aemilianus and disagreed at nearly every opportunity. Now they were on opposite sides in the discussion over Gaius Marius' future.

"The people have elected Gaius Atilius Serranus as consul. Marius is just another in a long line of generals who have failed to bring Jugurtha to heel," claimed Scaurus, supported by a round of clapping and stamping of feet.

"You cannot possibly be suggesting that Serranus will succeed over Marius," Rufus scoffed. Looking around at the seated senators who supported Scaurus he continued. "Serranus has little to no military experience. You simply wish to put another patrician in charge, in place of the *novus homo* who threatens your fragile egos. Have none of you learned from Carbo and Silanus? Both of them nobilitas and completely outmatched and outsmarted by the northern tribes? Have you forgotten the long list of nobilitas that have returned to Rome without victory over Jugurtha?" Rufus looked directly at Metellus Numidicus. "Marius outstrips us all with his military genius and you know it; Serranus isn't fit to shine Marius' armor."

Serranus lept to his feet. "I will not be insulted in this house, certainly not while I am consul!"

"My apologies consul," Rufus mocked, bowing. Scaurus banged his staff on the floor, unheard over another outburst of angry voices that flowed out the open door of the Temple of Jupiter Capitolinus and to the ears of the people who gathered below its steps.

Scaurus continued to bang his staff, calling for order unsuccessfully. Finally, a senator walked onto the floor of the senate unbidden and stood silently, waiting for the room to quiet. Quintus Caecilius Metellus Numidicus, the most recent commander of the war in Numidia, raised his hand and waited patiently for attention. Slowly, the other senators took notice and gradually the noise lessened until it finally came to a stop. He allowed the silence to continue for several long moments before he began to speak.

"All of you know me," he began softly. "You know that I have no love for Gaius Marius. He and I have been political enemies for many years. We disagree on many things. We certainly have never been able to see eye to eye on politics, and I will never support his election as consul. But there is no man more qualified to bring this war in Numidia to an end. I have known Marius for nearly thirty years. He has spent almost all of that time in the army, and much of it in battle.

"He served with me, and Rufus, and some of you under Scipio Aemilianus in Numantia where we finally pacified the Celt-Iberians after twenty years of war. He fought under my cousin, Quintus Caecilius Metellus Balearicus who defeated the pirates of the Balearic Islands and brought security back to our shipping lanes. He was a distinguished cavalry commander when Ahenobarbus defeated the Arverni and Allobroges in Gaul resulting in the new province of Gallia Narbonensis. As propraetor and governor of Hispania, Marius defeated the local tribes of bandits and brought peace to the region, allowing silver and gold to flow from the Iberian mines. He is an intelligent and thoughtful military commander. He has never lost a battle, and he has often been the reason that battles were won. When I was elected consul and given imperium to bring Jugurtha to justice, he was my first choice as legate, along with Publius Rutilius Rufus." Metellus gestured to where Rufus sat. "Now, as I have said, I will never support Marius for consul. But as much as I personally dislike the man, this senate can do no better than appointing him proconsul to bring this back-and-forth war with Jugurtha to an end."

"Here, here," said Rufus. "As Numidicus has so graciously stated" he said, referring to Metellus' recently awarded cognomen, "Marius is the best weapon that Rome has in its armory. I call for a vote!"

Despite the support of two of Rome's most influential senators, Marius won by only a narrow margin and was assigned proconsul to continue the war against Jugurtha. The senior consul Quintus Servilius Caepio was sent north to avenge Longinus and to restore Tolosa to Roman rule, while junior consul Serranus was left to a quiet consulship in Rome.

When the meeting adjourned Rufus caught Metellus by the arm and pulled him aside. "What are you up to Metellus? You are one of Marius' biggest enemies, why did you defend him like that?"

Metellus gave a wan smile and feigned offense. "Why Rufus, I said nothing untrue. Marius is in fact a brilliant general. I truly believe that he is our best option to defeat Jugurtha. Like me, he is not susceptible to Jugurtha's overtures. Yes, he went out of his way to injure my reputation," he acknowledged, "this is what happens during elections, but as you can see I have survived just fine. But your friend Marius is not as politically astute as he is militarily. He benefits from your endorsement while he is away, you are a good friend to him."

Rufus caught the sly tone in Metellus' words. "It serves your interests for him to remain out of the city, is that it?"

Metellus merely smiled and turned away, disappearing into the crowd that had broken up into cliques of patricians, plebians, and provincial senators. While the senators filed out Marcus Aemilius Scaurus stood beside junior consul Gaius Atilius Serranus and Metellus Numidicus openly staring at Rutilius Rufus. When Rufus stepped toward the senate door, he saw them and returned their looks with a confident smile. Rufus noted to himself that these three powerful enemies would bear watching in the future.

CHAPTER TWENTY-THREE

Gaul

April 106 BC

After his return to Narbo, Vulca bided his time with garrison duty until the new consul arrived with the mission to punish the Volcae Tectosages and recapture Tolosa. When Quintus Servilius Caepio arrived with his consular army, Vulca immediately requested to be re-assigned.

"I am told that you are the centurion that held off the Volcae Tectosages when they attacked the garrison at Tolosa last year."

"I am sir. I can only wish it would have turned out better."

"Yes, well, don't we all," Caepio said. "Why are you here centurion?"

"I am eager to take the fight back to them when you ride north, Consul."

May 106 BC

Caepio had surrounded Tolosa and cut it off from reinforcement. He emplaced two of his legions facing the city, and two facing away in order to keep from being surprised like Longinus had been.

The consul emplaced his siege engines and immediately began battering the walls of the fortress. He had no interest in negotiation, the enemy knew why he was there, and he would let the *ballistae* do his talking. The first night his tesserarius reported that two Volcae Tectosages had approached the line requesting to see the commander.

"We do not wish our city to be destroyed," they said. "We did not participate in the uprising; we are simple merchants, and we only want the city to be returned to its former status and for the war to stop."

"Tell me," Caepio said, "why would I stop? Your people helped destroy a Roman army and humiliated the survivors."

One of the men stepped forward. "I know consul, that it seems as though all of the Volcae Tectosages hate Rome, but that is simply not true. There are many of us who see our relationship with Rome as a boon." He gestured at his friend and to himself. "We know of a passage into the city that would allow you to get a few of your men inside. Once they are inside the city, they could open the gates and allow your men in. This would prevent a lengthy siege where many of our people would die from starvation and sickness and grant you the victory within days of when you arrived. All we ask is that you spare the citizens from slaughter."

"Tell me more." Caepio demanded.

Caepio placed Vulca in charge of a small force of soldiers, selected for the special mission. The consul detained one of the two men who had told him of the secret entrance in the camp as insurance, and the other led Vulca and his men along the river that passed near the fortress. True to his word, the Gaul showed them a small door that was hidden in the wall and used to collect water from the river.

The Gaul softly gave a password, and they could hear the bolt being lifted from the other side, then he quietly pushed the door open. Vulca took the lead, and his men followed as the Gaul led them along the bottom of the wall toward the gate. A row of buildings created a narrow alleyway between them and the outer walls.

When they neared their objective, Vulca saw that they must cross a well-lit open area to reach the gate. There were two guards pacing at the top of the wall, and one leaning against the gate tower, his head nodding sleepily. Their attention was outward, toward the fires of the Roman camp. None were looking inside the fortress where they felt secure.

Vulca motioned for two men to come to him. He pointed at the first and whispered softly, "I will lead to the bottom of the nearest ladder to the walkway, two will stay with me, and you will take two to the other side. At my signal we will climb the ladders and trap them between us." He pointed at the second man. "Take the rest of the men to the gate and get it open. When we clear the walkway, we will wave a torch to signal Caepio, then join you to defend the gate. I don't need to tell you, to keep this as quiet as possible." Vulca questioned each man with a look, and they both nodded their understanding.

Vulca experienced a strong sense of déjà vu, remembering how the Gauls had taken the gate of his own castrum just months ago. He took a first nervous step into the light of the small courtyard near the gate. The men behind him followed silently and Vulca let out a breath of relief when they all reached their spot unnoticed. He signaled to the other group, and they began to climb the ladders at the same time, but luck had deserted them. About halfway up, Vulca placed his weight onto a rung whose rope had loosened. A loud creak sounded through the night when the rope stretched. At first, the men at the wall simply turned around, expecting to see someone coming to check the guards, then, realizing they were being attacked rushed toward Vulca's ladder.

A loud crash rang out when a Gallic sword swung and struck Vulca's upraised gladius as he awkwardly tried to defend himself. The blow knocked him loose and Vulca fell sideways off the ladder, landing on his back like a sack of grain, the wind knocked from his lungs. The man behind him climbed further up and managed to reach the guard's ankle with his gladius, crippling him. When the guard fell to a knee, the Roman thrust his gladius through the man's chest.

The men on the other ladder reached the top before the sleeping guard realized what was happening. He awoke to a sword stroke across his throat and was pushed off the walkway. But as the Roman turned to attack what he thought was the last guard, a spear was thrust from the darkness of the guard tower. There had been another man sleeping inside the tower.

A quick scuffle broke out and the two men following up the ladder managed to kill him, but the warning had been sounded and they could hear shouts and running feet coming their way.

Below, the rest had gotten the gate open, and Vulca was slowly rising to his knees. "Wave the torch," he croaked, still gasping for air. "Wave the torch!" someone echoed.

The four remaining men on the walkway quickly joined the men at the gate and together they formed a defensive half circle, prepared to defend the gate with their lives. They had not brought shields and were at a disadvantage, but they took the shields and spears from the dead Gauls, set their feet in the packed dirt, and prepared for the worst.

Fifty Gauls burst from the darkness into the light of the torches, charging directly at Vulca who stood in the center. He still gulped air, then finally belched loudly, a result of the gasping. It seemed to relieve him just in time as the first Gaul reached him with a wild swing. Vulca ducked below and sunk his gladius into the Gaul's body just below his solar plexus. Half a moment later, five more Gauls smashed into their meager line, one driving a spear through one of his men. Vulca turned and drove his gladius into the side of the spearman's chest under his armpit. He quickly withdrew, searching for another target.

The remaining Gauls facing them suddenly stopped in their tracks. Fear etched on their faces, they turned and ran back into the darkened fortress, screaming an alarm. Momentarily stunned at their unexplained salvation, Vulca did not understand until the roar of the charging Romans behind him reached his ears. He shoved his men aside as the first of an entire legion streamed through the gate, the light from a thousand torches brightening the fortress like day. Vulca leaned his back against the wall until the pain in his abdomen subsided and his breathing returned to normal. Of the twelve men that he had brought with him, four had been killed and two were wounded.

Caepio's legions rushed in and put the entire city to the sword. The streets ran red as Caepio's soldiers avenged the loss of Longinus and the humiliation of Laenus' surrender. Caepio ordered his men to secure all the temples and storehouses where the city's riches were kept and left the rest for them to plunder. Their victory was complete. The city was burned, nothing was spared. The rebellion was crushed.

CHAPTER TWENTY-FOUR

Gallia Narbonensis

June 106 BC

Consul Quintus Servilius Caepio contemplated his situation, while sitting atop a tall chestnut stallion, its lustrous coat reflecting the morning sun. He was on a small rise outside the gates of Tolosa. It had been several months since Caepio had been sent north with the senate's imperium to punish the Volcae Tectosages for their uprising last year and to recapture the city of Tolosa and return it to Roman oversight. He had done so quickly and efficiently.

A few weeks after taking the city, Caepio walked along the edge of the Garumna River with one of his tribunes. Gnaeus Pompeius Strabo was elected that year as one of the military tribunes to accompany Caepio on his expedition to punish the Volcae Tectosages for their rebellion. Strabo had grown up on the stories of his father who had perished while fighting the Scordisci in Macedonia. For this reason, he was thrilled to be in Gaul fighting the barbarians.

Caepio had tasked Gnaeus Pompeius Strabo with finding and recovering the fabled treasure of Tolosa. It was Gaulish tradition to throw their riches into a body of water to be given to their gods in return for their favor, and Caepio was determined to investigate the rumors. Tolosa was known to be the richest city in Gaul as well as a religious center. The river flowed by in the valley below the fortress and there was a long pier that reached out into the river. It was decorated with animal skulls, feathers, and sacred objects, and was obviously used for ceremonial purposes. Strabo's engineers had begun the laborious process of building a diversion dam across the river upstream of the pier.

Caepio was drawn forward by the steady thump of a pile driver. A pair of oxen lifted a heavy stone by a rope threaded through a pulley suspended on a large A-frame support above the log barrier. When it reached its highest point the stone dropped on the upper end of the log, pounding it into the riverbed.

Upstream of the dam, a detachment of soldiers had built a watergate and dug a canal behind it that would accept the rising water as the dam widened, thus lowering the water level while both groups completed their task. As the dam neared completion, the river would be diverted to the canal. When the dam was complete, the bottom of the river would be revealed, where it was rumored the Gauls had deposited their rich offerings.

Strabo was pleased to tell the consul of his progress. "You can see that the water is already several feet lower, and the water is beginning to be diverted," he said proudly.

"Yes, you've made good time," said Caepio. Turning to Strabo, he said, "I understand that you have a new son."

Strabo, who left for Gaul months ago and had not heard about the birth yet struggled to maintain his composure. "Sir?" was all he could manage.

Caepio, seeing his discomfiture, explained, "Your wife's mother is a distant cousin to my wife, Caecilia. They have been close friends since they were children. I received a letter from my wife just yesterday and she was going on about your son and how plump and healthy he is, and how pleased she is for you and your wife. I was told to pass on the news. I try to never disobey my wife," he chuckled. "In any case, congratulations!" Caepio clapped the tribune on the back, laughing at the man's uneasiness at the familiarity of his consul.

"Thank you, sir."

"Have you decided on a name yet?"

"Gnaeus Pompeius, sir."

"Of course, of course. Say, isn't your mother related to that satirist that causes such a ruckus in the theater with his plays?"

"He's my uncle, sir. Gaius Lucilius. My mother is his sister."

"Hmmm, well, not my taste in entertainment, but he is popular with the plebs. He makes fun of many powerful men, and that's not wise. Anyway, soon we'll be at the bottom of the rivers and lakes and hauling up treasures beyond belief. Keep up the good work and you will be rewarded appropriately."

"Thank you, sir" Strabo replied, as Caepio turned away.

Scores of engineers were also in the process of draining several nearby lakes and within a week their efforts were rewarded with the glint of gold when the water receded. Strabo was present when the first hoard was discovered. He immediately ordered the men that were standing by to get into the muck and begin digging. By the end of the first day, piles of gold and silver ingots, jewel encrusted helmets and weapons, beautifully constructed jewelry, and rust covered swords, spears and shields of all shapes and condition had appeared.

Strabo immediately sent word to the consul who arrived late in the afternoon. "Well done!" he exclaimed. "Leave the weapons and such and load the rest onto the wagons. Get them back to the camp where they can be guarded and keep a guard on this site until you are satisfied you have recovered it all. The temples and treasuries in the city have been emptied and there will be more finds such as this, I am sure. We'll all be rich men, and the senate will be pleased that the war will be paid for twice over." The men within earshot cheered their commander as they bent to the task with renewed vigor.

Word had reached me that Caepio was returning to Gaul to punish the Volcae Tectosages. Using the vast wealth I had accumulated I had begun paying for information years ago, and through a network of traders and travelers, I received regular reports of what transpired in Rome, Gallia Narbonensis, Africa, even Pannonia; anywhere that Rome had it's tentacles. I no longer solely depended on Vallus' visits for information. Caepio's imperium had been announced publicly and within weeks, I knew of it in the far-off land of the Belgae.

My spies watched as Caepio looted the entire countryside of its wealth. Suspecting that Caepio would take the treasure of Tolosa back to Rome, I developed a plan.

July 106 BC

Vulca led the large caravan of reinforced oxcarts laden with the gold of Tolosa down the trade road to Narbo. Fifteen thousand talents of gold bullion. The first shipment of riches of the Volcae Tectosages was on its way to the treasure vaults of Rome. It was accompanied by thousands of captured slaves, fine horses, carts of grain, olives, and other foodstuffs. It was by far the richest caravan to have travelled the roads of Gaul, and more would soon follow laden with silver, statuary, jewelry, and other treasures.

Caepio, as conquering general was entitled to the lion's share, but custom dictated that his men would receive part of the plunder for themselves, after the senate claimed its share to pay for the war. Still, the men would be left with more money from this hoard than they could ever imagine in their lifetime. Caepio sent four maniples, around five hundred men, plus a strong cavalry escort to guard the caravan on its way south. From Narbo, it would be loaded onto ships and transported to the port of Ostia near Rome and then taken to the city by cart.

Deep in the wilderness between Tolosa and Narbo, an army lay in wait. The battlefield had been chosen to limit the effect of the Roman tactics and take full advantage of the type of fighting the northern tribes preferred. Borrix was now a master at choosing his ground. Four days out from Tolosa the caravan began the slow climb into the southern reaches of the central massif of Gaul, following the Atax River. The river plain narrowed between the limestone cliffs of the central massif to the north, and the foothills of the Pyrenees Mountains to the south. The treasure caravan camped outside the village of Eburomagus before entering the canyons that led to the Volcae Tectosages oppidum of Carcas on the other side of the pass, which heralded the slow descent toward Narbo and the Mare Nostrum.

On the second day past Eburomagus the sound of thunder seemed to emerge from a clear blue sky. Except that this thunder continued endlessly. The caravan guards soon realized that it was not thunder they were hearing echoing from the cliffs, but the sound of large drums that followed them deeper into the pass. The sound of battle horns soon followed, and a surge of barbarian warriors burst from the trees, running at them with abandon, screaming, and shouting insults and threats.

Vulca shouted orders to rally his men, but they were quickly overcome by the overwhelming horde of warriors. Fighting desperately, Vulca briefly glimpsed a large warrior sitting atop a fine warhorse, his loose red hair blowing in the slight breeze, observing the battle from the edge of the tree line. Then, Vulca's body spasmed when a heavy spear pierced his mail, just over his heart. The long and narrow iron spearhead was slowed by the mail, but not stopped. It severed the arteries of his heart and Vulca fell, never to fight another battle. His last thoughts were of his wife and son, as darkness crowded his vision, and he succumbed to his fatal wound.

The warriors quickly dispatched the caravan guards, and by the end of the day, the largest treasure ever amassed had disappeared back into the north.

"What!" Caepio was beside himself with fury.

"The . . . the entire caravan, sir. It's gone," the terrified tribune managed to stammer. He had been sent by Caepio to investigate the report that had come in.

"If you were not my son . . ." Caepio began, shaking his fist at the young man.

Caepio the younger, of course, had had nothing to do with the ambush. But he knew that informing his father of the catastrophe would mean facing the consul's wrath.

Caepio stormed away, whipping his cape when he turned about. "A fortune in gold, stolen by these damnable savages! How will I explain this to the senate?"

PART IV

BETRAYAL

106 – 105 BC

JEFF HEIN

CHAPTER TWENTY-FIVE

Gaul

August 106 BC

I awoke when Frida rose from our bed. "I'll come with you," I said. I had become accustomed to her walking in the night to relieve the pain in her back that had developed with her second pregnancy. "No, stay. There is nothing to worry about and nothing you can do." She leaned down and kissed me on the forehead, and I drifted blissfully back to sleep.

"Mama?" ten-year-old Lingulf questioned from his sleeping pallet in the corner.

"Hush child, go back to sleep."

She quietly slipped out the doorway and down the path to relieve herself, followed by a small, unseen figure that blended into the shadows. The Cimbri had settled for the fall and winter in a beautiful area deep within the canyons of the central massif of Gaul, directly north of where they had wiped out the treasure caravan. The area was safe from enemies as most of the tribes had paid tribute or allied with the Cimbri in their uprising against Rome. The hill tribes were savage, and Rome seldom ventured into the area.

The night was bright enough for Frida to see well as she walked the familiar path, pausing from time to time to stretch her back. Suddenly, a huge shadow stepped from the darkness beside her.

His large hands grasped her in an iron grip and the sausage-like fingers squeezed the arteries in her neck as he lifted her to the tips of her toes. She was so startled to be attacked within the safety of the camp she did not think to scream before the blood was cut off to her brain and she went limp.

Her attacker yelped when a dark shadow leaped at him, slicing his thigh with a small blade.

"Drop my mother!" Lingulf cried and lunged at the man again. The kidnapper backhanded him across the face and the boy crumpled to the ground.

"Bring him with us," came a voice from the darkness.

Within a few moments the attacker faded silently back into the night with his burden and the pair slipped away between the sentries.

When her senses slowly returned, Frida found herself being carried over the giant's shoulder, her hands and feet bound tightly, a cloth forced between her teeth and knotted behind her head. The man who carried her seemed to hardly notice her weight as he trotted swiftly down the trail they were following. She could see Lingulf, also bound and gagged, carried effortlessly under her abductor's other arm.

Another man followed but she could only lift her head high enough to make out his feet in the darkness. Fear's icy fingers gripped her when she realized what had happened and she began to struggle and scream behind the gag. She thought she heard the soft whinny of a horse before the man behind struck her soundly and she returned to the merciful embrace of unconsciousness.

The sun was brightening the sky in the east when she awoke again. Her body bounced with the gait of a horse as it cantered quickly down a packed road, her pregnant belly pressed uncomfortably against the beast. During the night, her captors had reached a more traveled road that would cover the tracks of their horses and confuse anyone who followed them. The warmth of the rising sun on their left told her they were traveling south but toward what she could not know. The smaller man now led the way, Lingulf slung across the withers of his horse, and turned off the road to follow an old trail that led to an abandoned farmstead. The giant pulled her roughly from the saddle and dropped her in the corner of the half-collapsed house while the second man deposited her son beside her.

"Do you know who I am?" He pulled back his hood and revealed his face.

She glared at him defiantly and made no response. There was no recognition in her eyes, but she felt revulsion when she saw the skull-like face and clouded pupils of her captor. When she recoiled, he saw the swell in her belly.

"You are pregnant?" he said, astonished. "Oh, this is even better than I imagined. Your husband will be driven mad when he discovers your disappearance. I have no doubt he will come for you and his children, and when he does, he shall suffer as I have suffered because of him."

His voice was familiar to her, and her mind raced to try and place the sound. When the man stood and walked away his tattered shirt fell from a shoulder and revealed a dark red scar on his back that resembled the tangled branches of an oak tree. The question tormented her, but no answer came during the long hours of the sleepless night she spent shivering on the ground.

Dawn. I awoke in a panic, seeking to assure myself by feeling under the bedding for Frida's warm body. The scar on my forehead throbbed and I felt a stab of fear deep in my chest. It had been hours since she left and now the sun was coloring the sky in the east. I jumped out of bed and quickly glanced around the cabin, hoping against hope to see her in the shadows. I rushed out the door calling for her, while my heart sank, fearing the worst. I had experienced this fear once before when Frida, Lingulf, and Hilgi had been kidnapped in the hills near Haimaz. Now, Frida and the child she carried were gone. When I returned to the cabin my chest tightened with another stab of panic. "Lingulf! Lingulf! No!" I shouted when there was no reply. A cry of anguish escaped my throat as I sobbed their names.

"Hrolf!" I shouted, running to my friend's home. "Hrolf, alert the camp, find Rurik. Frida and Lingulf are gone!"

Wiping the sleep from his eyes, Hrolf quickly dressed and sounded the alarm. Within minutes the wiry old tracker, Rurik, appeared before me. "Where did you last see them, Lord?"

"She got out of bed sometime in the night. When I woke, I realized she had not returned. Lingulf is missing too."

Rurik immediately recognized the small footprints at the door and began following them down the trail. "Give me time to get ahead, then bring some men," he said.

"Hrolf, search the camp. Look for anything out of the ordinary," I ordered. "I'll go with Rurik, gather some men and follow behind."

Rurik was moving quickly down the path following Frida's footprints. He stopped abruptly, staring intently at the ground. "Here," he said. "A large man stepped from the side of the trail and Frida's prints disappear. "Lingulf attacked him and drew blood, but his footprints also vanish. The man's prints are deeper when he walks away. He's carrying them." Rurik stepped off the trail and parted the bushes, carefully following the sign. "Broken branches," he said absently, pointing them out to me. "Here's a strand of long brown hair, probably Frida's. He came this way; here he was joined by a second man," he said pointing to the tracks. "This one has a lame leg, see the drag mark? They're moving quickly."

The man known simply as "The Prophet" had returned. He had been carefully watching and patiently waiting for months for this opportunity. The thought of salving the wounds that had festered and corrupted him for years was nearing reality. In his madness, the memory of why he hated Borrix was dimmed, he only knew that the prospect of vengeance consumed him.

On the second day of their flight Frida saw that the skull-faced man wore a familiar bear-claw necklace and bronze torque. She had been so astonished at his appearance that she had not noticed it in the dark of the first night. She recognized them both as her husband's and realized that this must be the man that he had spoken of that had been involved in his capture several years ago. She was confused, and she had no idea why this man hated Borrix so or why he had returned, but she knew that she and her children were in danger. The man was obviously mad and the large man that carried her and Lingulf seemed to be an unintelligent oaf that simply followed The Prophet's orders.

She caught Lingulf's eyes and silently reassured him. *Your father will find us.*

Bravely, Frida pushed her fear down and began observing, looking for opportunities to escape. She began by keeping herself calm. At first, she had resisted, struggled, kicked, and screamed, but now she was determined to make them think she had accepted her fate. She wanted them to relax their guard.

"I know who you are," she said that night. "You are the Prophet of Fenrir. You captured my husband and turned him over to the Romans, but when it was time to fight, you ran like a coward."

"Your husband is a formidable man, but I did not run from him. I ran from certain death at the hands of thousands of his warriors. My time on this world has a purpose. I had not completed that purpose yet."

She shot him a look of disgust. "What is that purpose?"

"You will know at the proper time," he said simply. His head twitched oddly to the side.

"He will kill you; you know."

"Perhaps, but not before I have achieved my revenge. After all, his death is not my ultimate goal," he said ominously. "With death, comes peace. I do not wish him peace. I wish him to know pain, to suffer guilt, to be tormented as I have been tormented. He can only feel these things if he is alive."

Turning away, The Prophet said, "That is enough talk for now. We have far to travel, you will need your strength."

Rurik's pace was swift, but the kidnappers were now on horseback and did their best to hide their tracks. He memorized the hoofprints of their horses, but on the second day the kidnappers had found a paddock and switched mounts. The pursuers lost a day following several different trails until Rurik recognized The Prophet's dragging print at a campsite. Hrolf and Ansgar caught up with a party of fifty men. Now a group of heavily armed mounted men pursued the kidnappers.

On the morning of the fourth day, we were attacked by a small group of warriors. We rode straight through the ambush with minimal injuries and continued our pursuit.

After splashing through the Garumna River we entered the foothills of the Pyrenees Mountains that separated Gaul from Hispania. We were harassed by small bands of hostile warriors every day, delaying us and keeping us from catching up to the kidnappers. Rurik was sure he was on the right trail and if the daily attacks were any clue, he was correct. I grew ever more anxious worrying about Frida and our children. I would not eat, and I could not sleep. Hrolf was worried and tried to reassure me.

"We'll catch them."

"Not soon enough," I snapped. Since Frida had been snatched, the headaches had returned in earnest and the pain was driving me closer to the brink.

Hrolf was silent. He had never seen me so close to losing control. Hrolf knew that ever since I had suffered horrendous wounds from an enraged bear I experienced severe headaches and now I had begun to feel numbness and pain that tormented every nerve in my body. The episodes were becoming more frequent. They seemed to last longer and were more intense each time. With the added stress brought on by the kidnapping of my family, I was in constant pain.

A week after abducting Frida, The Prophet slowed his pace and began searching for something. They had left the more populated areas and well-traveled roads, and their path led uphill as they neared the gray mountains. He was now paying more attention to covering their tracks and made more of an effort to disguise their campsites.

Finally, he conferred with the giant warrior he called Oda. "The entrance is just ahead," he spoke softly. "Walk in the river and follow it inside and wait for me. There are torches near the entrance."

After Oda left carrying Frida and Lingulf, The Prophet walked down their back trail and took great care to erase their tracks completely, leaving no sign of their travel as he worked his way back up the river.

Swaying with his movement, Oda carried her on one muscular shoulder. Frida tried to look ahead of them as they traveled along the river. Ash and beech trees covered in moss and vines created a peaceful scene that belied the ominous implications of her capture. Now she saw that the river disappeared into a great black hole in the hillside ahead.

Frida sucked in her breath in fear as the giant carried them into the black maw of a limestone cave entrance, splashing steadily in the shallow waters of the river that flowed from the bowels of the earth. At first, the coolness was a welcome change to the summer heat, but in her mind they were being taken down into the world of the dead. The cave looked utterly black from the outside but once she was inside the entrance her eyes adjusted to the light that filtered in from the opening. The giant flopped them down onto a rock ledge, hands and feet still tied. He was taking no chances that they could escape.

With a grunt, he turned away and found the torches that had been stacked conveniently nearby in a crack in the wall. From his belt pouch he pulled out a flint and steel and expertly brought a torch to life. Lingulf's eyes grew wide in fright at the flames flickering off the walls, casting weird shadows that moved about as if they were awakened by the light.

As darkness fell The Prophet joined them in the cave and with another torch, led them deeper into the cave. Frida, now walking on her own between her captors, shivered as the river narrowed and the water that had carved this grotto across a million years became deeper. The smell of the cave was surprisingly fresh and cool, and the only sounds were the slosh of their movement and the occasional grunt of effort as they climbed over and around rocks in the stream. Her trepidation grew with each tenuous step further into the darkness and she wondered how far they would walk into the earth. She felt a strange twinge of victory each time The Prophet stumbled with his lame leg, and it made her feel better to witness his weakness.

The light from the entrance disappeared when they rounded a bend and darkness fell like a blanket, only held back by the pitiable light from their torches. They scrambled out onto a narrow gravel beach, soaked from the waist down and continued along the beach until a large grotto appeared on the left. They turned into the cavern and the river disappeared into a black void behind them. Frida and Lingulf marveled in fright at the sight of giant stalagmites and stalactites that surrounded them like the teeth of some enormous monster who had swallowed them alive. Frida started when The Prophet turned. His skull-painted face glowed whitely in the torchlight. A wicked smile crossed his face when he saw the fear in her eyes, and it steeled her resolve.

Reading his thoughts she said, "I am Frida, the wife of Borrix, king of the Cimbri, and this is his son Lingulf. We do not fear you."

He looked at her intently, his head cocked to one side. "You will," he said threateningly and turned back to his path.

A wooden ladder appeared from the darkness and The Prophet climbed awkwardly to the top of the cave wall where a hole barely wide enough for Oda to squeeze through led to a small chamber. This led in turn to a narrow passageway that forced them to turn sideways to traverse. Oda had to relax his chest to give himself enough room to pass through without wedging himself in. He caught his weapons and clothing several times until the tunnel finally opened up and allowed them to stand up comfortably.

Another rabbit hole appeared, and they scrambled upward until they arrived in an upper chamber, a third level in this mysterious and terrifying cave system. Old bones reflected whitely in the torchlight, showing gaping jaws with huge teeth. White crystals winked back at them, and more stalactites reached down to meet stalagmites rising from the cave floor, like columns supporting the mountain above their heads.

The shadows from the flickering light revealed ripples in the clay floor and when Frida looked closer, she could see that they were the footprints of adults and several small children. The sign of some ancient people who had passed this way long before, the image of their bare feet pressed into the ancient clay for all time.

They continued on and Frida wondered if they would ever stop. The Prophet halted abruptly and stepped to the side. "Welcome to your new home," he said, grandly sweeping one arm. "This is where you will spend the rest of your days."

Frida caught her breath when she entered a large chamber. The fear came back, and cold fingers clutched at her heart as the full impact of his words reached her. Lingulf looked around fearfully.

In the center of the room a rock outcropping rose from the floor. From the entrance she could see the images of two bison sculpted onto the rock so skillfully it was as if the miniature animals could be breathing.

The room pulsed with an aura that she knew must come from those ancient sculptors. The bison were positioned in such a way that they appeared about to begin the mating process. Perhaps this was an altar of fertility, a place for the ancient creators of these wonders to honor their gods and ask for their blessings. Perhaps that is why they dragged their children so far into the bowels of the earth, and its enveloping darkness. Frida laid her hand gently across her belly and thought of her baby. She had not eaten in many hours, and she was weak from the effort to arrive here. In answer to the unspoken question, The Prophet tossed a leather wrapped packet onto the ground. "Eat." He stuck the end of his torch into a crack in the wall and sat, while Oda remained near the entrance.

Rurik was beside himself. He had lost the trail and for the last two days he had cast for sign in all directions. He had returned to the last place he saw their tracks but could not pick up the trail.

After following them for more than a week, Frida, Lingulf and their captors had disappeared.

I was mad with fear and helplessness, lashing out at everyone, worst of all Rurik. Hrolf stepped in and tried to reason with me, and we very nearly came to blows. "They're gone!" I cried out and collapsed into the arms of my friend. "I promised her I would always protect her and our children, and again she is taken from me, this time right from my very side. I have failed her as I have failed my people. What have I ever done to deserve the gods' punishment? What has she ever done?"

"They are near, I know it in my heart," Hrolf said. "They are alive, her captors would not have bothered to drag them this far with us close behind if they didn't want them alive. Someone is using them as bait. They want you. They have found a place to hide. Somewhere they already knew, that's how they've disappeared. We will keep searching until we find them."

I despaired and dropped to a seat on a fallen log. "I never wanted to be chieftain. It was forced upon me by circumstance. I was content to be a nobody. Why was I chosen, Hrolf? There were many others more capable than I."

"The gods do not explain themselves, Borrix. You were chosen, that is all we know. And it was a wise choice if anything is to be said about it. You were chosen by Donar and Wodan themselves. You have held together the greatest tribal alliance in history, and you have defeated every enemy you have ever faced."

"All that means nothing if I cannot protect my own family," I said miserably.

"Listen to me! We will find Frida and Lingulf, and you will avenge yourself upon whoever dared to take them in the first place. And then we will return to the tribe and together we will conquer the world. Anyone who chooses not to bend the knee to Borrix will be crushed. Do you hear me? We will find Frida."

I slumped dejectedly on the log and looked sidelong at my friend. The men were setting up camp a short distance away, reluctant to look our way, yet straining to hear our words. "Leave me be, Hrolf," I said, holding my throbbing head in my hands. "Just leave me be for a while."

I woke before the sun and wandered off into the dense woods. My headache had faded to the background of my consciousness, allowing me to think more clearly. *There only seem to be two kidnappers. The warriors we fought along the way were obviously just harassing us to give the captors time. Who did this? Why? Where are they going? They wouldn't go to this trouble just to capture a woman and a child. As Hrolf said, someone is using them as bait to get to me. But who? Ah, it doesn't matter who, or why. It only matters that I find them and kill whoever took them.*

Wandering about the forest, I came across a small river of cool, clear water and stooped for a drink. A yellowish glow caught my eye, and I reached out and plucked a small stone from the shallow river. I turned it over in my hand and saw the hole that I myself had drilled into the polished stone. This was a piece of the amber necklace I had made as Frida's marriage gift. My heart leaped. *Frida!* "Frida!" I shouted. No one heard but the trees. I looked about, marking the place in my memory and ran back to the campsite.

"I've found them," I shouted. "Rurik, I've found them. They walked into a river and followed it to cover their tracks. Look! This is from her necklace," I said excitedly. Hrolf appeared at my side.

"Show me," said Rurik.

I led Rurik back to the river at the head of the men. When we arrived, Rurik saw a partial imprint left in the water and another piece of amber a few steps upstream, confirming that they had followed the river.

Rurik led us up the river to the mouth of the cave where the men immediately prepared to enter.

"No," I said. "Rurik will lead Hrolf and I into the cave. The rest of you stay here and guard the entrance. Wait for our return but remain on your guard. We do not know if it is just the kidnappers we face or if others will come."

Searching about Rurik discovered the cache of torches just inside the entrance and by their flickering light we stepped into the darkness; Rurik in the lead, followed by me and then Hrolf. The sound of the water echoed from the walls as it flowed past rocks that had long ago fallen from the ceiling. Pinpricks of light sparkled when the firelight found droplets of water that filtered through the limestone and trickled their way down to the river.

Rurik saw the indentations where Frida and Lingulf stepped onto the gravel beach and led us into the grotto. Rurik was fifty feet ahead of me when he let out a grunt of pain and fell to the stone floor. His torch cast a large shadow on the wall as a giant charged from the darkness.

His deadly club whistled past my head. I ducked, saved by my reflex to the moving shadow. It struck against a thin stalactite and shattered the brittle structure. It would have shattered my skull if it had connected.

I jumped back and bumped into Hrolf who was coming up closely behind me and for a moment we were entangled, until Hrolf stepped past and drew his sword. The giant took advantage of the moment, landing a glancing blow to Hrolf's shoulder. Hrolf's fingers went numb, and his sword clanged on the rock at his feet. The monster stepped in for the kill, but now his swing was hampered by the closely formed mineral pillars. He dropped the club and moved toward me, ignoring Hrolf for the moment. The giant's speed was unexpected for so large a man and before I had time to draw my sword he was upon me, closing his massive fingers about my throat. His mad chuckle echoed off the walls as he lifted me to the tips of my toes. I tried in vain to separate a finger from the rest, to bend it backward and force the giant to let go. But the strength in his hands was enormous and the fat fingers clamped down even harder. I could feel myself fading. The last I saw was a burst of light and the giant warrior screaming right before everything went black.

Hrolf had picked up one of the torches that had been dropped in the attack and pressed it against the tail of Oda's shirt. The tattered material ignited easily and spread up his back, reaching into his long greasy hair that burst into a bright flame. Oda's screams echoed throughout the cavern as he went mad with the pain. Oda dropped Borrix and charged toward the creator of his agony, engulfing Hrolf in a bear hug as his skin was seared by the flames. Oda bent backwards and bounced up and down in an effort to break Hrolf's ribs and as he was lifted up Hrolf managed to get a foot against one of the stalactites. With the last of his strength Hrolf gave a mighty push, sending the two men over the edge of a pit and into a dark crevasse.

Frida looked up sharply when the hideous scream reverberated through the tunnels and finally reached the cavern of the bison. The Prophet jumped up, looking toward its source. After a moment of indecision, he snatched up the torch and hastened down the tunnel, leaving Frida and Lingulf in the terrifying darkness. But Frida was unafraid. She knew that the scream came from Oda. It could not have come from any other being; it was so horrible. That scream of indescribable pain could mean only one thing.

"Mama?" Lingulf said in sudden fear.

"It's alright son, your father is here, and he will make them pay with their lives."

I awoke to total blackness and the stench of burning flesh. My neck and throat ached with terrible pain, but as I began to move, I realized I was not injured. Searching about in the darkness, my hand touched the end of a warm torch. I reached into my belt pouch for a flint and steel and with a few strikes re-ignited the torch. The chamber lit up.

"Hrolf," I called hoarsely. There was no answer. "Hrolf!"

"Down here," came a weak reply.

I moved toward the sound and found Hrolf beside the giant's body, whose hair and scalp were still smoldering, his head at an impossible angle, neck broken. They were at the bottom of a pit, twenty feet down. His body had broken Hrolf's fall. "My leg caught the edge or something, I think it's broken," he said, sucking air between his teeth in pain.

"I have no rope, I'll have to go back," I told him.

"No. If this man was here, then Frida must be near. There's only one way out of this cave. You must go on. There's only the cripple now, the one who was dragging his foot. Hey," he said, suddenly reminded of Rurik. "Did you see what happened to Rurik?"

"No. I'll be right back."

"I'm not going anywhere."

I found Rurik's body where it had fallen, his skull crushed by the giant's club. I picked up the torch that lay beside him and lit it from my own, then walked back to the edge of the pit.

"He's dead," I told Hrolf. "Here, catch." I dropped the torch into the pit. "I'll be back as soon as I can to get you out of there."

"Go get your wife, I'll be fine. I've got enough to eat," he said, nodding at the body.

I smiled grimly, then turned away.

As The Prophet neared the cavern of columns, he could hear voices, and he could smell the burned flesh. So, Oda was dead, but he had stopped two of their three pursuers. *He will stop at nothing to find his wife, and when he does, I will have my revenge,* he thought.

The Prophet turned and scrambled back the way he had come.

I continued through the cave system. I found a torn scrap of cloth from Frida's dress, and it restored my failing energy. Warily, I made my way ever further into the earth until I noticed a faint glow coming from the far end of the tunnel. I paused, listening.

"Come," said an ethereal voice. "Come forward Borrix, king of the Cimbri. Come and claim your wife and child."

"Borr!" shouted Frida. "Be careful, my love."

"Father!"

My heart jumped. "Frida! Lingulf!" I rushed forward and into the light of another chamber. When I entered the chamber, I saw Frida sitting on a stone outcropping across the room. Lingulf sat beside her. Behind her stood the man who kidnapped her.

"You!"

"Yes," The Prophet hissed. "I took your family." His face was painted like a skull, and he was so emaciated, he looked like a skeleton. His skin was pulled tightly over his bones, his clothes hung in tatters, and he held most of his weight on one leg while favoring the other. "I have long waited for this moment, and I intend to savor it."

I crouched, watching The Prophet intently, ready for anything. "Is there anyone else, Frida?"

"Just the large man," she said. "The idiot."

"He's dead."

The Prophet shrugged a bony shoulder. "He served his purpose." Then after a pause he asked, "Aren't you going to ask why I brought you both here?"

"So we could watch you die?" I snarled.

The Prophet chuckled dryly. "You still have no idea who I am, do you *nephew*?"

I was confused. *Nephew?* Then it hit me like a thunderclap. The familiar voice that I recognized when The Prophet first kidnapped me three years ago. The cryptic references that he made. Memories came rushing back of the warning from the draugar; *Beware the traitor who lies in wait.*

Frida stared at him in horror. "Grimur?" she said, astonished. "But . . . you're supposed to be dead."

"You left me for dead; and I did die, once, but I lived again. When my family died and you drove me out of our tribe, I nearly gave up on life. I traveled the mountains for many months, until finally realizing that I did not wish to die. I desired revenge; I burned for vengeance upon you. I darkened your path for years, fomenting resistance to your passage, creating conflict in your path, and you never knew. I turned the Scordisci against you and they drove you out of Pannonia. I was there at Boiodurum when you emerged from the mountains and convinced the Raetians to resist you at every opportunity. I stood in the front ranks of the Vindelici at Manching, when they would have defeated you, but for the cursed luck that Teutobod showed up at the last moment. After that battle, I traveled north to lose myself in the great forests. Wandering alone for months, fasting and praying, I found a new purpose. Despite my efforts, you seemed to always pull victory from defeat. You seemed to be blessed by the gods. Then one night, Fenrir, the wolf god came to me in a dream and requested my assistance. He wished me to hasten the conditions that would bring about *Ragnarök* and release him from his eternal bonds. For this he promised that I would lead those who lived in the new Valholl that would be created after the chaos. Like me, he yearned for vengeance on his tormentor. I hated you, as he hated Wodan. So, I accepted his offer, and I encouraged the wild tribes in the great uprising that attacked westward across the Rhenus River, to create the chaos and the endless wars that would lead to *Ragnarök*.

"You are not the only person who bears a mark of the gods. So fearful of my efforts was Donar, that he tried to kill me three times. The first bolt from the heavens left me marked with the sign of *Yggdrasil*, but I lived. The second left me nearly blind, but I lived again. The third succeeded, but when my soul found its way to the underworld and the goddess Hel met me at the gates, she knew that her brother Fenrir favored me. She sent me back to the world of the living to continue his work.

"Yet again, what did I find but you. You! Again, you foiled my plans and drove that invasion back across the Rhenus and forced me into exile and out of favor with Fenrir. Once again, I disappeared into the wildlands, until an opportunity presented itself. Your rampage in Gaul made you one of Rome's most hated enemies. I sent a proposal to the Roman governor of Gallia Narbonensis, and I promised to deliver you in chains, so that he could claim the distinction of defeating you and your vast army. He promised me wagons of gold, but my real reward would be your defeat and public humiliation and eventual death at the hands of the Romans.

"Unbelievably, your men thwarted me again when they rescued you from my grasp. The slaughter of two Roman legions now left me out of favor with the Romans. Driven by equal parts rage and despair, I determined to sow distrust in your own ranks. I recruited spies within your army and gained the information I needed to get close to you, to make this final attempt for my revenge. I wanted to bring you here, away from your friends, away from any chance of you being rescued by your luck once again. Here, deep underground, near the realm of the dead, where I will be the strongest. Where my gods will strengthen me and ensure that you are finally vanquished and removed from this world."

I was silent while Grimur spoke, my brain trying to make sense of what I was hearing. "You . . . you left us," I stammered. "No one knew where you went. You never came back; we thought you were dead. So . . . it's been you all along causing all this chaos?"

"It wasn't difficult. No one wanted a horde of enemy warriors and their families eating up their crops and livestock like a cloud of locusts. All I did was bring news of your approach. Their fear did the rest."

I looked to Frida and was filled with a sudden rage. "You kidnapped my wife and son!" I shouted at Grimur and took a step toward him.

"Easy," Grimur said, stepping behind Frida he produced a seax that glinted in the torchlight. He held the blade beside her neck and stared malevolently at me.

"Another step and you lose your wife and your unborn child," Grimur threatened.

"What do you want from me?" I pleaded.

Grimur released Frida and moved behind Lingulf. My breath caught in my throat, and I could feel my heart thumping against my ribs.

"I want you to suffer," he said. "To feel the pain when your heart is ripped from your chest, as I felt when my wife and my child were taken from me. I want you to admit the failure that you are. You call yourself king, and yet you doubt yourself. You were a weakling boy, and as a man you cannot even protect your own family. You never deserved to be chieftain, and you are not a king!"

"I will say whatever you want, just don't harm them," I begged.

"Oh, but you must feel their pain for me to be satisfied," he said lifting the knife above Lingulf.

Frida's eyes locked with mine in a final assurance of our love. She glanced up at the knife that gleamed in the torchlight and fell towards Lingulf's chest. Lunging upward she grasped Grimur's arm with both hands, her body knocking Lingulf sprawling. I leaped forward, even while Grimur, surprised by Frida's sudden action, grinned with satisfaction. "You first then," he said. Sudden strength flowed through his body, and he ripped his arm downward. Frida's face went slack. The knife bit into her neck before I could reach them, and she slipped to the ground.

"Nooo!" came my anguished scream.

"Mama!" Lingulf cried, moving to cradle her head in his lap.

Grimur's face split into an evil smile as he drank in the torment he had caused. He reached for Lingulf's hair.

I leaped across the room and bowled into Grimur, knocking him to the ground, the seax flying from his hand. The crack of Grimur's skull smacking against the limestone went unheard as the blood pounded in my ears. Picking Grimur up by his tattered shirt, I slammed him into the stone, again and again, screaming in rage. The satisfied smile never left Grimur's lips, even in death. My fury finally spent, I slumped to the ground beside my wife and son, sobbing uncontrollably.

Oda's hideous scream had carried to the mouth of the cave, where Ansgar and the rest of the men waited. Ansgar took half of them to investigate and found Hrolf and Rurik. Leaving several men to care for Hrolf they continued on in search of me when they heard my cries from deep within the cave. Too late, they arrived to find me weeping on the floor beside my dead wife and our son.

The mottled sunlight filtered through the brightly colored leaves of the beech and oak trees that surrounded the mouth of the cave when I emerged bearing Frida's body close to my heart. Tears streamed down my scarred visage as I waded through the knee-deep water to where my men stood, silently waiting for me on the riverbank. Lingulf struggled to keep his composure walking beside me, glancing occasionally at his mother's body.

These men were my companions, my retinue, my closest friends, sworn to my leadership and to a man willing to give their own lives in my defense. We had faced death together dozens of times, yet now they stood helpless. We had pursued her captors across the length of Gaul and failed to save her. These men, these savage warriors, tall and strong, wept openly, feeling their king's grief in their own hearts.

Hrolf stood with the help of a crude crutch, his broken leg splinted and bound, his head hanging in sorrow. Ansgar, my giant friend, the commander of these men, drew his sword and slapped it against his shield in a slow rhythm. His men joined in as spears, axes, and swords clashed on wooden shields and echoed across the hillside in a final salute. Rurik's body lay to the side covered by his woolen cloak, and beside him, I gently laid Frida on my own bearskin cloak and covered her.

Two weeks later the party arrived back at the main camp of the Cimbri. I had spoken little since the funerals and eaten less. My face was gaunt, and my eyes were hollow. The memories of Frida's funeral pyre kept repeating in my head and the headaches had returned with a vengeance.

"I'm worried about him," Hrolf spoke softly to Ansgar. "He hasn't slept well since they were kidnapped."

"He's been using that weed that Vallus gave him in excess. He's numbing the pain."

"Hmmph," Hrolf grunted in agreement.

"What do we do?"

"I don't know."

CHAPTER TWENTY-SIX

I was lost in my grief. I stayed in my cabin, not emerging for anything. Samhain passed, then Yule. I lay in the darkness, trying to bury the pain in tankards of ale and ate only a few bites of bread. Through each night I could be heard moaning in mental and physical anguish as the pain overtook me, body and soul. Hrolf and his wife cared for Lingulf while the boy struggled with the loss of both parents.

People left food outside of my door which went mostly uneaten. Only Vallus had been admitted and then only to provide something new when the cannabis no longer satisfied me. "This is from the poppy," Vallus told me, revealing a plum sized ball of a sticky tar-like substance rolled up in a grape leaf. "Roman doctors use it for pain. It must be used very carefully and in small amounts." He inserted the tip of a small knife into the ball and mixed a drop into a cup of spruce tea that he had prepared. "You can mix it into a drink like this. It will make you drowsy, but it will dull the pain."

I leaned forward, eyes bright in anticipation, focused intently on the cup.

"Borrix," Vallus said seriously. "You must be careful with this. You can become addicted, and it will eventually kill you. Only use it in very small amounts and only when you really need it."

I gulped the tea and snatched the rest of the opium from Vallus, then retreated to my sleeping pallet.

Vallus sighed and walked out.

The opium brought peace of a sort. The pain from the headaches was dulled and I no longer saw Frida's death over and over again in my dreams. I slept the days away and talked to no one.

Hrolf brought Lingulf to try and break through to me. "Father," the boy called at my bedside. "Father." Lingulf grasped my tunic and shook me. He called again, his voice plaintive, "Father!" I mumbled angrily, "Go away!" and swatted at the small hands that pulled at my shirt.

"Come, Lingulf." Hrolf turned the boy away. Lingulf looked over his shoulder at the pitiful being that was his father. He did not understand. How could he? Through a haze, I silently wept at the pain and shame that I felt.

One day as spring neared, a committee of people visited me, concerned for me and the future of our people. Eldric came, accompanied by Skyld and Hilgi, Hrolf and Ansgar, as well as Caesorix, Lugius, Claodicus, and other clan leaders. Vallus stood to the side.

Outside the cabin the group waited while Ansgar and Hrolf came inside and dragged me out into the light, protesting weakly. I was haggard. My eyes were dark and sunken, and my hair was greasy and tangled. I stank of my own excrement and sweat. I blinked at the light that I had avoided for so long and tried to cover my eyes as my friends restrained me.

"Borrix," Eldric began. "Many on the council feel that you should step down as king. You have not attended a council meeting in months, and you have missed several important ceremonies. The people wonder where their leader is. Soon, it will be time to move on and you are obviously in no condition to lead. The people worry that you put their lives at risk by your absence."

I stood silent, held between my two friends. My head hung in shame. A sob escaped my parched throat, but I could not reply.

"Then I have no choice but to recommend to the council that you are no longer fit for your duties."

"Wait!" Vallus broke in. "I have brought a solution to his sickness."

"Like the one you brought for his pain?" Ansgar questioned, his tone accusing.

"No," said Vallus. "This is a plant that helps the body break away from the effects of the poppy. I beg you, give him some more time. Allow me to care for him. Please. I think this will bring him back."

"You have two moons," Eldric said. "After that the council will elect a new chieftain."

Vallus sat by my side for a week, administering his herb concoction and monitoring my recovery. At first, I spit it out and refused to take it, but my good friend was persistent and eventually won me over. I cursed him and lashed out at him, and he took it all, his guilt for bringing me the drug driving him to see me through.

I had more bad days than good. Today was an exceptionally bad day. It was hot, and sticky. My hair was plastered to my scalp and my bedding was soaked through. The nightmares had caused me to lapse back into despair and self-pity, grieving for my wife and even wishing that the gods would strike me down.

My cravings for the drug had lessened, but the physical pain that had been my reason for using the stuff still racked my body, and the memories were just as strong. I had cried and sweated out the poison, vomiting up everything that I managed to eat or drink, and then cramping and heaving when there was nothing left.

The pains in my belly competed with the headaches and muscle aches for which was the worst.

A low rumble of thunder in the distance carried into the darkened hut, warning of a coming storm. Weakly, I rose from the bed and staggered to the door. The sky was a leaden gray, with low clouds scudding across below the darker clouds above. A cool breeze struck my sweat soaked skin and chilled my body. A sudden downburst of rain fell violently from the sky. Large pellets of water spattered in the dust and quickly formed puddles and rivulets as it sought the easiest path.

I knew that this was the answer to my prayers. I would not go to Valholl, the destination of heroic warriors who died in battle, to eat and drink and fight until the end of time, but rather to *Helheim*, where those who have died by murder, or disease, or old age go to live on. This I knew deep in my heart. I would see my father again, my mother, Nilda, and best of all, Frida. It would be an escape from the pain and misery I now endured.

I stepped out into the downpour, and when I did, I was struck a mighty blow on top of my head. I fell to my knees. Chunks of ice were falling from the sky and splattering into the mud. Blood washed down my face from the wound, and I looked up. "Yes, yes! Punish me Wodan, punish me Donar! I have failed you; I have failed my people." I was battered again and again by the avenging ice of Niflheim until my shoulders and back became a bloody pulp.

The hail subsided and the large droplets changed into a deluge that obscured the nearby buildings and trees. A chilling wind blustered through, swaying the branches of nearby trees. The veil of falling water before me parted and a blurred image focused, then became clearer as it came near. I covered my head in fear at the vision that materialized. "Donar!" I cried. The storm god had appeared before me, and I was terrified.

"Do not fear me, Borrix. The Cimbri are still the favored people of my father, and you, Borrix, are my champion. This is why you bear our marks, and this is why we have given you the strength to fight your enemies. Now, I grant you the strength to end your suffering. Know that your loved ones await you, but now is not your time. You have battles yet to fight. Your people need you. Feel my strength course through your veins, expel these demons that have taken hold of your soul. Arise. Hold your head high with honor and prepare yourself. Your enemies will seek to destroy you yet again, but you shall rise above."

The vision flickered as the god of thunder turned away. The curtain of water closed again, and the wind stopped, leaving me on my knees, my blood streaming into the mud. As if the heavens reached the bottom of their bucket, the rain abruptly stopped. The silence was complete, only broken by the sound of water trickling from the rooftops and the steady drip, drip, as the last droplets fell from the leaves.

Vallus appeared at my side and helped me to my feet. "What are you doing out here? I left you alone only for a minute and you try and kill yourself?"

I straightened, standing to my full height and towering over Vallus. He was shocked. "What has happened?" he demanded.

"I have a reason to go on," I said. "Come, my friend, I am famished."

Over the next few weeks, I put back on most of the weight I had lost. I exercised with Hrolf and Ansgar. My color returned and so did my strength. I never looked back. The headaches had vanished, as had the pain I suffered throughout my body. I slept better, and I felt invigorated. I burned for vengeance against the Roman, Quintus Servilius Caepio, who had betrayed me and set the stage for Frida's death. As the weather warmed, I called for an assembly.

CHAPTER TWENTY-SEVEN

Spring 105 BC

There was growing unrest that threatened to fracture the alliance. I had begun to lose the iron grip I had maintained for years. My absence had caused many to lose faith in my leadership. They did not understand why I would make peace with a foreign god and wondered if I were still worthy. Some still chafed under the idea of kingship and openly complained of the change. Others wondered why we did not cross the Alpes after defeating Silanus to claim our new homeland in the fertile ground of northern Italy.

"We do not care for your need for personal vengeance," said Lugius, hunno of the Bear Clan. He had been a loyal follower, but my difficulties of late had created doubts. "You have not been present for months. Our young men have returned to raiding the Gauls, and now you want them to stop so that you can pursue a war with this Caepio? We stole his gold already, what more do you require."

"The gold will be returned," I said.

"Returned," he said in disbelief. "Returned? Why would we return it? That treasure is ours."

"No, it is not. It belongs to the Volcae, it is their heritage. We have more gold than we can ever use. It is more valuable as a gesture of good will to our allies."

"Good will," Lugius scoffed. "You really have gone mad."

"I made a promise to Lugos that I would ally with the Gauls, to push the Romans back into Italy. My quest to Lugos was the result of a vision from our own priestesses. You all swore an oath to me for life, will you renege on that oath?"

Lugius looked down, then back at me. "I will not break my oath. But you must be here for our people now. You must lead them. They believe in you, but you have to earn back their trust. You have to communicate what you want them to do, and why. They need to know they can trust you again."

"Even our allies are talking of leaving the alliance," Caesorix broke in. "The Ambrones whisper that they should break off on their own. The Teutones haven't joined us in years."

"Our allies now include the Gauls as well," I said. "We all have a common enemy in Rome. More specifically in Caepio. He is not just my enemy, what I propose is not just for my own vengeance. Njoror's curse keeps us from pushing our way into Italy and the only recourse we have to finally find a new homeland is to convince them that their only choice is to invite us into their lands. They must be forced to do so. We have defeated Rome in every battle we have engaged them in. We can do it again and give them no choice but to cooperate."

"How do you propose to do that?" asked Caesorix.

"By attacking them where they will feel it the most. Their coin purses."

The supply caravan from Aduatuca arrived with fresh oxen, cattle, and other goods necessary to supply us for the coming summer. When they returned they would take the wagons laden with Roman goods, arms and armor, as well as slaves and prisoners of war taken during last year's battles.

At the head of the column rode Glum, my father-in-law. We embraced and wept for the death of his daughter, my wife. "You must not blame yourself," he said. "I know it is your way, but you did not cause it, and you did your best to prevent it."

"She was my anchor. The only thing that kept me grounded to this world," I said. "I miss her so much. But I have found new purpose, and I am determined to finally bring our people home."

Glum had not changed. His tangled mass of dark hair stood out in all directions, and despite the sadness in his eyes, he still had the old humor. "Grandfather!" Lingulf ran to him and was engulfed in Glum's embrace.

"I've brought you something," Glum said, a smile breaking through the tangle of mustache and beard. He produced a seax, a real one, suited for a man. Lingulf's face lit up with joy. He looked at it wondrously, admiring its carved handle and leather case. "Gorm made the blade," he said. "I made the handle and case. It's a gift from the both of us." Gorm was the clan's blacksmith back in Aduatuca, and a close family friend.

The weapon was large in his hands, and he held it reverently. This was a gift for a man, and Lingulf knew it. "I will carry it always, Grandfather, thank you. Please give Gorm my thanks when you return."

We enjoyed a comfortable visit and passed the time with stories of events since we last saw each other. Glum had brought barrels of ale and good birch wine with him. "I tried making the grape stuff, but I can't seem to get it right. It usually turns to vinegar." He made a face and stuck out his tongue.

Glum watched joyfully as Lingulf went through his warrior training, using the oversized seax whenever possible, and Lingulf enjoyed the attention. Frida's death and my addiction had changed him. We had lost the close connection we held before. He knew I loved him, and he loved me. But when I had pushed him away and chosen the drug over him, he had changed. Who could blame him?

One day, Glum and Lingulf went to the forest and returned with a medium sized linden tree cut into three-foot lengths. Together, the two split it into boards and scraped and shaped them until they had what they needed for a new shield. "It's time you threw away that boy's shield you started with. You'll be eleven this summer, you're becoming a young man. You're not ready for a man's shield yet, but this will do until you are."

Glum took the boy to the butchering site to collect what they needed. They took some cattle hooves and boiled them down until a gelatinous substance formed. Then with the boards laid out on a flat surface, he slathered the glue on the edges of each board. Using sinew from the same steer he bound the boards together tightly and set them aside.

When it was dry, the pair cut the board slab to size. Glum produced an iron boss and edge banding, also made by Gorm just for this purpose and when the glue had dried and the boards were scraped again, Glum showed the boy how to nail the iron band in place, and then the boss that would cover the bearers hand and strengthen the center of the shield.

Two short boards were also glued and nailed across the back of the long boards to stiffen and strengthen the whole shield. Lingulf was charged with carving the wooden crosspiece that he would use to hold the shield. When the crosspiece was complete, it was fastened across the back of the boss opening, leaving enough room for Lingulf's knuckles when he held the shield.

Lastly, Glum walked with Lingulf to collect the woad, weld, and madder plants that would be used to make paint for the shield. It was Lingulf's responsibility to come up with the design and his grandfather showed him how to make the paint. The boy boiled each plant in a separate pot, adding urine to the woad when the color was extracted, and the leaves removed. Once the dyes were ready animal fat was warmed and added to the mix, with a bit of cow's milk in each pot. This would help the paint bind to the wood. Once cooled, the grease that formed became an effective paint.

That evening at supper, Lingulf walked in with hands that had turned shades of blue, yellow, red, and green from dipping them into the dyes and paint. He had several streaks of color on his face and his clothes. The boy was beaming. "The shield is complete," he announced, proudly holding it out for all to see.

"Wonderful!" exclaimed Glum, who had left the final design to his grandson.

"A wolf," I said proudly. "Well done." Lingulf had painted the shield red, with a black wolf's head silhouette in the center, over the boss. Accents of yellow, blue, and green completed the design.

Hrolf and Freki looked on proudly. "You can begin using it right away," Hrolf said.

"It needs a good week to dry first," Glum advised. "Then you can use it as you like. I'm proud of you Lingulf."

The next day, the caravan left to go back to Aduatuca. Glum hugged Lingulf tightly, then ruffled his hair. "You take care of your father," he said.

"I will."

Glum looked at me next and held out his hand. I grasped his forearm tightly. "Remember what I said."

"I will," I echoed Lingulf. "Watch for us in the fall."

"We watch for you every day. And pray as well."

I sent warriors east to find the passes that led over the Alpes into Italy, and west along the coast to find a route across the Pyrenees Mountains that separated Gaul from Iberia. We might not go this summer, but one day I knew we would cross one of those mountain ranges. Maybe both.

"Where do we go this year," asked Hrolf one night over a shared meal at his fire.

"East," I said bluntly, then softened my tone. "East out of the massif, then south along the Rhodanus toward Massalia."

"What about Teutobod and Amalric. Will they join us?"

"I don't know. I sent a messenger and instructed them to come south along the Rhodanus and we would meet them at mid-summer north of Massalia. I haven't heard back yet."

Hrolf frowned at the use of the word *instructed* but ignored it. "Massalia has formidable walls. We don't have the siege machines required to take it."

"No, we don't." I didn't share that Massalia was not my target. It was the bait.

Teutobod received the message at his hilltop stronghold atop the Donarsberg. "Apparently, Borrix now thinks he can order me around like I am one of his king's guards. Now that he is no longer living in a drug induced haze he has a new plan."

"What is that, Lord?" asked Teutobod's companion.

"He wants us to meet him along the Rhodanus and then strike south against Massalia."

"That is absurd. How would we defeat their walls? And to what end? We cannot hold such a place. The city sits on a promontory that reaches out into the sea; we cannot stop them from resupplying by ship. They could hold out there until the end of time, or until enough reinforcements arrive to defeat us."

Teutobod considered for a moment. "If I know Borrix, he already knows all this. Why would he plan a siege that has no prospect of success? Unless . . . it is not actually Massalia that he is after."

Teutobod sent for the messenger. "Return to Borrix. Tell him that we will meet him as he requested."

PART V

TERROR CIMBRICUS

105 BC

JEFF HEIN

CHAPTER TWENTY-EIGHT

Rome

January 105 BC

Publius Rutilius Rufus had finally won election as consul, with Gnaeus Mallius Maximus as his co-consul. Now, the senate met to decide what the consuls would be tasked to do in the coming year. With the Jugurthine war finally at an end and the Numidian king in chains, Gaius Marius was no longer a concern. Marius' political enemies focused their efforts against his ally Publius Rutilius Rufus.

The previous year, then Consul Quintus Servilius Caepio had put down the rebellion of the Volcae Tectosages and returned Tolosa and the surrounding region to the control of Rome. After much discussion on the loss of the treasure of Tolosa, rumored to have been stolen by the Cimbri, the senate decided it was time to finally put an end to the wars in the north. To do that, they created the largest Roman army to be fielded since Hannibal invaded Italy one hundred years ago.

The coalition against Marius and Rufus successfully shut out the new consul, Rufus, and secured an extended governorship of Gaul for Caepio, while Maximus was assigned to Gaul as the commander of a combined army that included Caepio's legions as well as his own two consular legions, plus two more supplemental legions and their auxiliaries: a combined strength of more than eighty thousand fighting men. Among the citizens, there was much consternation as to why Maximus was chosen to lead this large army, rather than the more experienced Rutilius Rufus. Surely Rufus would have been the better choice, but for some reason, the senate had voted to send Mallius Maximus, the new man.

Rufus, however, was not the least bit surprised. While they were not successful with interfering in the election of the popular Rutilius Rufus, his enemies held great power within the senate. He believed they had wielded that power to keep him in Rome, rather than out on the battlefield where he would have been more effective. He knew that Metellus, Scaurus, and Serranus had influenced enough senators to vote against him in retaliation for his support for Gaius Marius the year before.

Sidelined, Rufus used the time to focus his effort on the army, as he and Marius had discussed many times. While Marius experimented with the tactical organization of the new army, Rutilius Rufus established a new training regimen. By law, Rufus was also responsible to raise two consular legions. To reform their training, he incorporated a cadre of retired gladiators, *rudiarii*. These were men who had survived the arena and were honored by receiving the *rudis*, a wooden sword symbolic of their courage and skill.

While the army would continue to use the tactics of a compact mass of soldiers fighting in unison, Rufus and Marius recognized that many of the recent battles against the Germans had broken down into individual combat. They realized the knowledge of how to fight as an individual was just as important as how to fight in a unit.

Meanwhile, Consul Gnaeus Mallius Maximus received his imperium and was ordered to march as soon as his consular armies were trained. Caepio's legions were currently winter quartered at Narbo. The senate directed him to bring them to meet Maximus north of Massalia and turn over command to the new consul when he arrived.

While Rutilius Rufus focused his efforts on improving the army, the machinations of the Roman elite marched on. The rich and powerful always tried to curry favor with those in positions of authority. Many wealthy men were involved with public works projects around the republic and found that the relationships they kindled with senators and magistrates often brought them lucrative contracts for roads, bridges, apartments, aqueducts, and sewers. Sometimes it only took flattery and attention, other times an evening of food, drink, and women did the trick. But the language everyone understood was money. Bribes in the form of real estate, cash, and future incentives were the most effective, and there was always someone willing to grease a palm in order to get what they wanted. Becoming a magistrate and climbing the *cursus honorum* was the quickest and most lucrative way for a politician to become rich through the back door deals that took place.

Quintus Servilius Caepio had returned to Rome for the elections and to lobby for his position as proconsul in Gaul. While there, he attended one of the many lavish banquets held in the city after the new magistrates had been appointed for the year.

The light tones of a harp blended with the continuous babble of voices that sparred back and forth on the issues of war, politics, finance, and civil unrest. This party was being held at the luxurious home of the Princeps Senatus Marcus Aemilius Scaurus. There were small cups of olive oil and wine for guests to dip their bread in. Bowls of olives, figs, and an assortment of steamed vegetables sat beside platters of baked fish and roasted fowl with garum, a pungent fermented fish sauce. Ornate tables held artfully constructed pyramids of golden citrons from Syria, bright yellow lemons from the foothills of the Himalayan mountains, and orange kumquats and brilliant green limes that traveled by ship and caravan from the markets of India, whose merchants had traded for them with the Serens of a far-off land even farther east. The cost of these exotic fruits was exorbitant and was meant to impress.

Spoons for every guest was a luxury at only the best parties. Utensils were usually made of iron, bronze, or silver and expensive, but Scaurus spared no expense. Romans were accustomed to eating with their fingers and sopping up liquids with a piece of bread, and the lower class ate from wooden trenchers or earthen ware plates, but the upper class ate from bronze and silver plates and bowls.

A transparent spiral of smoke issued from several tall braziers that burned fragrant wood to keep the January chill at bay and added a slight haze to the comfortable atmosphere.

"I don't know what the senate is thinking," Caepio said to no one in particular. He was surrounded by a small group of sycophants who had been trying to attach themselves to the hem of his toga and were hanging on his every word. "Rutilius Rufus is the obvious choice to send to Gaul. He and I could work together to bring about a victory over these barbarians. Rufus is an experienced soldier and a *nobilitas*, not a new man, like this Mallius Maximus who has little military prowess."

The men around him nodded their heads vigorously and made incoherent noises of agreement.

Caepio continued, "I will never subordinate myself to someone like Mallius Maximus. He has never fought these northerners and I'm not about to take second place to a wet-behind-the-ears *novus homo* who will likely get all his men killed."

Furious at the senate's decision, Caepio soon left Rome and returned to Narbo, still stewing over the fact that the senate expected him to turn his army over to Maximus when the new consul arrived.

June 105 BC

Consul Gnaeus Mallius Maximus marched his legions north from their training camps in Italy along the Via Aemilia and across the Alps, then down the Durance River valley to the bank of the Rhodanus River and then north to a river plain near the city of Arausio. While the camp sprang up around him, he called his senior officers to his praetorium, the army commander's headquarters tent, to discuss a strategy to deal with the barbarian tribes. The clamor of his men setting up the camp served as an appropriate background to the voices of his commanders and staff officers discussing the situation.

Maximus pushed aside the privacy curtain from his sleeping quarters and entered the room. The group came to attention and saluted. Maximus nodded his acknowledgement and stepped up to the map table as his officers gathered around.

A tribune facing Maximus from across the table began with a summary of the enemy situation. "We know that last year the Tigurini and their allies vanished back into northern Gaul after then consul Caepio retook the city of Tolosa," he said, placing his finger on the map. "The Cimbri, Teutones, and Ambrones have not been heard from for several years, but now we are receiving reports from refugees that they are again pushing southward along the Rhodanus River toward Massalia, and that they have been campaigning throughout southern Gaul, probably re-allied with the Tigurini as well. But their tactics have changed. They are no longer attacking everyone they encounter. They are accepting tribute and adding to their alliance. They have turned their focus to attacking Romans and tribes that are securely allied with Rome. Roman estates along the frontier have been captured or destroyed, dozens of Roman citizens and thousands of allied Gauls have been murdered. Whole cities have been burned and looted. Unconfirmed intelligence tells us they have established an oppidum in northern Gaul that they return to periodically. This may be where they disappeared to in recent years. As you know this is the group of tribal people who defeated

Carbo at Noreia and four years later destroyed Silanus just a few miles north of where we currently stand. Two years ago, some of them were involved with the defeat of Longinus near Burdigala, and then again a year later when the Volcae Tectosages rose up against the Roman garrison at Tolosa. They are primarily made up of three northern tribes, the Cimbri, Teutones, and Ambrones, accompanied by thousands of Tigurini, a sub-tribe of the Celtic Helvetii. These outsiders are now allied with the Volcae Tectosages, the Arverni, and others from southern Gaul. Their estimated number is two hundred thousand total, of which perhaps half are fighting men. They are growing in number as local tribes join them and pay tribute rather than be conquered. If there are no questions, Tribune Marcus Mallius will give a summary of the current disposition of friendly troops."

The first tribune stepped aside and allowed Marcus, the eldest son of the consul, to take his place at the table. "Sir, our main body is currently occupied establishing a castrum at this location. Senior Legate Marcus Aurelius Scaurus commands a force of twelve hundred citizen cavalry as a forward screen a day's ride north of this camp. Per your orders he will make initial contact and provide warning of the enemy's approach.

"Proconsul Caepio, governor of Gaul, is marching toward this location now with four full-strength citizen legions and four auxiliary legions, plus several hundred allied Gallic cavalry. We expect his arrival within the week. After reestablishing control of Tolosa from the Volcae Tectosages last fall, Proconsul Caepio withdrew to Narbo for the winter, fortified the city and awaited the arrival of the new consular army, with the orders to combine forces to seek out and destroy the Cimbri alliance. Proconsul Caepio has made it clear that he expects to command those forces." The tribune paused at those last words and there was an audible intake of breath at the mention of Caepio's demands. Maximus gave no reaction, and his son went on. "The two armies will consist of eight legions of citizen soldiers and eight of Italian auxiliaries, more than eighty thousand fighting men when combined, plus several hundred allied Gallic cavalry and several thousand Gallic infantry, with approximately forty thousand support personnel and camp followers. There are twenty-three men in the infirmary with various illnesses and minor injuries. Three deserters have been caught and are awaiting punishment. Weapons and armor are in good condition. Morale is high, and the men are ready for combat."

Maximus nodded and turned to the army's quartermaster and camp commander. "Prefect, your report."

"Sir. The camp's defensive walls and ditch will be completed in a few more hours, work is progressing normally. Artillery is emplaced to defend the camp. Scout patrols are out, and the area is secure. The supply trains have arrived and are entering the camp as we speak. More have left Massalia with grain and supplies that I purchased while on the way here. There are no losses to report. We currently have two weeks supply of grain on the carts as well as the several days' worth the men are carrying. I will send out foraging parties first thing in the morning. The mules and oxen are in good shape and the blacksmiths will begin repairs on any damaged equipment as soon as they are set up." The group shared a smile when the distant ringing of a hammer striking an anvil confirmed those last words.

"Communications?" Maximus inquired.

A third tribune stepped forward. "We maintain good messenger communication back to Rome, and with the cavalry forward under Legate Scaurus. We are waiting to hear from Proconsul Caepio."

"Then how do we know what he is doing?" Maximus asked, turning back to his son.

"Sir, we received a messenger from Rome that passed on the governor's demand to assume command of the consular armies. He sent no direct communication to us. That's how we learned he is moving this way."

Maximus frowned. "That's a very roundabout way of getting information. Unacceptable. Prioritize getting direct communication established with Caepio."

"Sir," his son was obviously distraught. "Proconsul Caepio has made it clear, he will not cooperate with you or speak directly with you, unless it is as your commander."

Maximus' face flushed with anger. In an uncharacteristic outburst he shouted, "That man is impossible! How can the senate expect me to carry out a war when they saddle me with --". He caught himself and swallowed his fury. "Thank you for your reports. We will meet again in the morning. You are dismissed." The consul retired behind the privacy curtain to his personal quarters.

The law supported Maximus' claim that the currently serving consul was superior in rank and should command the two armies. But the senators themselves supported Caepio over him, simply because of their same prejudices. And yet, they had chosen him over the more experienced consul Publius Rutilius Rufus, who remained in Rome. Rufus also came from a patrician family and had served an illustrious career in the army, distinguishing himself in Numidia and Hispania. Rufus should have been the obvious choice. Nevertheless, Maximus was here now, with an army at his command, and an imperium from the senate to block the marauding horde from entering Italy and if possible, destroy them.

Taking a deep breath, he calmed himself. "Titus!" he called to his youngest son who had also accompanied him as his personal attendant.

"Yes, sir?"

"Take a letter." Maximus dictated yet another message to Caepio, claiming his right to command as the senior magistrate. He laid out his wishes that Caepio should bring his army to Maximus' position just east of the Rhodanus and establish a camp. From there the two armies could block the route to Massalia and the mountain passes into northern Italy, forcing the enemy onto a battlefield of their choosing. After finishing the letter to Caepio, Mallius began a message to the senate, urgently requesting they intervene and order Caepio to cooperate.

JEFF HEIN

CHAPTER TWENTY-NINE

Near the oppidum of Vienne

August 105 BC

I had never seen so many people gathered in one spot. The wagons and tents stretched to the horizon and beyond. There were warriors beyond count, and camp followers beyond that. The Ambrones had come south along the Rhenus from Aduatuca, bringing the Treveri. They joined the Teutones, Vagiones, Raurici and other tribes who had fought the Suebi with us. The Tigurini came from their mountain strongholds, leading other tribes of the Helvetii. Warriors of the Arverni and Volcae Tectosages joined us, as well as many other groups of unnamed warriors. All had responded to my call. All with a single purpose. To drive Rome out of Gaul.

A great council fire was lit and the hundreds of chieftains and hunnos sat or stood around the clearing. Eldric led a ceremony of prayer and sacrifice before I stepped to the front, atop a wooden platform that had been built for the occasion.

I was known to all. My shining red hair, scars, and eyepatch was legend. Even the slight limp was noted as the story of Borrix had been spread far and wide through the poems and songs of Aldric the bard. My friend who had saved my life when I was mauled by a bear. He had travelled with us many miles and stood by my side in many battles, until he was killed one day by a Roman lance.

A great cheer arose as I climbed the steps and became visible to the throngs beyond the inner circle. My heart thrilled at the accolade, and I looked down at my son who stood at the side of the rostrum, looking back with pride.

I raised my hands in acknowledgement and the crowds gradually quieted.

"For a generation Rome has imposed its influence upon you," I began loudly. "Each of us here has lost someone or something to that vile city. We have all been touched by those lying, pampered, traitorous pieces of dung!" I emphasized each of those last words, rising in volume until my voice echoed across the clearing and the crowd responded, cheering loudly.

"Only a day's walk from here, the Allobroges and Arverni were conquered by the Roman General Ahenobarbus. How many were killed in that invasion? How many slaves were taken and sold at the Roman slave markets? They claimed this land and gave it their own name, Gallia-Narbonensis. Their traders bring things of luxury and many Gauls accept these things, they change their lives to accommodate the Romans, they cut their hair, they accept their rules, they bend the knee. I will NEVER bend the knee!" I shouted to another chorus of shouts. When they quieted down I asked, "Will you?" They responded with a thunderous, "No!"

"Then will you join me?" I challenged. "Join me to drive this pestilence out of Gaul!" They roared their agreement for minutes. I stood on the rostrum, overwhelmed by their acceptance and faith. When I descended I saw Skyld standing nearby with a smug smile on her lips. She nodded at me in acknowledgement, then faded back into the crowd.

CHAPTER THIRTY

Cavalry Camp of Marcus Aurelius Scaurus

September 105 BC

Just before dawn, a warning horn blared and a cry came from the watchtower near the north gate, "Warriors at the north tree line!"

A cold rain was falling, making it difficult to see in the morning twilight. The blare of a cornu echoed throughout the camp and men scrambled from their dry tents to gather weapons and mount their horses in the strengthening downpour.

The swift response force, a turma of thirty horsemen kept on alert for quick reaction to an enemy threat, thundered out of the camp, splashing mud on the guards standing ready to close the gate after they passed. One turma kept their horses saddled and their weapons ready at all times. The duty rotated each night.

"Tesserarius!" Scaurus shouted. The night watch officer sprinted to report to his commander. "Report."

"Sir! There are warriors emerging from the trees and forming into ranks at the north tree line." The tree line was a full mile from the camp across a meadow of grass and small shrubs. *Plenty of room to form the cavalry*, thought Scaurus, standing under the awning of his tent, while the tesserarius stood miserably in the rain. *How did they get so close to the camp without being seen?* As quickly as that thought occurred, he dismissed it. That wasn't important. *There can't be that many of them or my patrols would have noticed their approach. It must be a small contingent that slipped between the scouts.*

"Get the turmae out of the gate and formed up, we'll wait for the report of the swift response force. I need to know how many there are."

"Yes, sir!"

A few minutes later, Scaurus cantered to the front of his cavalry on a magnificent white mare with silver trappings on his bridle and saddle. Scaurus wore a polished cuirass and helmet that was dulled in the gray light.

"Where is the response force commander? I need a report."

"They haven't returned, sir," said a young decurion sitting his horse nearby. "Neither have the two patrols that were out since yesterday."

Well, the patrols aren't due back yet, Scaurus thought.

The young cavalry officer's horse stretched out its neck, then its lips to gingerly pluck the purple bulb of a late blooming shoulder high milk thistle and chewed without a care.

Scaurus looked at the young man. *Why do they send these boys into battle so young,* Scaurus wondered. *They have too much pride and not enough experience.* "Keep your turma with me," he said. "You will act as my personal bodyguard and messengers."

"Yes, sir!" the young man fairly shouted at Scaurus, excited at his first opportunity to face the enemy he had heard stories of since he was a young boy.

Scaurus laid a calming hand on his mare's neck as she sidestepped nervously and tossed her head. The pouring rain softened while they waited. He shivered when he tipped his head, and a stream of cold water ran from his helmet edge inside the neck of his cuirass and down his back. Half an hour passed with no word from the missing turma. The tesserarius approached from the fort and walked up beside his commander, "Sir, the watchtower lost sight of the enemy when the rain strengthened. It appears they faded back into the trees as the first horses left the gate. We haven't seen anything since."

Just as the man finished speaking, their attention was drawn again to the tree line where a number of brightly painted shields appeared through the gloom. The rain stopped abruptly, and the low clouds parted on a stiff, cool wind. The light grew swiftly. The enemy warriors stood at the edge of the trees shaking their weapons, beating their shields, and shouting unintelligibly toward the Romans. There was still no sign of the missing men.

Scaurus' mare pawed nervously, feeling its rider's angst. The legate looked about, considering what he should do, while his men looked back to him for orders. Finally, he made a decision. "Decurion," Scaurus said. "Send two of your men back to the consul. Tell him we have made contact with the enemy's forward elements, and I will send a report when we determine the location of their main body."

"Yes, sir."

"Forward at the walk," Scaurus shouted, looking to one side, then the other. Holding his arm straight above his head he lowered it slowly, and their mounts stepped forward. Scaurus commanded a separate unit made up of all of Maximus' cavalry, consisting of twelve hundred men and horses, forty turmae of thirty men, each commanded by a decurion. Each turma was formed into three successive ranks of ten horsemen. Two were on patrol and one was now missing. That left thirty-seven turmae, more than a thousand mounted men, and he did not yet know what he was facing.

When they had closed half the distance, the barbarians began fading back into the wood line again. Scaurus frowned. A feeling of uncertainty crept into his chest. Suddenly a clamor arose from behind them and to the right. His head snapped over in that direction to see a large group of Germanic warriors that were moving toward the rear of his troops.

"Legate!" a decurion shouted, pointing to where the first band of warriors had been. They were back now, and their numbers had grown tremendously. Shields of every color and design were emerging from between the trees by the hundreds. A low rumble carried across the field when the enemy began their war chant, stamping their feet and striking swords and spears and axes against their shields.

Another shout, and a man pointed toward the left flank. Warriors had materialized in the open field and were jumping up and down, chanting, and shaking their weapons.

The horses began tossing their heads, their eyes rolling white in fear at the sound now coming from all sides. Their riders were having difficulty controlling them and the turmae were losing their formation.

There was no use trying to get back to the camp, it wasn't defensible against this. He was vastly outnumbered while still more steadily appeared.

The warriors behind him were closing in, and Scaurus realized his best option was to break through the line of surrounding warriors and use their speed to get away. He gave the order to charge and spurred his mare forward. His troopers followed, charging straight ahead. The bright yellow flowers of woundwort were trampled beneath their hooves. A bevy of quail burst from the tall grass, startling several of the horses on the right. The line of enemy warriors stayed in place, while hundreds of horses pounded forward. Clods of wet earth flew skyward, fountains of water splashed high as they came with their lances leveled at the enemy.

Yet the warriors stood their ground. Scaurus glanced aside at the young officer beside him, urging his horse a step ahead of his commander's, a look of pure exhilaration on his face as he galloped toward the enemy, his lance held close under his arm, ready to make his first kill. *Why aren't they moving?* Scaurus asked himself. The answer was revealed as he raced headlong when he saw before him a small, intermittent creek that crossed before the enemy warriors.

It was dry the day before when his scouts reported on the lay of the land surrounding his camp. But the recent downpour had left standing water that concealed hummocks and hollows that caused the horses to stumble and fall. It wasn't big, but the fresh muck was enough to mire the small cavalry force. The first riders went down into the shallow water and those in the second rank followed. Most of the third rank managed to stop their horses in time, the beasts sliding to a halt, many rearing up and unseating their riders. A shower of spears fell upon them, and the screams of wounded men and horses added to the din. A great cheer went up when the German warriors rushed forward into the disorganized cavalry force. The pursuing tribesmen caught up from behind and the slaughter began. Romans drowned beneath their horses or were injured in the fall. Those that managed to gain their footing faced an onslaught of ten men to one. Scaurus' leg was pinned by the weight of his mare. The Romans had no chance against the overwhelming number of warriors. A few were spared, including Scaurus, who was easily identified by his armor and superb mount. His struggling mare died quickly when a huge warrior brought an axe down on her neck. Scaurus was dragged from beneath her carcass, stripped naked and beaten severely, until a senior warrior intervened, knowing that Borrix would want to speak with him.

The swift response force had been drawn into an ambush just beyond the clearing, and one of the two patrols had been wiped out. The other patrol somehow avoided the roving bands of warriors and returned to what was left of their camp. The bodies of their comrades lay strewn about the small battlefield, beside the bloating carcasses of their horses. Their commander's body was nowhere to be found. The survivors mounted and rode hard through the night to reach the consul's camp and report the disaster.

Shortly after Scaurus sent the first messengers, his entire force had been destroyed. Later, when the survivors arrived at the main camp, word of Scaurus' defeat sped through the soldiers. Centurions and optios were challenged to stop the gossip, and they put the men hard at work reinforcing the camp, foraging for food, maintaining their equipment, and training for combat. The men were so tired by the end of the day they prepared their supper and went to sleep. There were few that sat around the campfires to discuss their fears.

The next day, Caepio arrived.

Caepio's legions established their camp on the west side of the Rhodanus, across the river from Consul Gnaeus Mallius Maximus. Each of the four legions of citizen infantry and four auxilia of allied infantry, five thousand troops each, was accompanied by their ala of three hundred cavalry, associated artillery and support troops, and tens of thousands of camp followers.

Caepio rode beneath his oversized banners, resplendent in his polished bronze helmet with red horsehair crest and bronze cuirass shining in the afternoon sun. He never once glanced across the river in the direction of Mallius' camp, and deliberately kept his back turned in that direction.

In Caepio's eyes, Maximus was beneath acknowledgement. He sent no messages, no liaisons to Maximus to arrange a meeting. By law Caepio was subordinate to Maximus, but he wasn't about to take second place to the *novus homo* with no serious military experience. "Let him come to me," Caepio told his legate when the man inquired about sending liaison officers to the senior officer's camp, which was the proper military protocol.

JEFF HEIN

CHAPTER THIRTY-ONE

Late September 105 BC

A delegation of junior senators arrived at Consul Gnaeus Mallius Maximus' camp during a slight pause in the week of rains. Rains that had turned the country roads to mud. The senators' journey in Italy and the south of Narbonensis had been on Roman roads that were paved with flat stones and curbed and drained to run water away from the road. But after they turned north along the Rhodanus, the delegation traveled on dirt roads that were full of potholes and cut by intermittent streams of muddy water that crossed its crooked path. Unlike the arrow straight Roman roads, these cart trails followed the lay of the land around swamps, across river fords, and over hills, meandering their way across the country. At first, the senators had all been excited at the prospect of being selected for such an important task, now they were realizing why the more senior senators remained in Rome.

Wet, hungry, and tired, they were happy to see the promise of the defensive wall and guard towers of Maximus' camp, even while the added insult of one more shower passed over them, whipping their clothing with a cool breeze.

All of them had seen military service of course, it was a requirement to enter political office, but not all military service was the same. Most had grown up pampered in the luxury of Rome's pleasant weather and marbled streets. Not only had they been selected for this mission due to their low standing in the senate, but they were also all members of the nobilitas and were likely to see things from Caepio's point of view, regardless of the legal rights of Maximus. The more influential senators were not about to cut the legs from under Caepio, one of their own. In keeping with political practice they sent a toothless delegation to settle the matter, this ensured that it looked like the senate was doing something, when in fact they were accomplishing nothing.

Maximus greeted them with enthusiasm, happy that the senate had answered his pleas. He hoped that they would put Caepio in his place and force him to cooperate. The two camps still sat on opposite sides of the river, isolating each of them and preventing them from supporting each other if necessary.

"We have prepared a comfortable tent for you where you can warm yourselves," Maximus told them. "There is bread and vegetables in the tent and there will be a banquet in your honor this evening. My son will show you the way," Maximus gestured grandly.

He was disappointed to see that most of the envoys were young, but he had no choice but to hope for the best. That evening, he entertained them and said nothing of the situation. That would wait until the next day.

"I cannot do the senate's bidding when Proconsul Caepio refuses to cooperate. He sits on the other side of the river, smugly thumbing his nose at me, all the while risking a disaster if the barbarians attack in force. We have already lost our cavalry contingent while waiting on him to get here, and now that he's here, I still can't begin a campaign because of his refusal to turn his army over to my command."

"We understand your predicament," said the lead envoy. "We will cross the river to his camp tomorrow and talk with him."

Gaius Julius Caesar, third of his name and brother-in-law to Gaius Marius, was an ally of Marius and thus a political enemy of much of the senate. Marius' marriage to Caesar's sister Julia had resulted in a resurgence of the ancient family of the Caesar's and Gaius Julius Caesar looked up to the military prowess of the famous Gaius Marius.

Although the Caesar's were also a patrician line, their support of the new man, Marius, made them very unpopular in Rome. Now that he was the lead envoy to support the claims of another new man, Caesar was in a difficult situation.

"I don't think you do understand," blustered Maximus. "I've been sitting here for months just waiting on him to get here, sending out patrols and pulling sentry duty. We've eaten up our stores and I've had to establish a market with local merchants to provide food. He's sent me no communication and he's been trying to undermine me in Rome. His orders were to subordinate himself to me and turn over command. He's dragged his feet all summer and finally arrived just days before you did, and still won't talk to me. I beg you, order him to follow his mandate so we can get this campaign underway before snow flies."

The next morning, the senatorial delegation left for Caepio's camp.

Caepio poured himself a cup of wine and began speaking with his back turned to the envoys, showing his disdain for them and displaying what he felt was his superior position.

"I know of course why you are here, and your journey, it seems, has been a waste of time. I have no intention of subordinating myself to Mallius Maximus." Caepio scoffed and shook his head, "I laugh every time the cognomen Maximus is applied to him."

Gaius Julius Caesar chose his words carefully, already knowing that there was nothing he could say that would change Caepio's mind. "Proconsul, with respect, as consul he has the support of Roman law, and the senate gave him an imperium that grants him command of both armies. Consul Publius Rutilius Rufus supports his claim, as does Marcus Antonius Orator and the princeps senatus Marcus Aemilius Scaurus. They are all of ancient patrician families like your own. Won't you consider abiding by the senate's decree?"

Caepio ignored the question. "Did you know that Mallius' entire cavalry force was wiped out just a few days ago? The man will get his entire army wiped out. No, I will not subject my men to his incompetence."

"But Proconsul . . ."

"I will say no more on the matter! You will do Rome a service by returning to Maximus' camp and convincing him that the only way out of this is to turn his army over to me. I will allow him to serve as my legate, but I will have overall command. That is the only way this will be resolved."

Caepio squinted one eye at Caesar. "Do you think that I don't know who you are? A once-great family that had to be pulled up from insignificance by the gold supplied by a *novus homo*. Your father should be ashamed to stoop so low as to marry his daughter off to a turnip-eater like Gaius Marius. Another upstart who has no place in the senate, or any business leading armies. Now go! My patience with you has ended." Caepio spun on his heel and dismissed the delegates.

Caesar and the rest of the delegation walked outside escorted by Caepio's guards like they were a group of commoners being evicted from a patrician banquet. Caesar was furious to be treated so. *Who does that man think he is? He just thumbed his nose at the whole senate,* he thought.

CHAPTER THIRTY-TWO

Scaurus faced me, unafraid. He drew himself up to his full height and stared defiantly. Ansgar, the commander of my retainers, saw the insolent look on the Roman officer's face and backhanded him across the mouth. Scaurus's head snapped to the side from the force of the blow, but otherwise he did not move. He looked up at Ansgar venomously and spat at his feet. The angry giant moved around him and kicked him behind the knees, forcing the Roman to the ground. Scaurus, on his knees, straightened his back and attempted to maintain his soldierly bearing. He looked up, returning his burning gaze to me. *This Roman's arrogance is astounding* I thought. I sat back in my chair and rested my chin on my hand, studying the prisoner. "Let him speak."

Scaurus licked the blood from his lower lip. "I am Marcus Aurelius Scaurus, senior legate of the armies of Consul Gnaeus Mallius Maximus, who has been given imperium by the Roman senate to destroy your army and send you scrambling back to your northern forests like the barbarian dogs that you are." Ansgar pulled back his arm to strike him again and stopped when I waved a hand.

"And yet, here you are," I said slowly, emphasizing each word. "Bound and helpless before the *barbarian dogs* who destroyed your cavalry. My people have been destroying Roman armies for more than a decade, and if you continue to get in our way, we will not stop until we have killed you all. Carbo, Silanus, Longinus; they all discovered what it means to betray us. Romans and liars, liars and Romans, they are the same."

"Your successes were no more than the blind luck of facing incompetent generals," retorted Scaurus. "You will never reach Italy. You will never defeat Rome. Your only hope is to turn around and go back into the wilderness that spawned you. You can never win against us. There are two Roman armies waiting for you," Scaurus boasted. Spittle flew from the Roman's mouth and his eyes bulged with rage, overcome at the humiliation he felt from being defeated and captured, yet defiant to the end. "You will not be so fortunate this time. Consul Maximus will destroy you. Your warriors will be slaughtered, your women raped and strangled. Your children will be sold into slavery and your names will be forgotten. You came from nothing, and you will return to nothing. Rome can never be destroyed by the likes of you! The Gauls tried. Hannibal tried. All have failed. Rome will endure forever!"

I watched in silence as the man raved. My men, watching the spectacle with interest, began to laugh. Just one man at first, then it turned into a ripple that traveled through the gathered warriors until hundreds of blood-spattered, wild-eyed warriors were laughing full-throated at the Roman as if they had just heard the best joke.

I glanced sideways at Hrolf, and then at Freki. Slowly, I stood. My sword hissed softly as I drew it from the scabbard. My one eye glared at Scaurus with primal anger and the Roman officer sagged as the bluster finally left him. Gathering his courage, he straightened again and looked up at me, pressed his lips together and accepted his fate.

"You have said your piece, and your words mean nothing to me. Know this, before you die Roman. The only thing that has saved your countrymen from being conquered, is the curse that stays our hand. If your leaders continue to send armies to attack us, they will continue to be destroyed. This I swear to Donar!" At the final word I thrust my sword into his heart. I kicked his body off my blade and chopped down to remove his head. My warriors cheered with abandon, lifting their weapons high in a salute, then beat them against their shields in an act of approval.

I pointed at the head and spoke to Ansgar. "Find a prisoner. Tell him to take that to Gnaeus Mallius Maximus. Tell him that we are coming, and if they stand in our way, we will crush them."

The next morning, I was up early to pray. I asked Wodan for his guidance and his strength in the coming days, and while I stood outside watching the rising sun light the horizon a streak of golden light crossed the still-dark sky from north to south. "Gungnir", I whispered in awe. Murmurs wafted through the camp as others saw the omen.

Legend told that when Wodan hurled his enchanted spear, Gungnir, toward an enemy he had blessed his people with victory. The light had flown south, toward the Roman camps. There could be no clearer message.

Maximus continued his barrage of orders, demands, and pleas to Caepio to cross the river so that they might combine forces. He no longer demanded that Caepio subordinate himself, but tried to coerce the proconsul to moving closer so that they could more easily support each other. Eventually, Caepio conceded the tactical advantage to having their camps in proximity and crossed to the east side of the Rhodanus, but he still refused to communicate with Maximus. He never replied to the letters, but he did move his camp to within a mile of Maximus'.

The northern alliance moved south for several days until my scouts came back with the message that there was a massive Roman army encamped along the Rhodanus, directly in our path. I halted the horde, and we established our own camp several miles north of the Romans.

CHAPTER THIRTY-THREE

Camp of the Northern Alliance

Near Arausio, Gallia Narbonensis

October 105 BC

A tribune arrived at our camp at sunrise. The man faced me without fear.

"Consul Gnaeus Mallius Maximus wishes you to come to his camp in order to discuss a peaceful resolution that is beneficial for both parties. Your safety is guaranteed. He requests that you bring no more than twenty men as an escort, and they may keep all arms on their person."

I was shocked to hear these words, then suddenly suspicious of a trap.

"Lord? Another messenger from the Romans has arrived."

I was confused. "Another? Send him in."

When the second Roman pushed aside the curtain and entered the tent, he was surprised to see another man wearing the armor of a Roman tribune standing to the side. Quickly recovering his composure, he delivered his message.

"Proconsul Quintus Servilius Caepio, Governor of Gallia Narbonensis, sends his terms for your capitulation. There will be no negotiation. Boiorix will surrender his sword to the consul, in person, and will remain as a hostage. In return, your people will be allowed to withdraw back to the north, beyond the border of Gallia Narbonensis. He does not care where they go, but they will never return to any Roman province or allied territory. As recompense for the Roman lives that you have taken and the destruction you have wrought, you will pay a tribute of twenty talents of gold and ten of silver, delivered to the city of Narbo on the summer solstice. You will release all Roman citizens that may be in captivity and all slaves taken in Gaul. Your reply is expected within three days."

I looked blankly at my advisors and burst into a fit of laughter that brought tears.

"Who does this Roman think he is?" I wondered aloud at the ridiculous demands, looking at Hrolf with a wide grin. "He butchers my name into something unrecognizable, then demands my surrender?"

"See that these men are treated well, but keep them separated," I told one of my guards. "I will have a reply to both of you soon."

"What do you think about this?" I asked Hrolf.

"I think it's a trap. This is just another attempt to confuse us with offering peace while threatening war."

"I disagree," Freki said. "They are vying for power. Caepio was governor of Gallia Narbonensis when we defeated Silanus. He served as consul last year, crushed the rebellion of the Tectosages and recaptured Tolosa. Now he is proconsul and governor again. He is a capable general and a Roman nobleman. He remains in Gaul as the proconsul because of our presence. This new consul, Gnaeus Mallius Maximus, has been assigned to Gaul to join with Caepio and lead his army against us. But apparently Caepio does not accept Maximus's command over him. He does not respect him as his superior. Apparently, this Maximus is what they call a *novus homo*. The first in his family line to hold the office of consul. Caepio comes from a noble family with a long lineage of consuls."

"So, they are fighting internally," I said thoughtfully. "Perhaps this can be to our advantage."

I sent word back to Mallius Maximus that I accepted his invitation, and I would send a delegation to speak with him tomorrow. I sent word to Caepio that I would send a reply in two days.

Camp of Consul Gnaeus Mallius Maximus

October 6, 105 BC

Mallius Maximus greeted Hrolf as befitted a delegation of a great nation. Two columns of legionaries stood at attention along the Via Praetoria, the street that led from the main gate to the Praetorium, or camp headquarters. Maximus himself waited outside the Praetorium to greet them, flanked by his subordinate commanders.

Hrolf strode confidently down the avenue and straight up to the consul. He was accompanied by a representative of Teutobod and Amalric and followed by several more imposing warriors. The Roman soldiers sneered openly at the barbarians that approached wearing a motley combination of leather and furs, iron, bronze, and copper helmets, and chainmail.

Camp of Proconsul Quintus Servilius Caepio

"Consul, our scouts have reported that a delegation from the

Cimbri has arrived at Consul Maximus' camp." Quintus Sertorius, a young cavalry officer under Caepio's command, addressed Caepio as consul instead of proconsul. Although his term as consul had expired and he was appointed by the senate as proconsul to continue the campaign in Gaul, Caepio insisted the title of consul be used. He could never see himself as subordinate to the *novus homo* that led the legions encamped across the river.

Sertorius was a decurion, the officer in charge of a contingent of thirty cavalrymen. Caepio had assigned his turma to keep an eye on the Cimbri encampment. "When?" demanded Caepio.

"Less than an hour ago, Sir."

The ugly specter of jealousy rose within Caepio, and his face flushed with anger. Fearing that he would not get the credit for resolving the Cimbri crisis, Caepio's head snapped toward his legate. "Ready the legions. We will march immediately. I will not allow this upstart my victory. We will attack while the barbarians are distracted."

Camp of the allied tribes

I could hear the approaching legions at the same time the reports reached me. The bugling of the battle horns alerted those who had not already realized what was happening and the hundreds formed to meet the Roman threat. The blocks of about one hundred warriors made up of clansmen and led by their hunno, formed a line of infantry between the camp and the approaching Romans. Freki assembled his cavalry to the left flank, opposing the Roman cavalry.

The alliance recognized the betrayal for what it was. Hrolf and the others were in the Roman's camp to talk peace, and now we were attacked. The hatred and rage spewed forth with such vehemence that it seemed to physically strike the lead ranks of the legions. The soldiers with their red cloaks appeared to falter, but came on, urged forward by their centurions.

Warriors of the allied tribes formed a huge mass of milling bodies that outnumbered the Romans three to one. Their line stretched longer and deeper than the legions with their auxiliaries. To the Romans it appeared as if every barbarian in the north had appeared before them. The garish sound of the Roman cornu trumpets signaling their commands mingled with the strident call of the Gaulish carnyx, the Germanic lur, and the bellowing ox-horns.

To the Romans, the barbarians looked much the same. Large, fearsome, wild-eyed warriors, each tribe identified in some way. Some with specific hair styles, or types of weapons; some by similar colors or patterns on their clothing or shields. But all were working themselves into a frenzy. Shaking their spears, axes, or swords in the air, clashing their weapons against iron shield bosses, and raising the din of the barritus, the battle cry of the northern tribes. The Germans were dressed in a mixture of animal skins, leather, and linen or woolen trousers; some wore tunics, most were bare chested. They had dropped their cloaks for the coming battle. The nobility of the Gauls wore fine mail coats and ornate helmets of copper and bronze. The wealthier had gold and silver chains or torques about their necks while the rest had iron or bronze torques. The younger wore no decorations, as they had not yet earned them. The many colors and designs on the painted shields reflected the afternoon sun.

Caepio's hasty attack meant he did not have the advantage of his artillery, which was still lumbering forward and would need time to emplace. But time was not on their side, Caepio's arrogance would be his undoing, but he could not back down now. A messenger arrived from Maximus pleading for Caepio to wait for him to arrive, so that they could face the barbarians together. Caepio angrily dismissed the man. "We will win the day, or we will die," he said to no one in particular. The reality of his situation was sinking in, but he still would not reconsider.

At double the range of a thrown spear, the Romans halted and dressed up their formations. The young Velites stood in a mass in front of the maniples of Hastati, followed by the Principes and Triarii. The Velites wore no armor, only off-white tunics and a variety of caps that marked their unit, usually a wolf, or a badger, and occasionally a metal helmet. They were of the poorest class of citizens to serve in the army and could not afford the expense of protective armor.

The Hastati, men who were a few years older and had a bit more money, wore metal chest plates over their tunics. Leather straps ran over their shoulders, across their back, and under their arms to hold it in place. They wore a bronze helmet with three upright feathers at the crown which had the effect of making them appear larger, with cheekpieces that tied with a rawhide strip under the chin to protect the sides of the face.

They carried two pila, heavy javelins slightly taller than a man, which were thrown in a volley to disrupt enemy formations. A gladius and pugio were worn for close quarters combat. They also carried a scuta, a long oval shield, for protection, and painted with the symbol of their legion. Some wore bronze greaves on their left shin if they could afford them and there were a few scattered chain-mail shirts in the formation that soldiers had taken from dead or captured Gauls in past skirmishes or had been handed down from a family member. Uniformity was less important than proper protection, but armor was expensive.

Behind the Hastati, the maniples of Principes stood ready. Their chain mail, heavier helmets, and larger shields provided them better protection than their counterparts. They were in their mid-twenties to mid-thirties, men in the physical prime of their life and could afford the better armor, though some still wore the chest plate of the Hastati. Along with the gladius short sword and the pugio dagger that all Roman legionaries carried, the Principes also carried two pila. These were the men that carried the success of most battles.

If the enemy did not break on the Principes or the battle began to turn away from their favor, the Roman commanders had one more weapon to employ. The last row of legionaries was the Triarii. The elder warriors who had survived many battles. The mature men who could be counted upon to stand to the last. If a Roman commander saw a weakness in the enemy lines that could be exploited, or saw the potential of his own line breaking, the Triarii were employed. Often, they were responsible for saving a battle that seemed to be lost.

"Ready the sagittarii," Caepio ordered. His order was immediately carried to the ranks of auxiliary archers standing at the rear of the lines.

"Forward!" I called with a sweep of my arm as I sprinted ahead. My voice was lost in the din, but those closest to me followed my example. We charged forward, the ripple following outward from the center, naturally creating the wedge-shaped formation we were famous for. Each clan followed suit along the line. A series of wedges formed, each behind their headman, the largest and bravest warriors leading the way. The war hounds were released. Jaws snapping savagely and trailing saliva, the hounds raced forward, ahead of more than a hundred thousand bellowing warriors.

"Target the third rank," Caepio ordered the centurion who commanded the archers, knowing there would be less misses if they shot into the mass, rather than at the front line. The archers stood at the ready, waiting anxiously for their order.

"Nock your arrows! . . . Draw! . . . Fire!" the centurion shouted. Thousands of bowstrings snapped forward launching their deadly missiles high into the air and over the heads of the legions, toward the ranks of the charging warriors.

"Shields!" I shouted when I saw the dark shadow of arrows rising above the soldiers to our front. Arrows thudded into the willow and linden boards held above our heads. The deadly rain wounded and killed, yet we rushed on, over and around those that fell or slowed. We endured three volleys before we closed to javelin range. The archers shifted their aim to the ranks farther back when the horde neared the first rank of Romans, the young Velites.

Each Velite carried a parma, a light wooden shield for personal defense, and throwing javelins called verutum, as well as a gladius and pugio. "Velites, launch verutum!" came the order. Thousands of young soldiers rapidly hurled their darts into the roiling mass of savage warriors, then faded back between the lines of Hastati, not needing another order and not waiting to see the results of their action.

"Hastati, launch pila!" the centurions in the front ranks of the Hastati shouted nearly as one, assuming control of the battle line just before the two sides clashed. Thousands of pila flew through the air, impaling warriors and lodging in shields. The weight of the iron tip drove its pyramid shaped head through wooden shields and into the arms and chests behind, breaking up the lead ranks. The weight of the javelins pulled downward on the shields and the length of the shaft made them awkward to hold in close formation, so that many cast down their shields.

As the Hastati stepped forward to throw, their arms came forward. In one fluid motion they drew swords immediately after casting their pila, bracing themselves behind their shield to absorb the coming impact. The impetus of the charge was so great that many of the warriors wounded by the pila or arrows closed the rest of the distance between the opposing lines and crashed into the Romans before they fell. Even as they died, they grasped at the soldier's shields, pulling them downward so the warriors behind could reach the Romans. Warriors in the front ranks were pushed forward by those behind, causing the front line of the Hastati to shudder with the force of the collision. Caepio's ranks stood fast, despite the vast numbers of enemy warriors, and the killing began in earnest.

This was the fight that the Romans were so good at. The deadly dance they had developed over centuries. Step, thrust, heave. Step, thrust, heave. But the front line of Hastati soon were unable to move forward. The immense force moving toward them had halted their forward momentum. Soon, both armies were fighting stationary. Both formations pushed the front ranks against each other. The men at the line could only push and stab between their shields. The Germans, whose longer swords and style of fighting exposed their chest and abdomen when they raised their arms to strike down. The Roman's took advantage of this to stab their shorter gladii between or over their shields, into their opponents torso; a quick stab to a vital area, then withdrawing their sword they searched for another target.

The Hastati were relieved to hear the trumpets blast the order for the Principes to launch pila. Many looked skyward to assure themselves that the javelins came. When the pila fell upon the enemy, the pressure on the front line lightened, giving the Hastati the opportunity to step back and allow the fresh ranks of the Principes to replace them on the line. The perfect order that the Romans executed this action with was lost on the enraged warriors. But they felt the energy of fresh men joining the line against them, even as they began to tire. The front ranks of the allied tribes wavered. Many fell from exhaustion but there were always more to take their place.

The Volcae Tectosages and Tigurini had fought the Romans on their terms before, but until now, the Cimbri had not experienced battle with an orderly Roman army. Carbo, Silanus, and other minor skirmishes had been ambushes. Battles that were won before the Romans could employ their superior weapons and tactics. While they still did not face the terrible force of their artillery and other heavy weapons today, the Romans fought in an organized manner, crushing the front lines of the tribes, like a millstone grinding flour. But a millstone could be stopped if too much grain was poured at once. And there was no shortage of grain this day. Despite their hopeless situation, the legions stood their ground. Caepio watched his soldiers being slowly ground down.

Too late he recognized the danger he had so blindly stepped into. While he fielded close to forty thousand fighting men, the vast army of barbarians stretched in a line twice as long and twice as deep as his legions. The tribes on the Roman right were forcing his men back, pivoting the formation as they stepped back to defend their flank.

From his vantage point, Caepio felt the first stab of uncertainty deep in his guts. He could see the ends of the barbarian battle line beginning to curl around. If they turned the formation, they would roll up the flanks and the battle would be lost. "Send the cavalry to assault their left," he shouted in a strained voice at his legate. "We need to relieve the pressure and stop that flank from turning." He grabbed a nearby tribune by his tunic and shouted, "Get to the left flank commander, tell him to wheel back, give up ground to keep the flank from collapsing."

Caepio's back was against the river and his men had nowhere to go. If the Germans turned the flank, they would be held against the river and slaughtered. The pressure of the massive army of barbarians was wearing on the legions. The Principes had suffered heavy damage but were holding. Their lines were thinning as the Velites dragged wounded men back to be tended. Shortly, the Triarii would have to rejoin the lines to bolster the Principes before they collapsed. The pile of bodies at the battle line had become high. The backward movement of the legions meant that the attacking warriors had to clamber over the bodies of the fallen to reach the Romans.

Quintus Sertorius rode at the front of his turma, his arm extended forward, pointing his spatha toward the enemy, directing his men to the spot he had chosen to assault. Sertorius' horsemen were flanked on each side by another thirty-man turma that smashed into the enemy's flank, causing momentary panic and confusion. But Teutobod held that flank and recovered quickly. He gave the order to set spears and receive the attack. The oncoming cavalry crashed into the line of blades, killing and maiming hundreds of horses and throwing their riders. The Teutones' vast numbers swarmed around the fallen horsemen, attacking them with their heavy spears and axes. Freki's cavalry raced past, charging the remaining Roman cavalry that had turned back.

The battlefield was a swirling maelstrom of movement as those who still fought tread on those who had fallen and slipped in the blood and entrails. The wounded reached out to grasp the legs of those above, begging for help, or trying to maim one last enemy before they died. Horns blared, horses screamed, young men called for their mothers while their life's blood seeped into the darkening soil.

Sertorius was thrown from his saddle when a Teuton warrior ripped his stallion's belly open with a long spear braced against the ground. Sertorius' last conscious thought was tumbling helplessly through the air toward the gaping maws and maniacal eyes of the fearsome north men.

Ansgar fought like a wild animal beside me, swinging a huge battle axe, chopping into the terrified Romans like so much firewood. An arrow had struck him in his tree-like thigh, but he seemed not to notice it as he brought the axe down into an upraised scutum, splitting the boards and deeply biting into the arm of the man holding it. The war dogs were savaging men to the left and right of the giant. The slaughter was creating a hole in the ranks. A centurion shouted for men to close the breach, and a surge of bodies responded even as Ansgar and I stepped forward, followed by a dozen others who began laying about them to widen the rift.

The Romans kept their bodies behind their shields, stabbing the point of their gladius out in an effort to impale the warriors that assaulted them, it was an economy of movement that the Germans did not use because their longer swords and fighting spears required more room to maneuver. Ansgar's bloodied axe swung through the air again, cleaving through the bronze helmet of the soldier in front of him.

CHAPTER THIRTY-FOUR

A centurion burst into Maximus' tent. "Caepio has attacked the barbarians!"

"Betrayer!" Hrolf shouted at Maximus, whose guards unsheathed their weapons when he leaped up.

"No!" he commanded them, holding out a hand to halt their advance. To Hrolf, he said, "I don't know what it is happening, but it isn't me."

"This negotiation is over," Hrolf said savagely.

His men were standing ready when they emerged from the tent, and they hurried toward the sounds of battle. They raced toward a tall hill rising above the stream that fed into the Rhodanus. The hill was covered in a patchwork of muted brown and yellow leaves that had begun to fall from the oak, maple, and beech that stood upon it. Its height offered a commanding view of the river valley where thousands of Roman troops were desperately fighting for their lives.

Low clouds had blown in on a cool, fall breeze. The air smelled like rain. From their vantage point, they looked down upon the battlefield where the crisp, controlled tones of the Roman cornu signaling to the legions mixed with the undisciplined blare of the carnyx and other signal horns of the allied tribes. The noise rose to their position on the heights, sounding for all the world as if the watchman of Asgard summoned the gods to do battle at the end of days.

A throaty roar rose to his ears when a surge of warriors rushed forward to meet the Roman lines. Like a wave breaking around a solitary rock along the seashore, the warriors flanked the red soldiers, whose rear ranks were backed up against the river. From their position, Hrolf could see centurions shouting, their voices lost in the din. The Romans' maniple formations collapsed and were compressed into a tight circle, facing outwards as the tribes pushed against the wall of shields. Before the warriors could close around them, a small group of mounted Romans burst forth, their red cloaks streaming behind them. In their haste they knocked over and trampled some of their own legionaries. Several fell when spears were launched towards them, but the rest got away.

CHAPTER THIRTY-FIVE

"Damn that man!" shouted Maximus. "We've lost all hope of talking our way out of this. Ready the legions!" Maximus ordered as the German delegation sped from the camp. "We must march to support Caepio, or all is lost."

Men who had been told there was no immediate threat while the negotiations were taking place, scrambled to extinguish their cooking fires, don their armor, gather their weapons and assemble in their units. The gates swung wide as the first maniple of the first legion stepped through. "Double time!" shouted the Primus Pilus of the first legion, leading the way toward the battle, calling a cadence that kept the men in step along the rocky trail that led toward Caepio's camp. Thousands upon thousands of soldiers followed; the stamp of their hobnailed sandals echoing across the meadows. They moved forward at a pace that ate up the distance yet conserved their strength for the battle to come.

As the lead units climbed the slight incline that separated the two camps, they witnessed a group of horsemen racing in panic across their path in the distance, as if Pavor the Roman god of terror gave chase. A low rumble rolled over the hill, a peal of thunder that turned into a roar of human voices and bronze horns as the first of the north men flowed over the crest. The great wave parted around lone trees and boulders without pause, each warrior seeming intent on being the first to reach Maximus and his legions.

The consul, a half mile back in the formation, looked forward in shock at the Germanic horde that raced toward him. On and on they came over the ridge.

Only a few hundred yards separated the armies, but the Romans were still in march formation, while the barbarians came as a massive, irresistible force carried downhill by their momentum and pushed on by those that came behind. The Germans barely slowed as they enveloped the column within moments. Maximus barely had time to react before his lead elements were locked in personal combat. The centurions in the front recognized there was no escape and determined to sell their lives as costly as they could. The soldiers could hardly miss a target as they hurriedly threw whatever missiles they carried, then drew their swords. The column curled back on itself. Men fell in the hundreds while others tried to turn away from the terrifying onslaught. Halfway back the columns turned their backs to the enemy and tried to reach the safety of their camp, but they were overrun.

There were so many warriors, that only a portion was engaged with the remaining legions while tens of thousands swarmed around those who tried to stand their ground. The rest chased down the fleeing soldiers and raced on toward the camp. So complete was the surprise and confusion, that warriors reached the camp before those inside were able to secure the gates. Within moments thousands were inside the walls. The slaughter continued all day as the tribes slaked their anger against the hated foes who had betrayed them again.

Amid the mutilated bodies of tens of thousands, Ansgar and I paused to catch our breath while the men attacked the last holdouts who gathered in slight clumps around a small hillock or a copse of trees. "What do we know of Hrolf and the others?" Ansgar asked. His blood slowing in his veins while his heaving chest returned to normal breathing.

I looked down, shaking my head. "I've had no time. No word. Search the camp for their bodies," I said, assuming they had been killed when the battle started. Turning away, Ansgar looked up when he heard a familiar voice. Several men were approaching on horseback.

"Hrolf," he called.

I ran to my friend, embracing him heartily. "We thought you were dead. I assumed they took advantage while you were in their camp."

"Maximus did not know of Caepio's betrayal," Hrolf began. "I believe he sincerely wished to negotiate. After we left, he joined the attack, but it was too late. You all saw to that," he said, clasping my shoulder, then nodding at Ansgar.

"We lost too many," I said sadly.

"That's not your fault. We went to them to negotiate a truce. We were betrayed and Caepio attacked. You had no choice. We watched from the hill there and joined where we could, but our warriors were already winning the day."

"You did well, Hrolf. I'm proud that you are a Teuton," said Teutobod, walking up. Turning to me he continued. "I'm going to find my people. We'll talk again soon."

I lifted a hand in acknowledgement and slung an arm around Hrolf's shoulders. "Come, let's discuss what we do next."

JEFF HEIN

CHAPTER THIRTY-SIX

When Sertorius slowly returned to consciousness, he could not open his eyes. His lashes were crusted shut with dried blood. The stench of spilled guts and blood and shit filled his nostrils. He retched loudly, adding to his misery. He lay still for a moment, listening. He could hear the battle still raging, but it was at a distance now as the Germans annihilated Maximus. His body ached terribly, but he didn't feel any broken bones. He lay under the weight of several men that were pressing on his chest, making it difficult to breath. The only thing that kept him from suffocating was the bronze breastplate that he wore, which allowed him room to breathe under the hundreds of pounds on top of him. He couldn't lift his left arm, but he worked his right arm free. Taking a chance, reaching up to wipe the blood from his eyes. When his vision returned, he looked about blurrily. Seeing no one standing near he pushed against the bodies that held him down. They slid wetly aside, and he wriggled his way painfully out of his bloody prison, finding that the reason he could not lift his left arm was because his shield was still strapped to it and another body lay on top. He winced at the sudden pain in his shoulder as he freed the shield, realizing he must have wrenched it in the fall from his horse. He slung the shield onto his back, picked up a fallen spatha and shoved it into his scabbard. His mouth was parched, and it was difficult to swallow. He searched for a canteen of water and found none, becoming desperate with thirst.

A sudden shout sent a spike of fear through him "Locian! Romisches!" He didn't need to understand the guttural words to understand their meaning. He had been discovered! He turned to see a group of women and boys scavenging the field, dispatching Roman wounded. They were pointing toward him and already several of the older boys were moving his way, armed with throwing spears quite capable of killing him.

Desperately, Sertorius looked about and saw his salvation. The Rhodanus River was a hundred paces away. Without a second thought, he sprinted toward the swirling waters. Forgetting his bruised muscles and the gashes in his arms and legs, Sertorius reached the water and splashed in, awkwardly lifting his knees until he was deep enough to dive in. Spears splashed into the water near his heels, but he was unscathed. The young warriors that had followed him were jumping up and down on the bank in frustration, but none chose to follow after one soldier that was sure to drown anyway. Panic granted him the strength to swim out to the center of the river before he felt fatigued and remembered that he was weighed down by the shield on his back and his breastplate. But it was too late. He must either swim the entire way or drown.

His legs became entangled with a submerged corpse. In a panic, he kicked violently to free himself as another one bumped into his shoulder. The river had become choked with the gore of the battle and the water ran red with blood.

Slowly the angry shouts behind him changed, and Sertorius realized they were cheering him on. Urging him to make it to the far shore, for the Germans admired nothing more than courage and strength, and Sertorius was showing them both. He turned on his side to give his injured shoulder a rest and continued, the effort of keeping his mouth and nose above the water was enormous. Just as Sertorius was about to succumb to his fatigue, his foot struck a sand bar in the center of the river, shallow enough for him to sit and rest as the current rippled around him. It provided just enough of a respite for him to catch his breath before he continued his escape. Sertorius reached the far shore with just enough energy to crawl onto the sandy bank, completely exhausted. When darkness slowly descended, he lay back, falling into a deep sleep.

When Sertorius awakened, the sun was low on the horizon. He had slept through the night of the battle and nearly the entire day after. He slowly got up and walked back into the river to slake his thirst and wash the sand from his wounds. The cold water had cleaned the blood from his body during the escape and his chest hurt with every breath. His probing fingers discovered several broken ribs and severe bruising to the tissue from the crushing weight that fell on him. He reckoned that the bodies that had covered him had probably saved his life by hiding him from the battlefield scavengers whose job it was to kill the wounded Roman soldiers. He whispered a prayer of thanks to Jupiter for hiding him from the barbarians and for giving him the strength to escape them.

Suddenly reminded of the battle he looked across the river at a field littered with Roman dead. There were so many bodies that he could see no ground between them. In the distance three columns of dark smoke rose toward the evening sky. A quick chill ran through him as he pictured the scene around those fires. Like most Romans, he had heard the tales of the Cimbrian priestesses and their human sacrifices. He hastily turned away, walking westward. His only thought was to return to the safety of Narbo, but first he needed someone to help bind his wounds, and he needed food.

The village of Arausio was several miles from the river. Sertorius started walking, shuffling on his wounded leg and resting often. At the first homestead he came upon, the door was barred. No one answered his hails. Further on, a man was driving a wagon along the path that Sertorius was following. As he approached, Sertorius fell to the ground with relief.

The farmer returned to Arausio and deposited Sertorius with four others who had reached the hamlet. One, a tribune judging by his kit, lay severely wounded. Barely conscious, he inquired of the outcome of the battle.

"We lost miserably," Sertorius told him. "It's horrible."

"I'm not sure that I'm going to make it. Please, tell my wife what happened. I have a newborn son. He must know that his father died bravely."

"What's your name Tribune," Sertorius asked.

"Gnaeus Pompeius Strabo."

"I will find your wife if you die, but you must not give up, you're not dead yet." Sertorius clasped Strabo's hand for a moment. "Let me see what I can do for your wounds.

Several hours later, a tall Gaul walked into their midst. His hair was cut short, and he was dressed in fine clothes. He was obviously someone of importance in the community. "The Germans have gone," the man announced. "After the battle they fell into an orgy of destruction. In every tree there hangs the body of a soldier. They built great bonfires within the Roman camps and burned everything. Tents, wagons, everything. They even threw the weapons and shields of the Romans on the fires, rather than keeping them. Many of the Roman wounded were thrown bodily into the raging flames to be consumed. They drove the horses and oxen into the river to drown them, then threw the gold and silver that was found into the river as well. They found the camp stores laden with wine and proceeded to get terribly drunk. In the morning, they returned to their encampment north of here and gathered their women and children, then continued northward. I followed them for twenty miles. I was nearly discovered several times, but you can be sure they have gone now."

Sertorius stayed at Arausio for a week. Then, with his mind made up, his wounds cleaned and bandaged, he set off for Narbo with the survivors, walking behind a wagon that carried Gnaeus Pompeius Strabo.

EPILOGUE

Borrix looked about the battlefield. Now thirty years old, his visage carried the effects of a man twice his age. The scars on his body were a testament to the many battles he had fought, but it was the unseen scars that caused him the most pain. The loss of his wife and unborn child had driven him to the brink of madness. Yet another betrayal by Roman generals had resulted in the most tragic loss of life for the Romans to date. Germanic warriors wandered the battlefield, dispatching the wounded and searching for booty amid the tens of thousands of Roman soldiers who had fallen this fateful day.

Not since Hannibal's victory at Cannae had such a loss been felt. News of the disaster spread quickly, reaching Rome within days. Terror of the Cimbri brought Rome to a fever pitch. The Senate began immediate measures to raise more men to defend against the Terror Cimbricus that surely must surge over the mountains into Italy at any moment.

Weary, disgusted with the treachery of the Romans, his blood lust sated but still fearful of the curse of Njoror, Borrix decided to forget Italy again. Instead, he turned west toward the setting sun. He would leave Gaul. Leave the Romans far behind. Take his people west over the Pyrenees Mountains into the land of the Iberians, where perhaps they would be beyond the reach of Njoror's curse, and he hoped to find the destiny he had so desperately sought.

HISTORICAL NOTES

The dormant volcano where Borr makes his sacrifice to Lugos in this book is Puy de Dome, one of a chain of dormant volcanoes in the Central Massif region of France. In 1872 a Gallo-Roman temple to Mercury was discovered at the summit. It is widely believed that Julius Caesar identified the Gallic god Lugos, as Mercury. In this story, the temple had not yet been built, but the site was one of several that were dedicated to the chief god of the Gauls.

The standing stone that the Cimbri encountered along the northern coast of Brittany is today called the Menhir de Champ-Dolent. It reaches more than thirty feet above the ground and is believed to have been erected around 7,000 years ago. It weighs an estimated 100 tons and was moved to its current site from where it was quarried 2.5 miles away.

The cave where Frida is killed is today called the Tuc d'Audoubert. Re-discovered in 1912 it is located in the foothills of the French Pyrenees. The cave is as described in the book and the incredible Bison sculpture dominates the gallery where they have stood, deep underground, for more than 12,000 years.

Dental treatment in ancient Rome is well documented. The Romans cared about their teeth and their appearance and sometimes used a whitening toothpaste made from human urine and goat's milk. Gold is known to have been used in dental work and the description of dentures is accurate to historical evidence. They were among the first to use painkillers in dentistry. The "tooth worm" was a common explanation for tooth aches. Vallus' dental treatment was the source for the opium that he eventually takes to Borr.

Cannabis and opium were known and used in the Roman world. Cannabis was grown throughout the mediterranean region and used as it is today for medicinal and recreational purposes. Opium was imported from farther east and used to treat insomnia, pain, and other illnesses. Vallus attempted to help Borr relieve his physical and mental pain by providing these substances, ultimately creating the lowest point of Borr's life.

In book three we begin to see the changes to the Roman army wrought by Gaius Marius. Many earlier historians attributed the changes in the army at that time to Marius and I have attempted to show how that may have taken place. Scholars today are less likely to give Marius all the credit and suggest that it was a process of necessary changes to address the differing threats that Rome faced in the last two centuries BC. I chose to do both, for certainly Marius was a man who could foresee the need for change and had the power to make those changes over the course of his seven consulships. Whoever was responsible, the changes implemented contributed significantly to the shift of power from the Senate to the generals and set the stage for the Social War, helping to bring about the end of the Republic.

Quintus Cassius Scaeva – A fictional centurion in this novel. A legionary of the same name is written about by Julius Caesar half a century later at the battle of Dyrrachium. I represent this Scaeva as his grandfather. The story of Caesar's Scaeva is a remarkable tale, and well worth the additional reading.

The treasure of Tolosa remains one of the enduring mysteries of ancient times. It was fabled to be one of the largest treasures ever amassed and was never accounted for after its discovery and theft by Quintus Servilius Caepio.

The battle of Arausio accounted for more Roman deaths than Hannibal's victory at Cannae, and by far eclipsed Vallus' loss in the Teutoburg forest. Yet, little can be found regarding that battle and there is no shortage of literature about the other two. I hope to have done that October day in 105 BC justice using the descriptions that are available. There are multiple sources to draw from and inevitably, someone will disagree with the order or outcome of events. Nevertheless, we can all agree that it was one of the worst days in Roman military history, and a turning point in the leadership, tactics, and approach that would be used by Rome to finally bring an end to the Terror Cimbricus.

I find the relationships that are represented in this time period fascinating. Many of the characters are significant in the role that they play later in life. For example, the many characters that served their initial service under Scipio Aemilianus in Numantia as younger soldiers, and the many young men who are just beginning their career. Sulla, who began his career under Marius winds up as his mortal enemy during the Social War. Gnaeus Pompeius Strabo who in this book serves as a tribune under Marius, will go on to become a general and significant player in Rome's wars. His father was the Roman officer in book 1 who died in Macedonia when Borr took the torque that he now wears from him. Strabo's son, born during this story, will grow up to become Pompey the Great, a contemporary, friend, and enemy of Julius Caesar the dictator, who is also the nephew of Marius. And finally, Quintus Sertorius. A young cavalry officer at Arausio, Sertorius would go on to become one of Rome's most intriguing sons and is a tale worth telling just in itself. Many of these characters will surface again in the conclusion of The Cimbrian War series and may find their way into more novels in the future, as they each have incredible stories to tell.

GLOSSARY

MAJOR TRIBES/NATIONS

ADUATUCI – A Gallic/Germanic tribe living in what is today Belgium during the late Iron Age. Fifty years after the Cimbrian War Caesar wrote: "The tribe was descended from the Cimbri and Teutoni, who, upon their march into our Province and Italy, set down such of their stock and stuff as they could not drive or carry with them on the near side of the Rhine, and left six thousand men of their company therewith as guard and garrison." Roman historian and senator Cassius Dio also mentioned that the Aduatuci belonged to the Cimbri race.

AMBRONES – A Germanic tribe whose homeland is unknown but suspected to have been south and west of Jutland. They joined the Cimbri and Teutones years after their journey began.

ARAUSIO – An ancient city near which the battle of Arausio was fought, now Orange, France.

ARVERNI – A Gallic tribe dwelling in the area today known as France defeated by Domitius Ahenobarbus and Fabius Maximus in 121 BC.

BELGAE – A large group of tribes living in northern Gaul. Vicinity of today's Belgium.

BITURIGES VIVISCI – Gallic tribe centered on their chief city of Burdigala, modern day Bordeaux, France.

BOII – A Gallic tribe in Cisalpine Gaul centered around modern-day Czech Republic, Bavaria, and Bohemia. Shortly after the time of this story they moved northward as far as Poland.

BRITONS – The indigenous Celtic people of Great Britain.

CELTS (Kelts) – The Celts migrated into the areas of central and western Europe in pre-Roman times. The term is generally interchangeable with Gauls.

CIMBRI (Kimbree) – An ancient Germanic tribe originating in Jutland, today's Denmark. They were possibly of Celtic descent and combined traits of both cultures. For unknown reasons, (Some historians wrote that it was due to an inundation of flood tides) they left around 120 BC, and migrated throughout Europe coming into contact with Rome several times in the second century BC.

CORNOVII – A Celtic tribe that lived in present day Cornwall.

CYMRU – The area known today as Wales.

GAULS – In the second century BC, the area today known as France was known as Gaul and the tribes from that area generally referred to as Gauls, though they referred to themselves as Celts.

GERMANS – The area north of the Danube River and east of the Rhine River was referred to by the Romans as Germania and the tribes from that area as Germans.

HELVETII – A loose confederation of Gaulish/Celtic tribes living on the Swiss plateau during the second century BC.

MARCOMANNI – A Germanic people east of the Rhine and part of the large Suebi confederation.

RAETIANS – A confederation of Alpine tribes who lived in present-day Tyrol in Austria, eastern Switzerland, as well as northern Italy on the south side of the Alps.

RAURICI – A small Gallic tribe living around today's Basel, Germany during the pre-Roman Iron-Age.

SCORDISCI – A Celtic tribe living in what is now Serbia, Croatia, Bulgaria, and Romania. They successfully resisted Roman incursions for decades.

SUEBI – A large confederation of Germanic peoples from what is now Germany and the Czech Republic along the Elbe River. Their members included the Marcomanni, Quadi, Hermunduri, Semnones and Lombards.

TAURISCI – A Celtic tribe that came down from the Alps mountains. They warred with Rome for several years which ended in their status of "Friend and ally of the Roman people".

TEUTONES – A Germanic tribe living south and east of Jutland among the sea islands and rocky shores of the Baltic Sea. They joined the Cimbri on their epic journey throughout the known world.

TIGURINI – A Gaulish tribe, part of the Helvetii alliance, living in what is today southern Germany and Switzerland. Allied with the Cimbri, Teutones and Ambrones to invade Gaul and fight Rome.

TOLOSA – Capital city of the Volcae Tectosages. Modern day Toulouse, France.

TOUGENI – A subtribe of the Celtic Helvetii.

VENETI – A seafaring Gallic tribe living in Armorica on the southern side of the Brittany peninsula.

VOLCAE TECTOSAGES – A Celtic/Gaulish tribe centered around Tolosa, modern day Toulouse, France.

IMPORTANT PLACE NAMES

ADUATUCA – Fortress of the Aduatuci. Caesar wrote that "Their stronghold was fortified by stones of great weight, sharpened beams, and walls built with manned stations. It was large enough to shelter at least 57,000 people."

AQUILEIA – An ancient Roman frontier city founded in the early second century BC. North of today's Venice.

AREMORICA – A region in Gaul including parts of Normandy

and the Brittany peninsula.

BOIODURUM – Oppidum of a sub-tribe of the Boii, located at what is today Passau, Germany.

BORREMOSE – Iron age fortress attributed to the Cimbri, located in present day Denmark near the village of Aars.

BRITANNIA – The island of Great Britain.

BURDIGALA – Modern day Bordeaux, France. The Battle of Burdigala took place in 107 BC between the Tigurini, allies of the Cimbri, and the Roman consul Lucius Cassius Longinus who was defeated and killed, along with most of his army.

CAMPUS MARTIUS – A military exercise ground outside the walls of Rome in second century BC. Later covered with large public buildings and temples.

CARCAS – An ancient oppidum near modern day Carcassonne, France.

CARTHAGE – Ancient capital of the Carthaginians. One of the most important trading hubs in the ancient world and hereditary enemy of Rome.

DONARSBERG – (Donnersberg) The highest point in the Palatinate region of Germany. The name is thought to refer to the Germanic thunder god Donar (the later Thor). A large oppidum was built on the Donnersberg around 150 BC. A part of the settlement's wall has been reconstructed.

EBUROMAGES – An ancient oppidum in Gaul, near present day Bram, France.

EIRE/HIBERNIA – The Celtic and Roman names for Ireland.

GADES – Modern day Cadiz, Spain. Founded by the Phoenicians possibly as early as 1100 BC.

GAUL – The area that is today France, Belgium, Luxembourg, and the Netherlands, with parts of Germany, Switzerland, and northern Italy. Generally, the area between the Alps, the Mediterranean Sea, the Pyrenees, the Atlantic Ocean, the North Sea, and the Rhine River.

GALLIA NARBONENSIS – Roman province in Gaul north and west of the Alps mountains. Today's Switzerland and southern France.

GERMANIA – The geographical area north of the Danube River and from the Rhine River to the Vistula River in the east.

HIPPO DIARRHYTUS – City on the Numidian coast. Now Bizerte, Tunisia.

HISPANIA – Today's Spain and Portugal.

JUTLAND/CIMBERLAND/CIMBRIAN CHERSONESE – Present day Denmark and the German state of Schleswig-Holstein.

LIMSFJORD – A shallow fjord that separates the mainland of Denmark from its most northern tip.

LUGUDUNON – Gaulish name for the fortress at what is now Lyon, France. The Romans renamed it Lugdunum in 43 BC.

MACEDONIA – Became a Roman province in 146 BC. Rome fought with the Celtic Scordisci and other tribes in the area for control of the mountainous interior for centuries. Corresponds roughly to modern day Macedonia.

MANCHING – A large Celtic oppidum near today's Ingolstadt in Bavaria, Germany. Capital of the Vindelici, a Celtic tribe in Gaul. It was destroyed sometime in the second century BC.

MASSALIA – Greek trading port on the coast of the Mediterranean Sea. Modern day Marseilles.

NOREIA – The capital city of Noricum and the Taurisci people near Klagenfurt in today's Austrian Alps.

NORICUM – Celtic kingdom located in modern-day Austria and

Slovenia.

NUMANTIA – An ancient Celtiberian town in Spain near the modern city of Soria.

NUMIDIA – An ancient kingdom located across much of North Africa.

OSTIA – Ancient port on the Italian coast near Rome.

PANNONIA – An area encompassing parts of modern-day Hungary, Austria, Slovenia, Croatia, and Serbia.

PORTUS CALE – Today's Porto on the west coast of Portugal. It was founded around 136 BC by the Roman general Decimus Junius Brutus Callaicus who had conquered the region.

PYRENEES MOUNTAINS – The Pyrenees were named in ancient times for the Greek princess Pyrene. The name has remained the same throughout history. They have long formed the border of the Iberian Peninsula.

RAETIA – A Celtic tribal area north of the Alps that was comprised of parts of modern-day Switzerland, Germany, Austria, and northern Italy.

SCANDIA – Ancient name for the Scandinavian peninsula that includes present day Sweden and Norway.

SISCIA – Celtic oppidum southeast of modern-day Zagreb, Croatia. Located on the Sava river.

STOBI – A city in the contested area of Macedonia that was fought over by the Scordisci and the Romans in the second century BC.

UENET – The capital city of the Veneti.

UTICA – One of the oldest Phoenician ports on the North African coast. Capital of the Roman province of Africa.

VAGA – The capital city of Numidia.

ROADS, RIVERS, and SEAS

VIA AEMILIA – The coastal road that led from Rome to Pisa. In 109 BC the road was extended to Genoa and then to Placentia by the Princeps Senatus Marcus Aemilius Scaurus.

ATAX RIVER – The Aude River in southern France.

BLAVEZH RIVER – The Blavet River flows from Central Brittany and enters the Atlantic Ocean near Lorient.

DANUBIUS RIVER – The Danube River is the second longest river in all of Europe rising in the Black Forest of Germany and traveling to the Black Sea. It remained the frontier of Rome for centuries.

DURIUS RIVER – The Douro River in Portugal.

GARUMNA RIVER – The Garonne River that flows through parts of France and Spain.

MUTHUL RIVER – A river in what is now Tunisia, North Africa. Site of the Battle of the Muthul River between Jugurtha and Quintus Metellus during the Jugurthine War.

RHENUS RIVER – The Rhine River flows from the Swiss Alps to the North Sea and is one of the major rivers in Europe, second only to the Danube in length.

RHODANUS RIVER – The Rhone River of Switzerland and France.

MARE NOSTRUM – Today's Mediterranean Sea.

OCEANUS ATLANTICUS – The Atlantic Ocean.

GODS/RELIGION/MYTHS/LEGENDS

Much of what we know of the Norse and Scandinavian religion is found in the Icelandic Poetic and Prose Eddas of the 13th century. At that time this was an advanced, developed religion that had its origins in Germanic paganism. In the Cimbrian War series, set about one thousand years prior to the Viking age, you will see references to the early Germanic beliefs that later developed into the better known Viking age religion.

BA'AL HAMMON – The Phoenician, and later, Carthaginian chief god of their pantheon and the god that made vegetation grow.

BORR – Mentioned in both the Poetic Edda and the Prose Edda, the Norse legends of gods and creation, Borr is the son of Buri, husband of Bestla, and father of Odin, Vili and Ve.

DONAR – The Germanic thunder god, later known as Thor.

DRAUGAR – An undead creature, usually the soul of a long dead king or great warrior.

FENRIR – The giant wolf-god who would bring about the end of the world by devouring Wodan/Odin and usher in Ragnarok.

HEL – Goddess who rules the land of the dead.

HELHEIM – (Hel) The Norse realm of the dead, presided over by the goddess Hel, daughter of Loki.

JUPITER – King of the Roman gods, god of the sky and thunder. Equivalent to Zeus in Greek mythology.

LUGOS – Early Celtic god. Known by other names on the continent including Lug and Mercury, and later Lugh in Ireland.

NJOROR – God of the sea and father of Freya.

RAGNAROK – The final battle before the end of the world of gods and men.

SAMHAIN – Pagan festival to mark the end of the harvest season and to usher in the dark half of the year.

SKOLL – Borr named his wolf Skoll after the warg Skoll that chases the sun through the sky each day.

SLAUGHTERER – The mystical flaming spear of Lugos. It was thought to be alive and its thirst for blood was unquenchable. The only way to put it to rest was to steep it's head in a tea made from poppy leaves.

VALHOLL – Wodan's mead hall where he receives the souls of his warriors. Later known as Valhalla.

WODAN – An ancient Germanic god of war and king of the gods. Later known as Woden, Wotan and Odin.

YGGDRASIL – The tree of life. The giant ash tree that supports the universe. When Yggdrasil dies, the world of gods dies with it.

YULE – Pagan Germanic holiday of the winter solstice, marking the beginning of the new year.

GENERAL

ACTA – Similar to today's newspaper. A source of news and goings-on in the late Republic.

ACTUARIUS – A Roman military clerk, usually for finance.

ALE – A type of beer brewed in ancient Europe.

ALPES MOUNTAINS – The Alps Mountains in central Europe.

ARMILLA – A gold, silver, or bronze armband awarded to Roman soldiers for bravery. Often shaped in the likeness of a serpent coiled around the upper arm.

AUGUR – A Roman priest who divined the will of the gods through his observation of the natural world.

AUXILLIARY – Non-Roman citizens attached to the army as cavalry and other special troops.

BARRITUS – Battle cry of the ancient Germans and Celts.

BATTLE OF NOREIA – Battle between the Cimbri and Roman Consul Gnaeus Papirius Carbo in 113 BC, near modern day Klagenfurt, Austria.

BALLISTAE – Torsion powered artillery weapons of the Roman army.

BOG IRON – A type of iron-ore found in bogs and wetlands. Common to northern Jutland, and the only local source of iron available, though it was poorer quality than the mined iron-ore.

CALIGAE – The leather shoes/sandals worn by Roman legionaries.

CAPITE CENSI – The common people who do not own property and are counted by head count.

CARNYX – A bronze trumpet used by the Iron Age Celts and Germans. The bell was usually styled as an open-mouthed boar or other animal.

CASTRA/CASTRUM – Roman military camp/fort.

CENTURY – A sub-unit of the maniple, about 60 men each.

CENTURION – Roman officer. Commander of a century, about 100 men.

CIMBRIAN WAR – A conflict/series of battles between the Cimbri and their allied tribes, and the Roman Republic that lasted from 113 BC to 101 BC.

COGNOMEN – The third name of a citizen of ancient Rome. Usually awarded for a feat or recognition, but later became hereditary.

COHORT – A unit of the Roman army that replaced the maniples of the earlier republican army.

CONSUL – The highest elected official of the Roman Republic.

CORNU/CORNICEN – The brass signal horns/players used by Roman legions to issue orders and communicate between units.

CURSUS HONORUM – The succession of political offices required for a Roman of senatorial rank seeking advancement.

CURULE CHAIR – The official chair used by Rome's highest magistrates.

CURULE MAGISTRATE – Executive officer of the Roman state.

DECIMATION – The practice of punishing severe crimes, particularly cowardice, by having every ten men beat one of the ten to death.

DECURION – Roman cavalry officer in charge of a Turma of thirty men and horses.

DELPHI – The ancient site of the oracle of Delphi. Located near modern day Greece.

DILECTUS – The process used by the Roman army to recruit soldiers.

EQUESTRIAN – The equestrian order of ancient Rome was a middle class of citizens who ranked just below the senatorial class. Often served as the Roman cavalry during the late Roman republic.

FRIEND AND ALLY OF THE ROMAN PEOPLE – A status that Rome used to incorporate former enemies or belligerent tribes into the republic, and later the empire, by recognizing their sovereignty and providing defense, while requiring them to pay taxes and be subservient to the Roman senate.

GALATIA – A geographic area in the highlands of central Turkey. Named for the Gauls who settled there in the third century BC after Brennus' invasion of Greece.

GLADIUS – Sword of the Roman legions.

GRAECIA – The ancient area of, as opposed to the modern nation of, Greece.

HASTATI – Roman legionaries who made up the front rank of the republican manipular legions once the Velites had launched their darts. Usually fought as spearmen.

HRETHMONATH – Early Germanic Pagan name for the third month, March.

HUNDRED – The "hundred" was a term used to denote the military unit formed from the Hunno's clan and stems from the fact that it was generally around one hundred warriors that made up the "hundred".

HUNNO – The leader of a Germanic clan or tribe that lived in a village or series of villages that made up a district. Also, the military leader of his district, responsible for raising his "hundred" in times of war.

IMPERIUM – A form of authority granted by the Roman Senate that provided the scope of a general's power as well as his military mission, such as removing the German tribes from Noricum.

LATRUNCULI – A strategic board game played by the Romans. Similar to chess.

LEGATE – A high-ranking Roman officer equivalent to a general officer today. During the Republic a Legate was usually second in command of a Roman Army. In later years a Legate was in command of a legion.

LEGION – In the Roman republic the legion consisted of 4,200 infantrymen broken down into ten cohorts and 300 cavalrymen broken down into ten turma. Each infantry cohort consisted of four maniples which were further broken down into two centuries, each divided into ten contubernia. At this time the four maniples were organized one as Velites, one as Hastatii, one as Principes, and one as Triarii.

LORICA HAMATA – The Roman mail coat used during the late Republic.

MANIPLE – A Roman military unit of 120 men during the late republic.

MEAD – An alcoholic drink made by fermenting honey with water, and sometimes adding various flavors by using spices, fruits, or other.

MILITARY TRIBUNE – An officer in the Roman army who ranked between the centurion and the legate. Usually, the first step on the cursus honorem.

NOVUS HOMO – Latin for "new man". The term used for the first in a family to serve as a senator or elected consul. Sometimes used by the patricians and old families as a derogatory term for someone up and coming.

OILLIPHEIST – The Irish/Celtic mythological serpent or dragon of Irish legends.

ONAGERS – A torsion-powered siege engine used to throw rocks and other items toward fortifications or enemy formations.

OPPIDUM – A fortified settlement in central Europe during the Iron Age. They were built as far apart as Spain and the Hungarian plain. Hundreds were built during the second and first centuries BC.

OPTIO – Officer second in command of a unit led by a Centurion.

PANNONIA – An undefined area north and east of the Danube. Roughly corresponds to parts of present-day Hungary, Austria, Croatia, Serbia, Slovenia, and Bosnia/Herzegovina.

PATRICIAN – A member of the aristocracy of ancient Rome.

PILLARS OF HERCULES – Large rock promontories at the Straight of Gibraltar that form the entrance from the Atlantic Ocean to the Mediterranean Sea; The Rock of Gibraltar on the north, and the Jebel Moussa in Morocco.

PILUM/PILA – A javelin/s used by Roman soldiers.

PILUS PRIOR – Commanders of the ten 1st-centuries within the legion.

PLEBIANS – Free Roman citizens that were not part of the aristocracy. The commoner.

PLEBIAN TRIBUNE – The tribune of the people was an election of a common citizen, who provided a check on the power of the Roman Senate and magistrates.

POPULARES – A political faction led by the Gracchi brothers during the late Roman Republic. They supported the agendas of reforming Rome's policies in favor of the plebeians, or common citizens.

PRAETOR – The commander of an army, or an elected magistrate. Often a governor of a province.

PRAETORIUM – The legion commander's personal tent and headquarters in a castrum.

PRIMUS PILUS – The senior centurion of the first cohort in a Roman legion.

PRINCIPES – Spearmen in the late republican army. Men in their late twenties and thirties. They were in their prime both physically and financially and could afford better equipment. They fought in the second battle line between the Hastati and the Triarii.

PRINCIPIA – The legion headquarters in a Roman military camp.

PRINCIPS SENATUS – A prestigious office that was awarded to the most respected and capable of Roman senators.

PROLETARII – The popular assembly, made up of those too poor to serve in the army.

PRO-PRAETOR/PRO-CONSUL – A Roman of senatorial rank who had served as Praetor or Consul the previous year. Usually assigned as governor of a province, or military general. The position was used to extend an individual's authority past the one year they were elected to office.

QUAESTOR – First step on the Cursus Honorum, the Roman political ladder to the top political offices.

RUDIARII – Gladiators who have survived the required number of fights in the arena and have successfully retired, earning the coveted wooden sword, the Rudis.

SCORPION – A Roman field artillery piece that functioned like a large bow and arrow. It fired bolts as long as a man at high velocity.

SCUTUM – The shield used by Roman legionaries.

SEAX – Usually associated with later centuries, the seax was a small sword, or large knife, also used by the Germanic peoples of the Migration Period.

SERENS – Ancient name for China/Chinese

SIGNIFER – A standard bearer in a Roman legion.

TABERNA – A Roman street tavern/pub/eatery.

TEMPLE OF JUPITER CAPITOLINUS – Ancient Roman temple on the Capitoline Hill dedicated to the Roman king of the gods.

TERROR CIMBRICUS – The phrase used by the Romans to describe the state of mass panic they felt over the possibility of the Cimbri invading Italy.

TESSERARIUS – Officer of the guard/watch officer in a Roman military camp/castra.

TESTUDO – A Roman military formation where soldiers used their shields to form a tortoise-shell-like protection against the enemy. Especially effective against thrown weapons.

TORQUE – A large neck ring made of rigid metal. Symbolizes the strength and virility of the wearer. Usually awarded for bravery or special action.

TRIARII – The third line of troops in the manipular legions of the Roman republic. They were the veterans, the oldest and wealthiest men in the army and could afford the best equipment.

TRIPLEX ACIES – The checkerboard formation of maniples that made up the manipular legion.

TRIREME – Roman warships with three banks of oars and a bronze battering ram.

UTISETA – An ancient Germanic pagan vision quest.

VELITES – The skirmishers in the Roman legions of the republic. They were light infantry and spearmen who carried thirty-inch wooden darts, a gladius, and a small shield. They rarely wore armor as they were the youngest and the poorest soldiers in the legion.

VITIS – A centurion's staff made from a grape vine about three feet long. Used for discipline in the Roman army.

A WORD FROM THE AUTHOR

DEAR READERS:

I invite you to join the tribe, and I am asking you for your help.

Thank you for reading book three of the Cimbrian War series, "Terror Cimbricus".

A word about creating a self-published book. Unlike being published in the traditional manner by a publishing company, the entire process is on the shoulders of the self-published author. All the costs of publishing are paid up front. Editing, formatting, cover and other art, website, advertising, social media and many other costs are the responsibility of the author. In traditional publishing, the author typically is paid an advance, and these costs are picked up by the publisher. A self-published author receives no payment until the book begins to sell and must cover all costs long before they see any profit.

So again, thank you for buying this book. If you enjoyed it, please help me by taking a few moments to leave a review on Amazon and Goodreads (see below) whether you bought the book on-line or in a store. Reviews on both will help if you have the time. Reviews are the way all books, self-published or traditional, gain momentum for more sales. Many readers buy books based on reader reviews, and the algorithms used by book sellers compound the sales and reviews to sell more books. Comments are always welcome, but you don't have to write anything if you don't want, you can just rate it using the five-star system. A few moments of your time will help me immensely.

Thank you for your help!

HOW TO LEAVE A REVIEW

Amazon

- Go to your order detail page
- In the US – Amazon.com/orders
- In the UK – Amazon.co.uk/orders
- Click the "Write a product review" button next to your book order
- Rate the item and write your review and click "Submit"

Goodreads

- Go to Goodreads.com
- Search for the author or book title
- Click on the star rating under the book cover and leave a review

LET'S STAY IN TOUCH!

Click the +Follow button on my Amazon author page.

Follow me at:

Facebook: https://www.facebook.com/JeffHeinAuthor

Twitter: https://www.twitter.com/JeffHeinAuthor

Instagram: https://www.instagram.com/JeffHeinAuthor

LinkedIn: https://www.linkedin.com/in/JeffHeinAuthor

Webpage: https://www.jeffhein.net

Jeff Hein was born and raised in Wisconsin and served in the U.S. Army for twenty years, then returned home to Wisconsin. He is now retired and lives with his wife Dawn and their lab/shepherd mix Daisy. Sadly, Daisy's sister Annie passed away during the writing of this book.

Jeff writes historical fiction based on ancient writings and modern archeological discoveries. He loves to weave the story together with known facts and plausible fiction that fills in the blanks and could very well have been how things happened, keeping the reader engaged, while staying as true as possible to actual history.

Watch for book four, the final installment and thrilling conclusion of the Cimbrian War series, coming in 2025.

JEFF HEIN